Hell With The Lid Blown Off

Books by Donis Casey

The Alafair Tucker Mysteries
The Old Buzzard Had It Coming
Hornswoggled
The Drop Edge of Yonder
The Sky Took Him
Crying Blood
The Wrong Hill to Die On
Hell With The Lid Blown Off

Hell With The Lid Blown Off

An Alafair Tucker Mystery

Donis Casey

Poisoned Pen Press

First Edition 2014

10 9 8 7 6 5 4 3 2 1

Library of Congress Catalog Card Number: 2014931625

ISBN: 9781464202988 Hardcover
9781464203008 Trade Paperback

Poisoned Pen Press
6962 E. First Ave., Ste. 103
Scottsdale, AZ 85251
www.poisonedpenpress.com
info@poisonedpenpress.com

Printed in the United States of America

For Chris and Donna

and for all the rest of my family in Enid, Shawnee, Tulsa, and especially Joplin, Missouri.

Nothing brings a family closer than spending an evening huddled together under a mattress in the bathtub, waiting for the storm to blow over.

The Family

Alafair Tucker: Wife and mother of many children, who never means to get involved

Shaw Tucker: her husband, a farmer, who is never surprised when Alafair gets involved

Their children:

Martha, age 24: engaged to Streeter McCoy

Mary, age 23: married to Kurt Lukenbach

Alice Kelley, age 22: married to Walter Kelley

One on the way

Phoebe Day, age 22 (Alice's twin): married to John Lee Day

Zeltha Day, age 2: their daughter

One on the way

G.W. (Gee Dub), age 19: worried about going to war

Ruth, age 17: a talented musician

Charlie, age 15: looking for adventure

Blanche, age 11: feeling better now

Sophronia (Fronie), age 10: always brave

Grace, age 3: knows things

Chase Kemp, age 6: Alafair's nephew and ward; he fits in just fine

Josie Cecil: Shaw's eldest sister, who takes charge

Charles, James, and Howard: Shaw's brothers, all of whom had better do as Josie tells them

Scott Tucker: Town Sheriff of Boynton, Oklahoma. Shaw's cousin

Hattie Tucker: proprietress of the Boynton Mercantile and the American Hotel; Scott's wife

Slim, Stretch, Butch, and Spike Tucker: their sons

Prospective Members of the Family

Trenton Calder: Scott's deputy, a music lover

Judy: a baby who was blown in on the wind

The Beldons

Mildrey: the mother

Jubal: her eldest son, who loves dirty secrets

Hosea: her second son, who hates everything

Ephraim, Hezekiah, Zadok, and Caleb: the rest of them
Lovelle: her daughter; the only one who really counts

The Eichelbergers
Mr. Eichelberger: a farmer; Alafair and Shaw Tucker's longtime neighbor and friend
Maisie Eichelberger: his wife
Rollo and Abra Jane: their adult children

The MacKenzies
Beckie MacKenzie: wealthy widow, music teacher, and mentor to Ruth Tucker
Wallace MacKenzie III: her grandson; he's a bit much
Randal Wakefield: Wallace's college friend and traveling companion

The Welshes
Marva Welsh: Beckie MacKenzie's housekeeper
Coleman Welsh: her husband
Sugar Welsh: Coleman's sister

The Doctors
Dr. Ann Addison: the town midwife; not really a doctor, but don't tell her patients that
Dr. Jasper Addison: her husband; really a doctor
Dr. Perry and Dr. Jepson: the other two doctors in town

The Critters
Charlie Dog: the Tuckers' family dog
Buttercup and Crook: Shaw's hunting hounds
Bacon: the illicit offspring of Charlie Dog and Buttercup
Penny: Gee Dub's horse; she has a sense of humor
Old Brownie: Trent's horse; he'd rather not be bothered
The White-maned Roan: for whom it was all too much and so he went crazy

A Note on Dialect

In Standard English Usage, the word "Scottish" refers to a nationality and "Scotch" refers only to a type of malt whiskey. To persons from Scotland the terms are not interchangeable. In the early twentieth-century Appalachian/Ozark dialect that Trenton Calder would have used, anyone or anything from Scotland was called "Scotch."

BEFORE

Trenton Calder

The summer that Jubal Beldon was killed was the same summer that we had the big storm in Boynton, Oklahoma. It was because of the storm that we found out that Jubal got himself murdered, even though he'd have probably met a bad end anyway.

There never was a more unpleasant fellow.

He drank and used bad language and relished making trouble for folks, but he was the only one of the Beldon boys who ever earned an honest nickel, as far as I knew. He was unpleasant to his neighbors and mean when he could get away with it, so nobody that I ever heard of liked him much. But he was tender with animals and I gave him credit for that. The calves out at his farm were sleek and fat and well cared for, and for years he had owned an old three-legged dog he had rescued from a scrap heap when it was a pup. It was just people that he couldn't get along with.

Trenton Calder is my name, and that June of 1916 I was deputy to Scott Tucker, the town sheriff. I'd been working for Scott for about five years when my ma sold the house and moved to Missouri, so I took up residence in the American Hotel, across the street from the jail, right above Boynton Mercantile. Conveniently, both those establishments were owned by Scott Tucker himself, and him and his wife, Hattie, let me live there for nothing. He told me it was part of the wages for being his assistant, and I believed it, whether it was true or not.

Scott had four sons of his own, so one more dragtail youngster didn't bother him none. It was him taught me to shoot a handgun, along with his younger boys, Butch and Spike. My own daddy had showed me the use of a shotgun, but he died before he got around to teaching me the fine art of subduing a knife-wielding drunk by shooting him in the kneecaps.

I liked being a deputy.

Scott was one of the Muskogee County Tuckers. There must have been a thousand Tuckers living around eastern Oklahoma. You couldn't hardly turn around without bumping into one. For a long time, my best friend was a cousin of Scott's by the name of Bill McBride. But Bill got killed back in '14, and after that, I kind of took up with Gee Dub Tucker, who was the son of another one of Scott's cousins. Ol' Gee Dub was three years younger than me and he never did have much to say, but what he did say was either right to the point or blamed funny. We used to go hunting together a lot. He was the best shot with any kind of firearm that I ever did see, right to this day.

Gee Dub had eight sisters and one brother. Some of them were older than me, married with their own homes. But most were younger and I had a devil of a time keeping them straight. Mostly I didn't even try.

Boys were slim on the ground over to that farm. There was Gee Dub's only brother Charlie, who was a mischievous kid, but likable as all get-out, and a mouthy little cousin named Chase Kemp who lived with them. Then there were the little girls, a passel of skipping, giggling little creatures who flitted around like butterflies, or dragonflies, or gnats. Gee Dub loved to tease and play with them, but I never had much to do with children, especially girls, so generally I just wanted to get on with it and never paid them too much mind.

I never even noticed when the girl just younger than Gee Dub moved into town to study music.

Alafair Tucker

Alafair Tucker's guiding philosophy was that there is always room in the house and in the heart for one more child. So adding another child to her brood of ten had hardly made a dent in her life when in the spring of 1916 she took her six-year-old nephew Chase Kemp to raise for a spell.

There were a lot of changes going on with Alafair's family that year, anyway, what with one child after another going off to take up his or her own life with hardly a backward glance or a how-do-you-do to the poor bereft parents, so Alafair rather liked having an unexpected ragamuffin to take in hand. Her eldest son Gee Dub was away at college in Stillwater so she tucked Chase right in to his empty cot in the corner of the parlor, next to her fifteen-year-old, Charlie.

Once upon a time, the two beds and two trundles in the Tucker children's bedroom were populated by eight young girls ranging from teens to infants. Now with three girls married and two living part-time in town, each of those still at home could easily have had a bed of her own. But it's hard to sleep alone when you're not accustomed to it. The trundles hardly ever came out from under the beds these days.

Chase was the only child of Alafair's youngest sister Elizabeth Kemp. Elizabeth had left home for a spell in order to go to law school in Tucson, and had begged Alafair to foster Chase until she could graduate and join her husband's law firm back in their hometown of Tempe, Arizona.

Alafair and her husband, Shaw, had looked at each other in perfect understanding after they finished reading Elizabeth's telegram. Of course they'd take him. He was family.

Chase had been under-parented and was in need of some civilizing, but he wasn't a bad child or a stupid one, either. When confronted with ten cousins who all knew how to handle themselves, he assessed the situation pretty quickly and fell into line without a fight. Within a week, anyone who didn't know better would think that Chase Kemp had grown up Tucker, same as all the others.

There was one cousin to whom Chase took a particular shine, and that was Alafair's second-oldest daughter, the newlywed Mary. Alafair didn't know why the twenty-three-year-old and the six-year-old had formed such an immediate bond, but she wasn't inclined to question God's plan. Mary was a naturally maternal young woman and Chase was in need of mothering.

As soon as Mary and her new husband Kurt Lukenbach returned from their wedding trip in May and moved into the big new house Kurt had built on his nearby farm, Chase would rise at dawn and run across the fields to Mary's house for breakfast. Most days he went to Mary's after school, as well, and spent the afternoon tagging along behind the laconic Kurt as he secured his animals for the evening. Eventually Chase began to sleep over on the weekends, and then, after school was out for the summer, he spent more time at the Lukenbach farm than at his aunt and uncle's place. Alafair would have thought that Kurt and Mary would be annoyed at having a chattering six-year-old intrude on the honeymoon weeks of their new marriage, but when she broached the subject to her daughter, Mary assured her that they both loved having the boy around.

So Alafair let it be. She expected Chase enjoyed the extra attention, anyway.

When her older daughters had married, Alafair had feared that she would lose the closeness she had always had with each of them. But the opposite had proven to be the case. Phoebe and John Lee Day lived less than half a mile away, on the farm that Shaw had built for them when they married. The day she moved into her bright new house, Phoebe began carving a path through the fields from her front door to her mother's.

Even before granddaughter Zeltha was born, Phoebe came to visit her mother three or four mornings a week, sometimes to bring her laundry or sewing to do alongside Alafair, but usually just to visit for a little while. She never stayed long. After all, she had her own place to run now, and a husband and child to take care of.

Phoebe's second child was due in a few weeks so when she trudged up the path that June morning, carrying a small covered pail, she was leaning on the arm of her husband John Lee. They found their girl Zeltha sitting on a box on the front porch, along with her three-year-old aunt Grace, paying rapt attention to their play-school teacher, Alafair's next-to-youngest, Sophronia, age ten. Grace and Sophronia leaped up and rushed to meet them, but Zeltha stayed where she was, sitting on her box with a puppy in her lap, a barn cat draped across her feet, and the old yellow house dog, Charlie Dog, at her side. She beamed at her parents.

Phoebe could see her mother and sister Blanche working in the garden. In midsummer there was no end of things to plant, cut, mulch, weed, and harvest, or bugs and mites to pick, spray, or drown in a jar of kerosene. They were so busy at their tasks that neither had noticed Phoebe and John Lee arrive, so Phoebe and John Lee went to them, three little girls skipping ahead and Charlie Dog plodding behind.

It was Blanche who saw them first. She waved and smiled from under the brim of her shady straw hat, her cheeks pink from exertion and glowing with vitality. Phoebe smiled back, marveling at her sister's newfound ruddy health following a winter of illness.

Alafair was bending over a row of beans with her back to the gate, but turned to see who Blanche was waving at. "How're you doing, darlin'?" she called when she spotted Phoebe.

"Good, Mama. Come to fetch Zeltha home. John Lee was set to do it by himself, but I told him I could use the walk."

Alafair straightened and removed her makeshift gloves, onetime socks with holes punched out for her thumbs. She whacked them against her skirt and bits of dirt went flying as she walked over to the fence. "The more you move around the easier it will be when your time comes."

Phoebe nodded. If anybody knew the ins and outs of childbirth it was Alafair.

Zeltha threw her arms around her father's overall-clad knees and he picked her up, while Sophronia and Grace clambered around the fence without any excuse but high spirits.

"Fronie, go get that basket of beans I just picked, and you and Grace take them up to the house and wash and pick them over. I'll be up in a minute to help you string them."

The look on Sophronia's face said that she regretted her ill-timed appearance, but she grabbed Grace's hand and came through the gate. Rather than complain, she contented herself with making faces at Blanche, who appeared entirely too happy to see her younger sister sentenced to kitchen duty.

Alafair was unconcerned with her offspring's opinions of their assignments. "Why don't y'all stay for dinner?" she asked Phoebe. "I don't know what I'm going to do with all these green beans. Cook up a big mess with fatback, I reckon."

Phoebe and John Lee exchanged an amused glance. Alafair was transparently tempting Phoebe with one of her favorite dishes. Considering the fact that she could hardly reach her own stove anymore, Phoebe was more than willing to be tempted. She held up the pail. "Well, we were hoping to be invited. I brought over a bucketful of new onions to cream, and there's half a dozen green tomatoes on top, too."

John Lee shifted Zeltha on his hip and gestured for the pail. "Give that to me, honey. I'll take the girls on up to the house before I go find Dad."

"Him and the boys are out in the cotton patch," Alafair called to his back as he led the parade of girls up the path toward the farmhouse.

The women followed more slowly, Alafair with her arm over Phoebe's shoulders and Phoebe with an arm around her mother's waist. "You reckon Mary and Kurt will come by?" Phoebe asked.

"I doubt they will tonight. Chase has been over there since dawn, and Mary likes to cook for her boys. They'll likely be over this evening. We can make ice cream."

"Oh, that sounds good! I declare I need to learn not to be having my babies in the summer. It was such a nice spring after that awful wet winter, but these past few days have been entirely too hot for my liking. Windy, too. I don't like that unsettled feeling."

"We were lucky to have such a calm spring, sugar. This is Oklahoma, after all. We have to have our wind and dirt. Can't get away with nice weather for too long."

"I expect not. So how's Ruthie like teaching piano lessons?"

"Oh, she loves it. And Miz Beckie loves having her there. No wonder, that poor thing rattling around by herself in that big old house. She's fixed up one of the spare bedrooms just for Ruth, and Ruth spends the night there about half the time now. She told me the house is a bit creaky and dark for her taste, but she stays over because she's so fond of Miz Beckie and hates to think of her lonely."

"She still plans to go off to Muskogee to study music next term, doesn't she?"

Alafair laughed. "Oh, yes. I figure that when Ruth leaves, Miz Beckie will just have to get herself a dog."

They reached the back porch and Phoebe paused to catch her breath before tackling the steps. "You think Ruth will be here for dinner? I'd surely like to see her."

Alafair shrugged. "I don't know, honey. When she left for town this morning, she didn't mention her plans for today. When it comes to you young'uns, I don't know anything anymore."

Trenton Calder

Here is how it happened that I fell in love with Ruth Tucker.

One of the big regrets of my life has always been that I have no musical talent at all. I can't carry a tune in a gunny sack, and when I go to sing in church, folks get the awfullest looks of pain on their faces. Never did learn to play an instrument, either, needless to say. But I love music. I love to listen to any beautiful sound, whether it be a lady with a fine singing voice or a chorus of birds on a pretty spring morning. It was that very love of music that set my life on a new course, just a few months before the United States entered the Great War. I was twenty-two years old.

Every morning on my rounds I passed by the Masonic Hall over on Elm Street. On that particular June morning it was hot and sultry, and the windows were open just enough to let in the fresh air. Now, at this time of day there wasn't generally anybody in the hall except for old Boot Murillo, the caretaker. So I was surprised when I heard piano music coming from the auditorium, and I stopped dead in the road to have a listen. I never did expect any mischief. The hall was always open and anybody could go in there for meetings, or to play checkers, or the like.

No, it wasn't the fact that someone was inside that stopped me in my tracks. It was the beautiful music wafting out of that window like a breeze from heaven. I knew the tune, and could have sung along if I'd had a voice to do it with.

Flow gently, sweet Afton, beside thy green braes
Flow gently, sweet Afton, I'll sing to thee praise
My Mary is sleeping beside thy green stream
Flow gently, sweet Afton, disturb not her dream.

For the longest time I couldn't move, waiting for that song to end. It crossed my mind that I was going to be late back to the jailhouse, which I never was, and Scott might wonder where I'd got to. But I couldn't have left while that music was playing if I'd wanted.

When the last note faded away, my body just sighed of its own accord, and my heart felt so happy that I was determined to find out who had given me such pleasure on a hot morning and tell him so. I walked around to the front door and went right in to the auditorium, where I saw a slim young woman sitting at the old upright piano over in the far corner by the stage. Her back was to me and she was paging through some sheet music, unaware that I had come in.

I couldn't see her face so it took me a minute to figure out who she was, though I could tell right away that she was one of Gee Dub Tucker's sisters. Every one of the eight girls in that family had her own look–some of them tall, some short, some red, or dark, or blond, but there were three who had a bunch of wild reddish curls, and this was one of them. The older one of the three was married and living on a farm outside of town, and the youngest was still a little girl, so I realized pretty quick that this was the middle one, Ruth.

I didn't want to startle her so I cleared my throat, and she turned around on the piano stool.

I was already walking toward her across the wide, wooden floor of the auditorium when she turned to face me. When she smiled, my foot just hung there in the air in mid-step for a second.

She looked happy to see me. "Trent Calder! Good morning. Mr. Murillo told me it'd be all right if I practiced here for a while. I hope I'm not bothering anyone."

Now, I'd known Ruth Tucker since she was a child. A sweet little old thing, all leggy and coltish, and I expect that's the way I thought of her until the instant she turned around on that piano seat.

I still think of that moment to this day, the memory as clear as glass even as other memories of my life fade. The hollow sound of my boots on the wooden floor, the dusty, leaf smell of the air coming in through the window. The bright, russet color of those curls that she had wound into a knot at the nape of her neck.

She had the strangest eyes. They were big and turned up at the corners, with red-gold lashes. But the thing that bowled me over on that day was that they were purple. She was wearing a blouse the color of ripe plums, and her eyes were a perfect match. It came to me that she was talking, and I figured I'd better listen in case she required an intelligent answer.

"How are you, Trent? I haven't seen you in ages."

I sat down next to her on the piano bench. "I'm just fine. Shoot, I just can't figure out why I haven't seen you around much lately. Where have you been keeping yourself?"

"I can't figure it out, either. Must be that you haven't been paying attention, because I see you out and about all the time, strutting up and down the street with your six-gun on your hip, rattling the doors on the shops at sunset to make sure they're all locked." Her fingers danced over the keys and she glanced at me with those purple eyes. "Every afternoon, you sit for a spell in a chair in front of the jailhouse after dinner and try to look all official, until some little nipper comes along and you run off after him in a game of tag. Makes it hard to take you seriously as the steel-eyed lawman, you know."

She was ragging on me, I knew, but all I could think was that she had noticed me. Something jiggled in the back of my brain. "I thought you were off in Muskogee studying music! When did you get back?"

She wasn't about to let me off the hook. "Why, Trent, I haven't even gone yet. I just went over to Muskogee last week to enroll at the Music Conservatory. I'll be starting in the fall. For the past few weeks I've been staying at Miz Beckie's off and on and helping with her piano students during the summer."

Miz Rebecca MacKenzie lived in a big, gloomy house just north of town, right on the road to Tulsa. Everyone called her Miz Beckie. She had taught piano to every church accompanist in the county, except for the Church of Christ folks, of course, who didn't hold with such things. She had even taught Ted Banner, who played the piano every Friday and Saturday night at the Elliot and Ober motion picture theatre, and as rumor had it, at the Rusty Horseshoe Roadhouse on the other nights of the week.

Miz MacKenzie was a good-looking woman with a neat figure and big blue eyes, always dressed to the nines in the latest fashion, even on days that she had no notion of leaving the house. She wore her silvery-gold hair pinned high on her head, like a crown. But even if she looked like a queen, she wasn't haughty. No, not a bit of it. Her life's mission was to donate money for public projects, or to help the poor.

Miz MacKenzie sang like an angel, and taught singing as well as piano. Not to me, of course. We couldn't afford music lessons, so I never learned anything. Even so, she gave all of us who grew up around there a gift that can't be valued.

"I'm surprised you remember me at all, much less remember that I'll be studying music." Ruth sounded a mite put out when she answered me. "All those times you've had supper out at the farm with us—who do you think it was sitting at the end of the table, passing you the mashed potatoes? Just one of the mob of Tucker kids, I guess."

I didn't say it, but something had sure happened to her over those few months and it didn't have to do with learning how to teach kids to play the piano. "Well, smack me with a two-by-four, Ruth. I deserve that tongue-lashing, because I must have been blind not to notice you. I promise to pay real close attention to you from this day on."

She glanced at me again, and her teasing expression faded. She stopped playing and shrugged. "Never mind. Things happen when they're supposed to, I expect."

At least I was smart enough to note the change in her tone. I stood up, my hat in my hand. "I'd better get to work. Sure was nice to see you. Next time I get invited out to your folks', maybe we can have a long talk and catch up."

She gave me a quirky smile, and I swear there was a look in her eye that said she knew things about me that I didn't know myself and she wasn't inclined to educate me anytime soon. "Maybe we can."

When I turned to leave, my mind was going like a rabbit with a fox after him. I hadn't been out to the Tucker place for three or four weeks, and I was already scheming how to get myself invited to supper as fast as I could.

How is it that the world can shift like that in the blink of an eye, and things that had been so ordinary and familiar become something you could never have imagined just the moment before?

Wallace MacKenzie

By the time Ruth returned to Beckie MacKenzie's house late in the morning, the day had turned windy and the sky was full of shredded, scudding clouds. The late Mr. Wallace MacKenzie Senior had been a man of means, one of the founders of the Francis Brickworks, and had left his wife Rebecca well off. Her two-story Victorian house was a monument to Victorian excess with its turrets and gothic windows, portico and balustrade. The MacKenzie manse stood in all its curlicued glory just outside the Boynton town limits. Impossible to miss, and impossible to miss the visual declaration that a very important family resided here.

Ruth had never quite understood why the MacKenzies had felt they needed all that space. Five bedrooms upstairs and servants' quarters in the back by the kitchen, and even at the height of Mr. MacKenzie Senior's working and family life, only three people at a time had ever lived there. And now only the widow was in residence. It must have been a lonely existence for such an outgoing woman. Ruth had once asked Beckie if she wouldn't be happier in a smaller house in town, closer to the society of others and handier for her many music students, to boot. But Beckie wouldn't hear of it.

"I must be near the ghosts of my happy past, Ruth dear," she had declared.

Ruth entered the house through the kitchen door at the back, and before she removed her hat, put the basket full of fresh greens that her mother had sent onto the counter. She made a half-hearted attempt to wipe her dusty shoes on the doormat before giving it up as a lost cause and taking them off.

Beckie's daytime housekeeper, Marva Welsh, was already seated at the kitchen table, shelling peas into a bowl. She looked up at Ruth and smiled a greeting.

"I was wondering where you might be, Miz Ruth. Did you stay the night at your mama's?"

Marva Welsh was a Negro woman of thirty or so, small and pleasingly rounded, with a gentle manner and a frightening competence in the arts of housewifery. She was the wife of Coleman Welsh, master carpenter and brother of Sugar Welsh and Carlon Welsh, who was himself a skilled handyman and the husband of Georgie Welsh. Georgie was Alafair's sometime chore helper and neighbor. It had occurred to Ruth that if it weren't for the Welshes, many of the white citizens of Boynton would be sitting in filth, starving, with their houses falling down around their ears and their gardens gone to seed.

"I did, Marva, but I came into town early this morning. I've been practicing my piano over to the Masonic Hall. Here. Mama sent a mess of greens for Miz Beckie's dinner." Ruth held up the dishtowel-covered wicker basket by the handle.

She set the greens on the table, where Marva uncovered and

inspected them with approval. "Why, thank you, honey. They'll be mighty fine for dinner with some dumplings."

Ruth smiled. "I'll go tell Miz Beckie I'm here. I've got Claudia Woodstock coming in for a lesson in a while."

"You better put your shoes back on, sugar." Marva's head was bent over her bowl of peas, but her voice held a hint of amusement. "Miz Beckie's got company."

"Miz Beckie, I'm back," Ruth called. She walked down the hall in her dusty shoes, toward the sound of voices at the front of the house. She was pleased to know that the garrulous Beckie had company. It made her feel less guilty for spending the previous night at her parents' house and leaving her friend alone.

She stopped at the sitting room door, dismayed when a young man stood up from the wing-backed chair in front of the fireplace and gave her an impish grin. Wallace was home.

Ruth had known Wallace MacKenzie the Third since she was a child. He was Beckie's darling, and his own estimation of himself was just as high as his grandmother's. He was a handsome fellow, everyone agreed about that, tall and fair, with sharp blue eyes. His blond hair was long on top and parted in the middle, falling nearly to his cheekbones on either side and cupping his cheeks like wings. Ruth suspected that Wallace wanted to cultivate a resemblance to some romantic English poet and enjoyed the fact that people thought him an intellectual. Which he decidedly was not.

Wallace had come to live with his grandmother after the grandfather died. So she wouldn't be so lonely, they said. But Ruth was of the opinion that his parents in Muskogee had had enough of him. Whatever the reason, the arrangement had suited everyone.

Except for Ruth. His overblown personality annoyed her no end. Fortunately, he had been studying medicine at Vanderbilt University in Tennessee for a couple of years, so she seldom had to put up with him. He loved to make a show and fancied himself quite the charmer. When he did manage to make a rare visit home, Ruth was careful not to find herself alone with him.

Beckie's already cheerful face was positively celestial. "Ruth, lass! Look who's finally decided to favor his old granddam with a visit!"

Ruth mustered a feeble smile. "Good morning, Wallace."

Wallace stepped forward, grabbed her shoulders, and gave her a wet kiss on either cheek in grand Continental style. She resisted the temptation to scrub her face with her sleeve as he held her at arm's length for inspection. "Ruth, I promise you get more beautiful every moment you live. Gran tells me you have a beau, that old classmate of mine, Trent Calder!" He released her and clapped his hands over his heart. "Say it isn't so, or whatever shall I do?"

Ruth's mouth dropped open, and she shot Beckie an exasperated look. "Wherever did you get such a notion?" She could feel her cheeks burning.

Beckie beamed back at her, unrepentant. "I'm not blind, Ruth dear. I see how you look at him as he walks his patrol, so serious and manly."

"Trent and I are friends." Ruth's acknowledgment was begrudging. "But I'd hardly call him my beau."

Wallace shook his head, but there was a twinkle in his eye. "Then there's still hope for me! I can't imagine that a jewel like you would prefer a fellow so tall and skinny and redheaded that he resembles a lit match. If you do, I'm desolate, but I suppose there's nothing I would be able to do but rail against my fate."

Beckie emitted a ladylike tinkle of laughter. Ruth was torn between feeling insulted on Trent's behalf and amused at Wallace's apt description of her friend.

"I thought you were spending the summer traveling with a college chum of yours," she said.

He gestured toward his vacated armchair, inviting Ruth to sit down. "I was. I am. And here he is."

To Ruth's surprise, a dark young man stood up from his seat on an ottoman next to her chair. She hadn't even noticed him.

He inclined his head toward her. "Randal Wakefield, ma'am." His voice dripped with Southern gentility. He was shorter than

Wallace, but just as elegantly turned out in a smart dark suit with a belted jacket and plus-four trousers. His brown eyes were warm and friendly, and Ruth liked him instantly.

"Glad to meet you, Mr. Wakefield."

"Randal, please." He grasped her hand briefly before he sat back down.

"Randal and I are on our way to Colorado," Wallace said. "Randal insisted that we take a detour through Oklahoma so that he could meet my grandmother. Seems that he had to see with his own eyes this paragon of whom I so often speak."

Beckie clasped her hands in front of her face, her blue eyes wide. "Randal is such a fine young man, Ruth! Of course, I am disposed to like anyone who brings my darling Wallace home for a visit!"

Randal placed his hand over his heart. "You are too kind, Miz MacKenzie."

Wallace tossed his mane out of his eyes. "I hate to leave so precipitously, Ruth, but for some reason, Randal insists on a tour of Boynton before luncheon, even though I've warned him that there's nothing worth seeing."

"Well, now, Wallace," Randal protested, "it would be unspeakably rude to leave this lady's company just as I am making her acquaintance."

"Oh, don't change your plans on my account!" Ruth's response sounded hasty, even to her. "We will have plenty of time to visit over the next few days."

Wallace leaned over and kissed Beckie on the cheek. "Since we have Miz Tucker's permission, we'll take our leave, Grandmother. I don't expect this will take long, and we'll be back long before Marva finishes cooking dinner."

Beckie MacKenzie

"Isn't this the most wonderful thing, Ruth dear?" Beckie said, after the young men had excused themselves.

"You must be very happy to see him. How long is he going to stay, did he say?"

The woman's face crumpled briefly as she pondered his departure. "Only a few days, I'm afraid. But you know young men. They must have their adventures. Besides, it may happen that we are drawn into the European war, and if that occurs, who knows what will happen? I feel that Wallace and his friend want to enjoy themselves while they can."

"Won't you worry if Wallace goes for a soldier?"

"If war comes, my Wallace will do his duty. America will gain a fine, brave officer if he is called, you can be sure of that. It's in his blood."

Beckie's father was born a Highlander, and according to her, he had also been a surgeon's assistant in the British Army and was a great hero in some European war. After which he had immigrated to America and become a surgeon for the Confederacy. Ruth doubted there was anybody in the county who hadn't heard Beckie's tales of his deeds and adventures, for she'd recount them to perfect strangers if she got the chance.

"I believe you have at least one brother of age, Ruth dear. Has he told you his plans should war come?" Beckie's expression made it plain that she thought all young men were bound to do their patriotic duty.

Ruth turned her head to look out the window. "My mother doesn't like war talk, ma'am, but if it happens, I think he would enlist, yes." She didn't say what she thought about that.

Beckie nodded, looking grave. "And now back to the business of the day, Ruth dear. Marva has planned a wonderful dinner for us. But I'm afraid that Marva is leaving early tomorrow. What shall we do about a nice repast for Wallace and his friend, not to mention ourselves? Do you suppose that I could telephone the Palace Restaurant and ask them to deliver a meal tomorrow afternoon?"

"You certainly could, Miz Beckie, but why spend your money? I'd be more than happy to fix up something, and I'm sure Wallace and Mr. Wakefield would rather have a home-cooked meal after so many months of whatever alarming thing they've been eating at college. I know my brother Gee Dub was so underfed when he came home after his term was over that he had to stand in the same place twice just to cast a shadow."

She expected a token argument, but Beckie accepted her offer with such alacrity that Ruth realized wryly that her landlady was hoping she would volunteer to cook. Ruth often made supper for the two of them, and she knew Beckie had a high opinion of her kitchen skills. Ruth wanted to do it, anyway. Cooking would give her an excuse not to socialize with Wallace and his friend until they actually sat down to eat. Ruth thought she might ask Marva's permission to prepare breakfast, dinner, and supper every day they were here, and clean up, as well.

"I'm sure I can fix something that will please your guests. Let's see. Does Wallace like pork chops and dressing, do you think?"

"Oh, my dear, pork chops are Wallace's favorite! And I must say that I quite enjoy them myself."

"Perfect, then. When I come in from home in the morning I'll stop by Mr. Khouri's market and see if I can buy some good chops from him." She had planned to stay over at Beckie's until after the church picnic on Sunday. But Wallace's arrival was making her reconsider that plan, which meant that she would be walking home after her last piano lesson this evening and walking back to town in the morning. "I only have two students coming tomorrow, so I plan to practice on the piano at the Masonic Hall for a little while more after they leave and before I start on the pork chops. I'd like to get better acquainted with that old upright before I have to play at the church picnic on Sunday."

Beckie leaned forward and put her hand on Ruth's. "Why don't you invite your young man to supper tomorrow, Ruth dear? I'm sure Wallace would enjoy seeing his childhood friend."

"You mean Trent? Miz Beckie, I told you…"

Beckie shushed her. "Don't fool with me, now. You do like him, don't you?"

Ruth felt herself blush. "Well, yes, I do, but I do not intend to be forward about it."

"Why heaven forfend, Ruth dear! Just tell him that I'm inviting him for Wallace's sake."

It was a transparent ruse, Ruth thought, but she said, "If I happen to run into Trent Calder beforehand, Miz Beckie, I'll mention that you suggested he come to supper."

"Oh, good. Wallace will be glad to see him. Trent and Wallace played together some after Wallace first moved here."

Ruth nodded, but didn't say that she doubted Wallace had spared Trenton Calder a thought in years.

Alafair Tucker

After her last student had finished his lesson late that afternoon, Ruth left Beckie to enjoy her visitors on her own, and walked the blustery, dusty, two miles from town back to her parents' house.

She was met at the gate by Bacon, the rambunctious, six-month-old pup who was the offspring of Shaw's prize hunting hound bitch, Buttercup, and the family's elderly shepherd mix, Charlie Dog. Bacon's littermates had all been pureblood English coonhounds, sired by Buttercup's hunting companion, Crook. But in spite of Shaw's diligence in keeping Buttercup penned the last time she was in heat, old Charlie Dog had managed one forbidden tryst. The pureblood pups had all been sold to eager hunters, but Shaw hadn't had the heart to drown the charming little mongrel. Besides, Grace took one look at the fluffy yellow scrap and called him Bacon (who knew why?) and just like that he was part of the family.

Grace, Chase Kemp, and Zeltha joined them halfway up the drive to the house, all chattering and skipping, as energetic as the puppy. By the time Ruth reached the picket fence that surrounded the house, she knew every detail of every event that had occurred on the farm that day.

She had walked into something of a family reunion. A picnic supper was in progress, and the entire Tucker clan was happily munching away at sandwiches, cold chicken, and potato salad.

Ruth's parents, Alafair and Shaw, were sitting side by side on the porch swing, and her four older sisters and their mates were arrayed across the porch in a semicircle of hard-backed kitchen chairs. Her two brothers, Gee Dub and Charlie, were splayed across the steps in loose-limbed comfort, leaving only a corner of the bottom step for the younger sisters, Blanche and Sophronia, to sit with their dinner plates on their laps. Three abandoned, fly-blown plates on the porch marked where the littlest ones had been sitting at the moment they spotted Ruth coming up the drive with Bacon romping beside her.

Grace flitted ahead and opened the picket gate for her, and Ruth waved as she walked through. "Hey, everybody!"

She was greeted by a chorus of "hey" and "howdy," but only her mother was willing to put down her supper and walk down the path to meet her.

"What are you doing back here so soon, sweetie? I figured you'd spend the night in town."

Ruth gave her mother a hug, then glared at the sky as though the wind was a personal affront. "I took a notion to come home tonight, Ma, but I kind of wish I hadn't now. It looks like it might rain and I don't fancy a muddy, wet, trip back into town in the morning."

"I'm glad you did, darlin'. I miss your shining face when you're not here of a morning."

They walked up onto the porch where Ruth hugged and kissed each relative in turn. Her eldest sister, Martha, raised her eyebrows. "If we'd known you aimed to walk back to the house tonight, Streeter and I could have given you a ride from town like we did Alice and Walter." She nodded toward her fiancé's Model T Ford parked next to the fence.

"I didn't know I was going to until I did, Martha." Ruth turned toward sister number three, lively, blue-eyed Alice, also expecting a blessed event any moment, and her husband Walter, the town barber. "I didn't expect to see you all out and about, Alice. Mercy, you look like you're about to pop!"

Both Alice and Walter laughed at Ruth's apt comment. "I feel I'm about to pop, Ruthie! We figured we'd better get out of the house while I can still walk."

"Besides, we don't like to miss an opportunity to eat your ma's cooking," Walter added with a wink.

Alafair accepted the compliment with a thin smile. Handsome, glib Walter Kelley was her least favorite son-in-law.

Ruth was quite aware of her mother's attitude and tried not to let her amusement show. "Is everybody going to the church picnic on Sunday?"

"We will," Martha said, and was seconded by Phoebe and Mary. But Alice shrugged.

"I will if I can waddle over there. Else Walter may have to go by himself. I hope to have increased the population by one before then. Mercy, I don't know how much longer I can stand feeling like a heifer! How are you feeling, Phoebe, by the way? You haven't said 'boo' since we got here." Phoebe and Alice were fraternal twins, and both due to deliver before another month was out.

"Happy as a clam." Phoebe sounded smug. "This second one is way easier than the first, if that's any comfort to you."

Alice laughed. "I've forgotten what comfort is."

Shaw stood up. "Come on, boys," he said. "If the ladies are going to be discussing childbirth, I aim to be missing." He raised the male half of the congregation with a gesture. "Let's mosey down to the stable and admire the stock."

The gentlemen rose and ambled away in a group. Not to be left out, the five youngest children and their four canine companions followed along.

"Don't be gone long," Alafair called after them. "We'll be making ice cream directly." She took Ruth's arm. "Come on inside with me, sugar. You can help me mix up the custard."

Alafair led her daughter into the house, through the newly mopped parlor and into the warm kitchen. "Sit down. I'll fix you a plate and you can eat while I cook up the makings for the ice cream. The girls will be glad to know you're back tonight. With you and Martha spending nights in town half the time, Grace wants to sleep with Blanche and not Sophronia and it's a big flapdoodle every night at bedtime until Mama or Daddy goes in there and knocks some heads together."

Ruth laughed. "There are enough beds now that everybody could have her own."

"That'd suit Blanche, but Grace will never have it." She gave Ruth a knowing look as she set down a plate of cold chicken and potato salad and a big mug of milky coffee. "I admit I'm surprised to see you. I figured you'd spend the night in town. Did Miz Beckie do something to set your teeth on edge?"

Ruth took a bite of drumstick. "Oh, no. Wallace showed up today, along with some college friend of his. Randal, his name is. I thought I'd make myself scarce tonight."

Alafair simply said, "Ah." She was acquainted with Ruth's opinion of Wallace MacKenzie the Third.

"I'll confess," Ruth continued, "if it was left to me, Wallace would make up with his father in Muskogee and not come home to Miz Beckie's at all. But Miz Beckie is so happy to see him again that I expect I can't begrudge her."

Alafair busied herself with milk, sugar, and eggs for a moment. "If you feel uncomfortable in that house while Wallace and his friend are there, honey, maybe you'd better stay here until they leave. You know we'll carry you into town so you can teach your lessons whenever you need to."

"Oh, that's not necessary, Mama. I'm sure Wallace doesn't have the slightest interest in me. I'm too common for the great MacKenzies. But he can't stand it that I don't think he's the finest young fellow in all Christendom. He's so used to worship and praise that he's downright insulted when he doesn't get it. I talked a while to his friend Randal and liked him, though. He seemed like a gentleman. No, I'll go back tomorrow, and it'll be fine. I offered to make pork chops and dressing for supper tomorrow. Miz Beckie told me I could invite Trent Calder. She's got it into her head that I'm partial to him. She is quite the matchmaker." Ruth sounded amused.

Alafair lowered her head so Ruth wouldn't see her smile. She was inordinately pleased that Ruth liked Trenton Calder. She had always had a soft spot for the red-haired deputy, so serious and thoughtful. He had always been good to his mother, and in Alafair's opinion that was a strong predictor of an excellent husband.

And if any of her kids deserved an excellent husband, it was Ruth. Ruth was an affectionate girl. She had spent more of her childhood in someone's lap than any two of the others together, and still was ready with a hug and a kiss. Circumstance had put Ruth in an oddly singular position, the middlest of middle children, the sixth of ten living. The eldest four were all girls, and made as nice a little group as may be. The youngest three were also girls, a tight gang of playmates. But Ruth was born between the two boys. Her mother's knobby-kneed, long-limbed little tree-climber, with stubbed toes and scratches on her arms, who had loved to ride horses, and dance, and sing, and play the piano. Never lost among her horde of sisters and brothers, but always going her own way. Alafair smiled at the memory. When had she become this soft-voiced, elegant creature? They always grew up when you weren't looking. If someone had threatened to drown her if she didn't choose, she might, just might, say that of all her much-beloved children, Ruth was her favorite.

Yes, if anyone deserved an excellent husband it was Ruth. If the previous experience of four daughters' romances hadn't taught her to keep her opinion to herself, Alafair would have been quite the matchmaker in this instance as well. "And did you invite Trent to supper?" she asked.

"I might, if I see him beforehand." She sipped at her coffee. "Mama, would you come to supper at Miz Beckie's tomorrow?"

"I wasn't asked."

"I'm asking you. I'm the cook, so I figure it's all right."

"Oh, no, honey, I just can't. Since all you older girls have left the house, I've got too many helpless mouths to feed." The idea that the men might feed themselves, much less feed the children, didn't cross her mind. "But if you want, I'll take you back to town in the buggy tomorrow after breakfast, and we can go to Khouri's together and pick up whatever you need to cook for supper. I can even help you fix it up, if you need."

"I don't need help cooking, Ma, but I'd appreciate it if you'd come with me to Khouri's. He likes you, I can tell. He always gives you the best cuts."

Alafair smiled and shook her head. "He's just a good, decent fellow. I don't buy enough meat or produce off him to keep him in collar buttons."

Ruth Tucker

After breakfast the next morning, Alafair drove Ruth back to town in the buggy. Chase had gone home with Mary, and Zeltha with her parents, but Alafair's three-year-old, Grace, came along, since she was particularly energetic that morning and had been distracting her older siblings from their chores. Instead of delivering Ruth straight to Beckie MacKenzie's, Alafair accompanied her daughter to Khouri's Market in order to lend her expertise to the choosing of pork chops. Khouri's Market carried meat, dairy, and produce all in one location. The quality of his merchandise was top-notch. He was so obsessed with freshness that he would never allow a wilted carrot top or a day-old egg in his store. Besides, Khouri's was located right next to cousin Hattie Tucker's Mercantile and so was convenient for all grocery-shopping needs.

"What can I do for you, Miz Tucker?" Mr. Khouri asked.

"Not for me today, Mr. Khouri. Today Ruth is buying, and I'm just along for the outing."

Mr. Khouri's black eyes locked on Ruth with a knowing expression. "I'm going to guess that Miz Beckie is still celebrating her grandson's homecoming, and you're here on her behalf to buy something special for dinner."

Ruth laughed. There were no secrets in Boynton. "That's the long and short of it, Mr. Khouri, and I'm impressed at your skill in putting one and two together and coming out with three every time. Marva is leaving Miz Beckie's early today so I volunteered to do pork chops and dressing for supper, depending on if you've got some nice fat ones you can let me have."

"Well, now, I believe you're in luck, young lady. Just this morning I acquired a couple of dressed shoats from your brother-in-law, Kurt Lukenbach. I was just about to trim them up. I expect I could find you some chops that would fit your requirements, nice and fat."

After much examination and discussion, Khouri wrapped six thick, marbled chops in brown butcher's paper for them. Ruth and her mother walked out onto the boardwalk and stood for several minutes reviewing the proper way to cook pork chops and dressing while Grace ran in circles around them.

It was some moments before they parted—Alafair and Grace to visit Alice, and Ruth to deliver the pork chops to Beckie's icebox before walking the five blocks to the Masonic Hall to practice on the ancient piano awhile.

Ruth waved good-bye to her mother and Grace as they headed toward Second Street, then turned just in time to see Wallace MacKenzie and Randal Wakefield emerging from the Williams Drug Store directly across the street. She stopped in her tracks and considered going back inside Khouri's Market, but it was too late. Wallace called her name and crossed the road to meet her with his friend trailing behind him.

The two men fell in on either side of her. Wallace put one arm around her shoulder and squeezed. "What delights have you purchased in yonder establishment, my darling Ruth? Something delectable for our supper, I'll warrant. Will you be preparing it with your own fair hand? I hope so, because that would enhance its flavor ten-fold."

Ruth shook his arm off. "You are quite the bag of wind, Wallace. Yes, I've bought some cuts of meat for supper, and you can thank your grandmother for the thought, like you can thank her for so many things."

Randal chuckled his approval. "*Touché*, Wally, you old bag of wind."

Wallace staggered and clutched his chest. "Oh, you wound me! Come Randal. Let us repair to the local alehouse where I can ease the pain with demon rum."

Randal looked surprised. "I was under the impression that a man can't purchase liquor in Oklahoma, Wall."

"Never believe everything you hear, Randal. Farewell, cruel maiden. Tell Gran we'll see her tonight at your much-anticipated supper. Come on, Ran."

Ruth rolled her eyes at Randal, who shook his head and smiled. What folly.

Trenton Calder

A few days before the church supper, I was heading to the Newport Cafe for a bite of dinner when I heard the music coming from the Masonic Hall. I knew it had to be Ruth practicing on the upright piano, just like the day before, when I fell in love with her. After that day I would have recognized her playing anywhere. I wafted into the hall like a cloud on a breeze, toward that music. She had finished playing a piece that I didn't recognize, something real high-class, and was turning the pages of her sheet music. I came to stand beside her piano bench and she looked up at me with the sweetest smile. She was wearing green that day. Her eyes were the color of the leafy woods on a summer day.

"Well, I'll swan," she said. "I suppose that if ever I want to see you, I should just come here and play the piano like it was a duck call and you'll come flying in. Did you know that Wallace MacKenzie is back in town? Miz Beckie asked me to cook up some pork chops tonight for him and his friend from college who came with him to visit."

I had known Wallace MacKenzie for years. Me and him had gone to school together for a while, after he got sent to live with his grandma and before I had to quit school and go to work. I didn't think much of him, but he thought so much of himself that my low opinion didn't trouble him none. Life was easy as rolling off a log for him. Him and his dad butted heads, but the old man never cut him off. Seemed to me like Wallace always landed on his feet whether he deserved to or not. He was even going to college, which I would have given my right arm to do.

I'm ashamed to think about the stab of jealously that went through me when Ruth said she was going to cook for him.

If he'd have been there I'd have punched him right in the eye and thought of a reason later. It must have showed on my face because Ruth's eyes got big and she laughed before she added, "Miz Beckie wondered to me if you might like to join us?"

I could have kicked myself around the building. "Well, I'd be pleased, if you'd like me to." I tried not to sound too eager.

She began to play "If I Were the Only Boy in the World." "I'd be pleased to have you," she said, "if you think you can behave yourself."

The Bedlam Boys

On her way back to Beckie's house just north of town and nearly to the brick works, Ruth was thinking about the menu for tonight's supper. She had been aware of the four men on horseback coming south on the road for some minutes, but as the daughter and granddaughter of horse-breeders, she had been paying more attention to the fine, healthy horseflesh than she was to the men on their backs—until they grew close enough for her to recognize them.

It was some of the Beldon boys. Jubal was in the lead, as usual, mounted on his big roan gelding with the cream-colored mane and the white blaze on its face. He gave her a wicked grin when he saw her expression change. She stopped in her tracks and looked around for an escape. The big, two-story, turreted and multi-windowed MacKenzie house was only yards away. So near and yet so far.

Shoot.

She was going to have to brazen it out.

Ruth didn't have much good to say about any of the fellows in that gang. They were called the Beldon boys because six of them were brothers, but there was also that Gibson lad from down by Council Hill; Dave Walker, son of old Mr. Walker that farmed east of town; Marshall Dix; and one of the Leonard boys. They liked to travel in a pack, of which Jubal Beldon was the top dog. All the boys in the Beldon gang were low characters—impulsive, cruel, spoiling for a fight. And stupid, in her opinion, all but

Jubal. He was sly, like a weasel, or maybe more like a rat, with his quivery pointed snout sniffing the air for something rotten he could get into. Jubal Beldon reminded Ruth of one of her mother's clothespins, with legs entirely too long for his body. He was all out of proportion in a lot of ways. Nothing seemed to go together. One of his eyes was the color of thunderclouds and the other was milky white. He had a bitter little pursed mouth with a snaggle of teeth. His forehead bulged out, but he had a manly square jaw. All in all, Jubal was a startling sight, and a startling kind of fellow, to boot.

The others followed him around with their ears pricked up, and Jubal was just looking for some reason to say "sic 'em". Her father's cousin Scott Tucker, the town sheriff, called them the Bedlam Boys, always looking to cause trouble. People were scared of them, and that was all right by them.

Determined not to give them the satisfaction of seeing her anxiety, Ruth lowered her head and quickened her pace, hoping against hope the oncoming rowdies were in a hurry to get somewhere that had nothing to do with her.

She wasn't surprised that they weren't.

One of the brothers—Hosea, the second-oldest, she thought—turned his horse and fell in beside her as she walked. Two of the others followed suit, but Ruth was aware that the leader, Jubal, fell back to follow from a distance. "Where you off to, Ruth?" Hosea said.

Ruth didn't answer.

"Why, you're not very friendly today, are you?"

"This gal is never very friendly," Dave Walker observed.

"Well, that's because she's a Tucker," Hosea said. "They're too good for the likes of us, boys."

Ruth plunged on through the laughter and unsavory comments, trying to lengthen her stride but finding herself squeezed in.

"How 'bout it, Ruth? You think you're too good for us?" Hosea dismounted and moved up beside her. "How about a little kiss to let me know there ain't no hard feelings?"

The men snorted with laughter, and one of the others dismounted as well.

Ruth began to feel alarmed, but she kept her eyes on the wide, dusty road. She was somewhat comforted by the thought that if they tried to offer her bodily insult, they'd all most likely disappear mysteriously one day. If her father and brothers had anything to say about it, anyway.

Hosea stepped in front of her, forcing her to a halt. No one had put his hands on her yet, but one or another of them kept bumping her shoulder, her hip, her leg. She finally looked up, straight into his eyes.

"Let me pass."

Hoots and catcalls. It was as though the very fact of acknowledging their existence had emboldened them. They were touching her now, her hair, arms, shoulders. *What was going on?* She had always been the little tomboy running with her brothers and no fellow had ever given her a second look. Something had happened recently. She had noticed people eyeing her differently, behaving differently toward her. But not like this. Nobody had ever bothered her like this before and she had no idea what to do.

Beckie had come out onto her front porch to see what the hoo-hah was all about. Ruth's eyes clamped on the woman as though she were a lifeboat in a storm. She was about to call out, but Beckie figured out the problem pretty quickly and ducked back inside. Not five seconds later she reappeared with a broom in hand and strode down the porch steps. "You boys leave that child be!" she called, brandishing the broom like a club.

Miz Beckie may have been an old woman, Ruth admitted to herself, but she knew how to handle a bunch of unruly yahoos and she wasn't afraid to do it, either.

The Bedlam Boys turned as a group to see who was intent on spoiling their fun. The sight of a small elderly lady bearing down on them with a broom didn't seem to daunt them.

Not that Beckie was deterred by their laughter. She took a swing and caught young Dave Walker on his right shoulder. He staggered and his hat went flying. The mood turned ugly in an instant. Ruth forgot her fear and balled up a fist. She'd go down fighting to defend her protector.

Jubal prodded his horse forward a few steps and spoke for the first time. "Forget it, boys." He extended his arms to hold off the pending anarchy. The Walker boy and the third Beldon deflated quickly, but Hosea shot his brother a look that would freeze fire. He ignored the order.

"I ain't in the mood to forget it. I said I'd have a kiss and a kiss I'll have." He took a step toward Ruth.

"You'd *best* forget it, you hooligan." Beckie inserted herself between them. "I'll sic the sheriff on you. Not to mention my grandson is in town, and he won't tolerate disrespect to a lady."

"Is that so?" Hosea's tone was sarcastic. "Well, if we happen to come across any ladies, we'll keep that in mind. Come on, you lot."

The boys remounted grudgingly as Ruth took Beckie's arm and the two of them headed for the house as quickly as was seemly. Marva was standing on the porch, now, watching with an expression of alarm. Ruth wondered why Jubal, the head troublemaker, had backed off when his henchmen became unruly. It wasn't like he disapproved of their actions. More like he wanted to get a good view of the proceedings. So why had he stepped in as soon as Beckie showed up and it looked like things might get ugly? Against her better judgment Ruth cast a look back over her shoulder as she mounted the steps to the house. The gang had spurred their mounts and were galloping headlong toward town. All but Jubal. He was still sitting on his horse in the middle of the road, watching them. His expression was calculating, and maybe a little disappointed.

Beckie MacKenzie

"I reckon you saved my bacon, Miz Beckie." Ruth was sitting on the very edge of her chair in the parlor, across from Beckie, who seemed remarkably unaffected by the incident. Marva scuttled around the room, fluffing pillows behind Ruth's back and pouring tea to soothe their nerves.

"Oh, I doubt if you were in any real danger, Ruth dear. Boys will be boys. But I won't have any truck with such unseemly comportment."

Marva refrained from comment, but she did emit a derisive snort.

"I don't know, ma'am," Ruth said to Beckie. "That bunch is trouble for sure. Cousin Scott says he's got to keep an eye on them all the time. They're always up to mischief. He's always got one or another of them in the jail overnight for vandalism or fighting. He says it's just a matter of time till one or two end up in prison. My money's on that Hosea."

Marva spoke up. "Well, you keep shet of that Jubal, Miz Ruth, honey. If there was ever anybody looking to do harm it's Jubal Beldon, always telling nasty stories about folks whether they was true or not."

Ruth was surprised at the rancor in Marva's voice. "What do you mean, Marva?"

The look Marva gave her suggested that she thought she had said too much and didn't intend to be drawn into any more open criticism of a white man.

Beckie waved her hand. "Oh, Marva, quit fluttering around and sit down. If you've heard something about Jubal that dear Ruth should know, you'd best tell us."

Marva relented and perched herself on an ottoman. Never had anything to do with the man, myself," she said. "But I expect he said something to some kin of mine that made her quit working for a white family she liked. Don't matter if it's her fault or not. A colored girl can't be too careful about that kind of thing."

"When was this?" Ruth asked.

"Oh, a couple of years ago, at least. I ain't thought about it since." And that was all she was going to say about that.

Beckie shook her head. "Now, Ruth dear, a young lady must take great thought of her reputation. Next time a lad gives you any lip, you just lift your head high and plow right on by as if he wasn't there."

"Why do you think they did me like that, Miz Beckie? I wasn't doing anything to bother them."

Beckie gave her a knowing look. "Dear heart, boys will do anything to get the attention of a pretty young woman, even if they're too jugheaded to know the right way to go about it."

Ruth was startled at this pronouncement. What kind of idiot scared a girl to make her like him? It was pitiful, in a way. But it was hard to maintain a Christian attitude toward Jubal and his gang when they took such pleasure in the fear of others. And when did she become a pretty young woman?

Jubal Beldon

After the confrontation with Beckie MacKenzie, the Walker boy peeled off toward home. The Beldons continued on together, riding south until they reached the road that led to Morris and turned west, heading for their own farm. Nobody said a word as they rode to the corral and unsaddled their mounts.

Jubal threw his saddle over the top rail of the fence. "Zadok," he said to the younger brother, "that feeder is low. Bring up another bale of hay."

Zadok headed for the barn without comment. Hosea turned to follow him, but Jubal said, "Not you."

Hosea halted in his tracks, his head lowered and fists clinched, until Zadok was out of earshot. He turned around to face Jubal.

"Don't you never sass me again." Jubal's tone was menacing. "When I say stop your mischief, you stop it."

Hosea was only a year younger than Jubal and much better looking, with his even features and clear brown eyes. And in his own opinion, infinitely smarter. He was also smaller in stature, though that had never daunted him. Jubal had ridden roughshod over him all his life and their father had always taken Jubal's side. In fact, their daddy had seemed to enjoy seeing Jubal beat the wadding out of his younger brothers. Not that Hosea hadn't given as good as he got. When they were boys, Jubal never failed to get the best of him, but once they grew up, their fights were usually fifty-fifty propositions. After the old man died, Hosea had briefly held out hope that all the brothers would be on a more even footing, but it hadn't worked out that way. The old man had left everything he owned to Jubal and the younger brothers were too cowed to say anything about it.

Hosea's nostrils flared with hatred. "Or what?"

His hostility seemed to amuse Jubal. "Or I'll knock your teeth so far down your throat that you'll be chewing with your belly button."

"You want to try it?"

A childish shriek caused them both to start. "Mama, Jubal and Hosea are fixing to fight again!"

They turned to see their five-year-old sister Lovelle hanging over the corral railing, her rag doll dangling in one hand. Jubal casually slapped her off the fence. "Git, you little brat!" She sped off toward the house, crying for her mother.

Hosea was distracted just long enough. Before he knew what had happened, he was on his back in the dirt, staring at the sky and seeing stars in the middle of the day. He didn't have time to register the searing pain in his jaw. He didn't have time to register anything; not to think or plan or consider how to defend himself. Jubal kicked him in the side and he rolled into a fetal position, gasping for breath.

There was a pause, long enough for Hosea to realize that Jubal could kick him to death and there wouldn't be anything he could do to prevent it.

But Jubal didn't kick him to death. He didn't say anything, only turned around and walked away without a backward glance.

Hosea lay in the dirt for a little while, trying to catch his breath, as tears of pain and humiliation dribbled down his cheek. Eventually one of the horses wandered over and nosed him, curious. Hosea lifted himself to his hands and knees, then slowly got to his feet and stood with his arm over the horse's neck for support. He could see his mother standing by the back porch, comforting his bawling sister. Jubal was nowhere to be seen.

The wild, formless, burning resentment that Hosea had lived with all his life was no different after the beating than it was before. But he had learned a lesson. Don't give your enemies any warning before you strike.

Trenton Calder

I would no more have gone to eat dinner with Wallace MacKenzie than with Kaiser Wilhelm himself if Ruth hadn't invited me. Of course, if Ruth had invited me, I'd have had supper with the Kaiser, the whole German Army, and the Turks, too, as long as she was there.

I don't believe I had ever set foot in Miz Beckie MacKenzie's house before that evening. Her and me hardly ran in the same social circles. The most important things in Miz Beckie's life were her family, her music, and having Scotch blood. I never knew anybody so proud of the folks she came from.

Miz Beckie herself was born in South Carolina before the War Between the States, if I remember right, and she sounded like it. Except that she was always using these strange Scotch words. I think she had an idea that it made her sound interesting, but as far as I was concerned it just made her hard to understand.

That evening she was as gracious to me as if I'd been a regular gentleman. For Ruth's sake, I expect. Wallace shook my hand and pounded me on the back like I was a long lost friend, but he spent the rest of the night making sport at my expense. His fancy education hadn't changed him any. He was still as annoying as he had been when he was a brat. His friend Randal was another story, though. A fine fellow, it seemed to me, quiet and good-natured with a sharp wit. Made me wonder how him and Wallace got to be friends.

Ruth had made up quite a spread for the five of us—the fattest, juiciest pork chops I ever saw, with pan dressing, little creamed onions with tiny new potatoes, and cucumbers in vinegar. After we had all eaten ourselves silly, Miz MacKenzie said we should adjourn to the sitting room before dessert.

We mostly talked about the war in Europe and whether America was going to get in it, a topic which I thought wasn't all that good for digestion. But Wallace was on a tear about it, and whatever Wallace wanted to talk about was what we talked about. Ruth never liked to hear about the fighting but Wallace's grandma seemed as excited about him going off on a great adventure as he did. I've known folks like that, who don't have much of a handle on how things really are. Randal had a comment or two but Ruth didn't have much to say. When she stood up to bring in the dessert, I went to help her.

We passed through the dining room on our way to the kitchen, gathered up some of the plates off the table and took them into the kitchen. She wouldn't let me help her do the dishes. I tried to tell her that I sure had plenty of practice since my mother didn't believe that a boy ought to sit on his backside when a meal was cleared up any more than a girl. Ruth just scraped and stacked the plates and cups nice on the cabinet, and I sat at the table and watched while she sliced pieces of cake. She put them on fancy little dishes to carry back into the sitting room, along with a silver pot of coffee and a bowl of sweetened heavy cream.

Miz MacKenzie gave her a sly look when we came back in, Ruth carrying the big silver tray and me trailing along behind her with my hands dangling by my sides like a blockhead. Ruth put the tray on the tea table and passed around cake and coffee before she sat down next to Miz MacKenzie on the blue velvet settee. I perched my long self on the only open seat available, an ottoman next to the fireplace, and balanced my plate on my knee.

I don't know what her and Wallace and his friend had been talking about while we were gone but I reckon the war talk was done, because as soon as we were settled Miz MacKenzie commenced to questioning me about my family and my plans for the future. I didn't mind. I figured I could use the practice. If things went between me and Ruth like I hoped, before long I'd be answering for myself plenty to her daddy and mama.

When she went to ask me if I planned to join the Army, though, I didn't rightly have a good answer. Lots of people I admired were dead set against us getting involved in any war, but I knew that if we got into it I'd probably have to join up sooner or later. And in fact, after the U-boat attacks on American ships had started the year before, I had told Scott that I was eager for the adventure. But in spite of all my big talk I wasn't as keen to fight any more. The idea of leaving Ruth just when I had found her didn't much appeal to me.

My half-hearted answer served to get Wallace to rattling his saber again. "I'm eager for the warrior's life, Trent. It's the best way I know for a man to test himself, to come face-to-face with his demons and do battle with them. To find out what he's made of."

I heard Randal sigh, but he didn't say anything. Neither did I. Boynton wasn't much of a Sodom or a Gomorrah, either, but since I had been a deputy I had seen enough violence and foolish behavior to do me.

"A soldier's life can be verra noble," Miz MacKenzie said. "It's a life of great sacrifice, laddies, for the peace and safety of others." She eased herself back into her big armchair. "Both your grandfathers were soldiers in their time, Wallace, and your father, too. All acquitted themselves proudly on the field. My Dada, your great-grandda Hamilton Bruce, was a field surgeon with the 42nd Regiment of Foot, and fought under General Campbell at the Battle of Alma in fifty-four."

"Was that before he became an Admiral along with Nelson and then King of Scotland, Gram?" Wallace had heard it all before. He was teasing his grandmother, but Randal leaned forward.

"In the Crimea?"

Miz Beckie's eyes got wide. "Aye! Do you know about the Battle of Alma?"

"Medicine is my avocation, but history is my passion," Randal said. "That battle was a turning point of the Crimean war, largely due to the Black Watch."

Wallace flopped back in his chair. He looked put out, but he sounded amused. "Here we go again! You'll be sorry you got him started, Granny."

"What is Black Watch?" Ruth asked.

Randal turned to look at her. "That's the nickname for the British Army's 42nd Regiment of Foot. They're called that because the tartan they wear is so dark."

As far as I was concerned they might as well have been speaking Chinese. I had never heard of Crimea or the 42nd Regiment of Foot, and when it came to tartan, I had no idea what they were talking about. I'd have asked if I weren't ashamed of being so ignorant.

"Mama has a little piece of tartan cloth that her I-don't-know-how-many-greats grandfather brought over with him." Ruth made a little square with her fingers. "It's about yea big, kind of gray-brown, now, all faded. We don't know exactly what it was for, but the family story is that he was forbidden to have it in the old country and kept it hidden under his shirt until he came over here."

"Isn't your mother's maiden name Gunn? That's a Highland name, you know."

Wallace clapped his hand to his forehead. "Oh, no, Ruth! You've opened the barn door! Neither Randal or Gran can be stopped now."

Randal laughed, but Miz Beckie was affronted. "Well, Ruth dear, apparently Wallace has heard enough about tartans to last him a lifetime."

"I don't know, Miz MacKenzie," I said. "I'd like to hear about it."

Wallace stood up. "That's it for me."

His grandmother waved him back down. "Don't be rude, Wallace. Don't worry, we won't bore you. Thank you, Trent. Perhaps you'll come back for tea someday and I'll tell you and Ruth all about it." She turned to face Randal. "I still have my father's Black Watch regalia, Randal dear. He kept his entire uniform, from bonnet to ghillies. I'd never part with it for anything."

Randal straightened up, interested. "Oh, I'd love to see it, Miz Beckie."

"So would I," Ruth seconded, and I put in that I'd be interested in getting a gander myself. We all shot Wallace a sour look, but instead of throwing cold water on the proceedings, he volunteered to go upstairs and fetch it.

"I know right where it is, Gran. After all, you've made me look at it enough times."

He brought down from upstairs an old cedar-lined wooden box about three feet by three feet and maybe two feet deep, and placed it on the tea table in front of his grandmother's chair.

She opened the box like it contained treasure, which I guess to her it did. It was late in the day and not much sun left to come through the tall windows. At first it looked to me like the piece of cloth she drew out really was black. But when she held it up I could see that it was dark green and blue checks.

"This is his *feile-beag*," she said. "In English it's called a kilt."

It looked like a short skirt to me, heavy wool with sharp pleats all across the back. I'll admit that I was a mite shocked to think of a man wearing something like that. Especially a soldier! I didn't say a word, though. Ruth and Randal both looked real interested and even Wallace acted like a man wearing a skirt was the most natural thing in the world. Miz MacKenzie draped the kilt over her lap and commenced to drawing out the rest of the outfit, piece by piece, and telling us about each one, her voice as reverent as if she was describing Jesus' swaddling clothes.

"These are his hose and flashes..." The wildest tall checkered socks I ever did see, and some rags I figured he used for garters. "His uniform shirt..." Old-fashioned puffy sleeves, but at least it looked like a regular soldier's blouse, tan, with regimental insignia on the shoulder. "His sporran..." Looked like a lady's handbag to me. "His ghillies..." Shoes with a bunch of holes punched in them! "...and bonnet."

A bonnet! I declare. It was a dark blue color, broad and shapeless, and had a round silver pin on one side. All I could think was that these old Scotch soldiers must have been the meanest, most vicious, most brawl-loving, sons-of-guns ever born to wear a getup like that, because they wouldn't be able to step out the door without somebody trying to beat them up.

But then Miz MacKenzie lifted something out of the box that looked like either a real short sword or a terrible long knife, maybe two feet long, and I revised my opinion of the outfit right quick. It had a fancy carved wooden haft with an amber stone on the end of it, and the black leather-covered scabbard was chased with silver. She drew it out to let us see the blade. I leaned forward all eager to look at it, and the other fellows did, too. I was aware that instead of leaning in, Ruth drew back. I expect that's the difference between fellows and girls.

"This is called a dirk," Miz MacKenzie told us. "It's just for fancy dress, though, lads. I reckon folks stopped stabbing one another with these a hundred years ago." She slid the blade back into its scabbard and laid the dirk on the table before she reached into the box again. "Now, this…" She held up another knife, much smaller, maybe eight inches long in all, with a bone handle and a flat leather scabbard. "This is the kind of a knife that means business." She unsheathed it and held it point up in front of her face. "Da called this a *sgian dubh*, a black knife. So called because you used it whenever you were in a black situation, children. Your knife of last resort. You keep it tucked into your hose, like this." She showed us by holding it down beside her calf.

We fellows clamored to have a look and she let us pass it around while she refolded the uniform and carefully put all the pieces back into the chest. When it came around to me, I ran my thumb along the wicked little blade. One edge was grooved and the other was razor-sharp, like a skinning knife, and it came to a point at the end. I recognized a fine weapon when I saw one and handed it back to the old lady with regret.

After she closed the lid, she sat looking down at the box on the table before her, lost in her memories. When she looked up again, she smiled. "This will be yours some day, Wallace. I hope you'll cherish it as much as I do."

I expected Wallace to make a smart remark, but to my surprise he said the right thing for once. "It'll be doubly dear to me, Gran, since it means so much to you."

Miz MacKenzie teared up for a second, but took herself in hand right quick. "I'm glad to hear it, dear. Someday I'll impose upon you to try it on for me. You resemble my dearest Da, in size and coloring at least, and I'd love to see how it looks on you once before I die."

"That would be an excellent idea, Wallace," Randal seconded.

Wallace grinned. "Perhaps that can be arranged, Grandmother, some dark night when no one is around and all the curtains are drawn."

Josie Cecil

The First Christian Church had moved around quite a bit since its founding shortly after the town of Boynton, Oklahoma, came into being in 1902. For a while the congregation met on the second floor above the Bank of Oklahoma. Then when the membership grew too large for that location, the church moved to the Masonic Hall. The hall was a perfectly adequate location for several years, certainly big enough to accommodate the church's growth. But after all, a church needs a permanent home, same as a person.

For the past couple of years, the elders and deacons had been raising money to buy land and raise a building. But the Lord does provide, and recently the North Methodist Church had consolidated with the South Methodist Church and the two congregations had moved in together, leaving the North location vacant. The church was a perfectly lovely little red-brick building with a bell tower and steeple on one end. The ground floor held the sanctuary, and the basement contained a fellowship hall and a couple of rooms just right for Sunday School classes.

The new pastor, Mr. Bennet, and Mr. Skidmore, the Sunday School superintendent, called an emergency meeting of the governing board the minute they heard that the North Methodists were vacating. The board voted unanimously to put in a bid on the building, and the Methodists accepted.

The first meeting in the newly dedicated church was scheduled for the first day of July, so to commemorate the last service in the Masonic Hall at the end of June, the ladies of the church planned a big picnic to be held after the last Amen was said.

Considering that it had been a cool, mild spring to now, the final Sunday of June was hot and dry and crackling. While the women unpacked the pies and soups and salads and cold meats they had carefully brought from home in crates and baskets, and laid them out on the long board-and-sawhorse tables under the trees, the men and children milled about, impatient and hungry, fanning themselves and talking too loudly. Mrs. Bennet stood at one end of the picnic table and Alafair's sister-in-law, Josie Cecil, stood at the other, directing the proceedings with the efficiency of a couple of sergeant majors.

You couldn't swing a cat, Alafair thought, *without hitting a Tucker.* Shaw's mother, Sally, and stepfather, Peter McBride, sat on hardback chairs under a spreading live oak, holding forth among the rest of the elders. Shaw and various of his brothers, cousins, and neighbors were arrayed along the side of the building and energetically discussing whether or not the United States should get involved in Mexico and how the European war had affected the price of cotton.

With their blessed events pending, John Lee and Phoebe had decided to stay home, as had Alice and Walter. But her eldest girls, Martha and Mary, were there, which pleased Alafair no end. The youngsters had organized a game of baseball in the field to the west of the building—all but Alafair's youngest, Grace, who was still unwilling to let her mother out of her sight after their month-long separation earlier in the year.

Ruth and Beckie were inside the hall, planning the post-picnic sing-along and hymns for the afternoon prayer meeting. Since Beckie was a Presbyterian, her presence at this special service showed in what high regard she held her protégée.

Alafair and Martha stood at the end of the table and sliced pies, chatting happily with Josie. It was quite a while before Alafair noticed that her helper Grace had acquired a playmate and abandoned her post at her mother's side. Grace was sitting in the grass, engaged in make-believe with a very blond child just a little older than she. It took Alafair a moment to recognize Lovelle Beldon, the youngest by far of the Beldon brood.

"Is Mildrey Beldon here?" Alafair asked her sister-in-law, surprised. "I never saw her during the service."

Josie's gaze followed Alafair's. "Oh, yes, Mildrey came in late and sat at the back with Lovelle. There she is yonder." The mother of the Beldon brood was standing at the center of the table, dishing out baked beans. Josie snorted out what could have been a laugh. "I don't see any of them boys, I'm glad to say."

Martha smiled. "Poor Miz Beldon. She's a nice woman. I never could figure out how such a kind creature managed to raise so many wastes of breath."

There were six Beldon boys in all; Jubal, Hosea, Ephraim, Hezekiah, Zadok, and Caleb. That's how many tries it had taken Mildrey to produce the golden-haired light of her life who was now creating a doll town with Grace. Lovelle was five years old. The youngest son Caleb was twenty.

"Well, I hate to speak ill of the dead," Josie said under her breath, preparing to do just that. "But I blame the daddy. It takes a good daddy to raise good men."

Alafair shook her head. "All Mildrey's affection seems to be lavished on that girl."

"Well, Mildrey long gave up her hopes of a daughter before Lovelle made her surprise entrance into the world." Josie sounded quite sure of herself. "Mildrey Beldon has a lot of love in her, and all those boys don't appear to be interested in anything about their mother except her cooking."

Alafair thought that was probably true. All the boys were grown, but not one of them had bestirred himself to marry. They all seemed happy enough to let their mother look after them. Except for Jubal, they were something of a worthless lot, as far as Alafair could see.

Mildrey Beldon

Josie waved at Mildrey. "Hey, Mildrey, come on up here and help us dish out pie!"

Mildrey looked surprised by the invitation. She may have been known around town as a good Christian woman, but she bore the taint of her hooligan sons, and few ladies went out of their way to befriend her.

She cast a glance behind to make sure that Josie hadn't been calling to someone else, and when she could find no other candidates for the invitation, made her way down the length of the table and squeezed in next to Alafair.

Josie Cecil was a force to be reckoned with; tall and buxom, black-haired, with warm, laughing, no-nonsense, hazel eyes. She had no truck with gossip and was skeptical of popular opinion. She had told Alafair more than once that she was perfectly capable of making her own decisions about folks, thank you very much.

Mildrey had probably been a pretty woman in her youth, but a lifetime of drudgery had ravaged whatever beauty she had once possessed. Her face was seamed and her blue eyes sad and faded, but the light brown hair rolled into a chignon was still thick and lustrous.

Alafair and Martha each gave her a welcoming smile and Mildrey answered with a tentative smile of her own. But it was Josie who broke the ice. "How nice to see you again, Mildrey! I swan, you've been making yourself scarce of late. What have you been getting yourself up to?"

"Nothing interesting, I guarantee," Mildrey said. "Y'all know how it is when you've got a farm to run and a passel of mouths to feed." She looked at Alafair for confirmation.

Alafair obliged. "I can attest to the truth of that."

Josie relieved Mildrey of the empty plate she was clutching and began to cover it with slices of pie and cake. The oldest of Shaw Tucker's several siblings, Josie had been mothering everyone she came in contact with since before she could remember. "I see Lovelle over yonder. My, but she has grown! What a pretty child."

The smile that lit Mildrey's face as she contemplated her darling made her look years younger. "She's a fine girl, too. Never has give me a lick of trouble in her life."

"Can't say that for boys, can you? They're always getting up to something and giving their ma cause to tear her hair." The mother of three boys herself, Josie felt entitled to offer the judgment.

Mildrey's smile was wry. "No, you can't."

"I heard that Mr. Turner fired your youngest from the livery stable after just two weeks."

Josie's comment stung. Mildrey's expression made that obvious. "That's so."

"Got in a fistfight when Hec Lawrence criticized the way he cinched a saddle," Josie continued, ever sympathetic but unaware of her effect on the embarrassed mother.

Alafair glanced at Martha, who nodded and slipped away.

"I expect your boy is back on the farm with you," Josie continued blithely. "Now, if he was my young'un...oh, look here!"

Martha was approaching with Josie's daughter-in-law, who was holding in her arms the apple of Josie's eye, her infant grandchild. Alafair took advantage of the distraction to put her hand on Mildrey's arm. "I see a couple of empty chairs over there under the hickory tree. Let's us go have a seat." Mildrey looked glad for the easy escape.

"Josie don't mean anything," Alafair assured her as they walked. "She'd give you her last nickel without you asking."

Mildrey nodded. "I know it. Miz Cecil has been mighty good to me since D.J. crossed over."

"How are y'all doing out there without D.J.?" Alafair asked, as soon as they got settled in their chairs. The patriarch of the Beldon clan had passed into the arms of the Lord earlier that year, leaving Mildrey to the tender mercies of their six unmarried sons.

Mildrey shrugged. "Nothing's changed much." She didn't seem overly upset about her recent widowhood. "I was afeared at first that all them boys would run amok. I mean even worse than they did beforehand. D.J. pretty much made them toe the line, at least when they was around him. He left the farm lock, stock, and barrel to Jubal, as long as I can live there for the rest of my natural life, so at least he done me that good. I about half-expected Jubal to kick his brothers to the road, but he didn't.

They ain't much in the way of farmhands, but they don't cost nothing and they're better than nobody, I reckon. That's what D.J. always said, anyway."

"Do they pay mind to Jubal like they did their daddy?"

"Well, they do. Somehow he manages to keep a lid on their shenanigans, though I don't expect they like it much. Especially the second one, Hosea. Them two always butted heads since they was little. I don't know why Hosea hasn't took himself off a long time ago. I guess working for Jubal is easier than having to find a real job of work. Not that any of them confide in me, don't you know."

Alafair looked down at her plate to hide her expression as Mildrey described her problematic sons. She hated to think how it would feel to be the mother of a bunch of bullies.

Mildrey seemed to read her mind. "Well, D.J. was always mighty rough with the boys. As soon as they started coming along, D.J. decided that it was his duty to make men out of them. He made them fight one another to settle their differences. He wouldn't let them stop whaling at each other until he seen blood or one of them was too beat up to go on. There was never any giving up or making peace. So I reckon I can't blame them much for being like they are. Now, Jubal, he don't enjoy violence like the others. Even so, when he got big enough, he hauled off and whopped his daddy and that was that. I think D.J. was proud of him for standing up for himself. After that it was like Jubal was D.J.'s deputy, and the other boys were the outlaws."

Well, that explains a lot, Alafair thought. As far as the Beldon boys were concerned, Jubal had taken his father's place as the new sheriff in town.

"So where are your boys now?" Alafair asked. "I didn't see any of them at church."

"They ain't very churchy. Jubal brought me and Lovelle in. Said he'd be back this afternoon to carry us home. I left the rest of them abed this morning."

Wallace MacKenzie

The conversation was interrupted by a sudden commotion among the congregation gathered under the trees. It sounded like laughter and good-natured whooping. Alafair stood up to get a better look. "What in the world?"

Ruth and Beckie MacKenzie had left the hall and were threading their way through the crowd, followed close by a dark, good-looking fellow whom Alafair didn't know. Ruth had noticed her mother standing under the hickory tree and was steering her companions toward them just as the crowd parted, and Alafair caught sight of a man with yellow hair, dressed in the most outlandish garb she had ever seen: kilt, blue bonnet, purse, tall socks, red ribbons, and all. She had never heard such hooting and hollering. A dozen men blocked his way, slapping his back and making bad jokes, but he took it in stride with a big smile, and gave as good as he got. He was still grinning when he made his way over to the women.

"I do declare!" Alafair exclaimed, and began to laugh. She turned to share the joke with Mildrey Beldon, but she had disappeared. Martha and Josie joined the knot of gawkers next to Alafair.

Ruth made the introductions. "Mama, you remember Wallace MacKenzie."

Alafair didn't, really. Or maybe she just didn't immediately recognize the elegant man with the floppy blond hair who was bowing over her hand. The last time she had seen Wallace he was an irritating and rather sneaky fifteen-year-old. "Sure, I do," she said.

Josie wiped the tears of laughter from her eyes. "I heard you were home, Wallace. You're dressed as fancy as the King of Diamonds, son! Whatever are you supposed to be?"

Beckie was surprised. "Why, Josie, this is the very regimental dress uniform that my father brought with him when he came to South Carolina back in the fifties. Wallace is wearing his great-grandda's kilt this afternoon just to please me, the dear bairn." She looked proud enough to bust.

Ruth leaned in and took her mother's hand. "Wallace is wearing the outfit Miz Beckie showed us when we had dinner at her house," she reminded her. "I told you about it, Mama."

From the wicked grin on Wallace's face, Alafair thought that he was more likely wearing the outfit because he enjoyed making a spectacle of himself. He winked at her, confirming her suspicions. "Anything to please Gran," he said.

Ruth pushed forward the more soberly dressed, dark-haired youth who had arrived with them. "And this is Wallace's friend from Vanderbilt, Randal Wakefield."

Dark-eyed Randal smiled and squeezed her hand gently. His quiet manner made Alafair look at him with a great deal more interest than she did the ebullient Wallace.

Ruth Tucker

The shadows were lengthening when the final prayer meeting in the Masonic Hall came to an end, and families were gathering themselves together, preparing for the trip home at the end of a satisfying day of fellowship. Ruth stood up from the piano and cast her gaze around the auditorium for a face she recognized.

Her parents were nowhere to be seen. She could just see the heads of her brothers topping the crowd in the far corner, Gee Dub's black curls and Charlie's straight dark-blond, both leaning in toward a copper-gold redhead on their own level. Nobody but Trenton Calder had hair the color of a brazen sunset. She smiled and started toward them, almost shifting course when she caught sight of Beckie. At the last instant she noticed that Wallace was standing with his grandmother, and she managed to veer back into the crowd without being seen. She ran right into Jubal Beldon.

A word occurred to her that would never have passed her lips. When did he show up? He must have come to take his mother and sister home after the service. Jubal gave a brief grin that revealed just a glimpse of crooked teeth. "Well, howdy, Ruth Tucker," he said. "We meet again."

She opened her mouth to tell him that it was no pleasure, but Beckie's advice about feigning disinterest popped into her head. She made an effort to move on without looking him in the eye, but Jubal wasn't so easily put off. He seized her arm. "You handled yourself good out there on the road the other day. I like a brave gal. How about stepping outside with me for a nip of something more refreshing than lemonade and we'll talk about it?"

Later, when she was pondering what better reaction she could have had, she realized that her sister Martha would have frozen Jubal to the ground with a glare, Mary would have laughed in his face, Alice would have spit in his eye, and Phoebe would have faded into the crowd like mist. But this was the trouble with being a well-bred and rather inexperienced girl. Her first instinct was to be polite. After all, it had been Jubal who had put an end to his brothers' devilment on the road earlier that week. He couldn't be as bad as all that.

"No, thank you, Jubal," she said. "If you'll excuse me, I'm going to meet my brothers."

She started to walk away but to her surprise he didn't release her arm. Her forehead furrowed, and she looked up at him. Another glimpse of those snaggle teeth. "Oh, I think you will." She was too surprised to resist when he hauled her by the elbow a few feet, through a bunch of chatting matrons into the relative privacy of a corner. She gathered her wits enough to shake his hand off of her.

"What are you doing?" she managed. "I said I don't want to…"

Jubal took a step toward her and Ruth took a step back. The wall halted her retreat. She looked away, but Jubal leaned in so close that Ruth could feel his breath on her cheek.

"You'd better be nice to me, Missy." His voice insinuated itself into her ear. He drew back enough for Ruth to sidle out of his way, but he grabbed her arm again before she could escape. "I could ruin your reputation real easy. Folks love to spread gossip. It don't even have to be true."

"Is this lowlife bothering you, Ruth?"

She whirled around to face Wallace, who was standing so close to her that she nearly bumped her nose on his chest. She didn't know whether to be relieved or dismayed.

Well, better the devil you know… "Yes, Wallace, thank you." Her voice was breathy. "I think I've had enough of this conversation so if y'all will excuse me."

Neither man moved and she found herself caught between them. She suddenly knew how a doe felt caught between two stags in rut.

"Mind your own business, fancy pants," Jubal growled. "Or should I say fancy no-pants? What kind of gimcrack are you supposed to be?"

"How would you like a punch in the eye, Jubal, just on general principle?"

People in their vicinity began to take notice of Jubal Beldon and Wallace in his silly outfit standing nose to nose and squeezing Ruth in the middle like a piece of cheese in a sandwich.

"Where's your girlfriend, MacKenzie?" Jubal was saying.

Ruth didn't understand. Was he referring to her? "I'm not his girlfriend," she said, and Jubal smiled his unpleasant smile without looking at her.

Wallace struck a boxer's pose. "Put up your dukes, Beldon!"

That was the last straw. Ruth felt the blood rush to her cheeks and she wrenched herself free just as Preacher Bennet and a couple of other men stepped in.

"None of that, boys," Mr. Bennet said as Ruth made her escape into the crowd. "This is a church meeting, and I'll have no brawling."

Shaw Tucker

After they had their fill of making sport of Wallace, Shaw and various other male members of the congregation returned to the business at hand: whether or not the United States would get into the European war. Only weeks earlier Congress had nationalized all the state militias and renamed them the National Guard, then immediately mobilized the Oklahoma organization for duty on the Mexican border. Several families had sons and fathers in Texas at that moment, and no one was happy about it.

Why nationalize the militias? Did this mean that war was imminent? But at the Democratic Presidential Convention last week Mr. Wilson had promised to keep us out of war. The Republican nominee, Mr. Hughes, said Wilson's policies made war more likely…

The almost-donnybrook between Jubal Beldon and Wallace MacKenzie interrupted the lively conversation.

At first, Shaw was alarmed to see his daughter Ruth caught between the combatants, but she extricated herself quickly and made away into the crowd. Shaw laughed as Jubal and Wallace circled one another. "Looks like Wallace's getup is causing him some grief."

His brother James Tucker was just as amused. "Aw, that boy always did hanker to be the center of attention. He'd be disappointed if somebody didn't kick up a row over him."

Shaw voiced his disapproval. "Leave it to Jubal Beldon to turn merriment into a big shindy."

His neighbor, Mr. Eichelberger, narrowed his eyes. "That fellow is mean as cat meat. I hate him."

Eichelberger's tone was so venomous that the joking ceased and his companions glanced at one another in surprise. The Tuckers and Eichelbergers had lived down the road from one another for nearly twenty-five years, since Shaw had first moved his family onto his homestead. The happy, energetic, little farmer had helped him build his house, and Mrs. Eichelberger was indispensable help to Alafair when the children were babies. Shaw loved the Eichelbergers like his own aunts and uncles. He had never known Mr. Eichelberger to say a bad word about anyone. Until now.

"Jubal is always on the shoot, it's true," Shaw ventured. "Has he been grieving you, Mr. Eichelberger?"

The question gave Eichelberger pause. He blinked at Shaw before responding. "Never mind, son. He's just mean, is all. He's the kind who'd pull the wings off flies."

Shaw's brother-in-law Jack Cecil shook his head. "I don't know. He's good to animals. Once I saw Jubal bust a guy's nose for mistreating his horse."

Eichelberger's face reddened. "Well, he's the kind who'd pull the arms off people, then. I wouldn't be broke up if young MacKenzie mashed in his ugly face."

James took the opportunity to lighten the mood. "How would you tell the difference?"

Trenton Calder

That old Jubal Beldon was a piece of work, all right. Me and Gee Dub and Charlie were standing over by the door. We fellows had been talking about going outside for a smoke, joking about how far away from the hall we'd have to walk to make sure our mothers never got wind of it. That's when Ruth came up to us, white as a sheet, and said that Beldon had been rude to her. But she didn't let on about his threats. Not right then, anyway.

Charlie didn't take it very serious, but Gee Dub got real quiet. He never had much use for any of them Beldons in the first place, and besides, him and Ruth were kind of close, them being the two exact middle kids in that pack of ten. Her tale upset me, too, a lot more than it would have two weeks earlier.

See, she was too good-hearted to realize that you've got to stomp on that kind of guy's foot to get him to leave you alone, or do something else about that plain. I offered to rearrange Jubal's face for him, and I was serious, too. For some reason she laughed. I was affronted, at least until I saw that my offer had made her feel better.

Gee Dub was perched to take action, too; take her home, or give Beldon what for, or tell their daddy about it. Ruth said she was sorry she had told us if it was going to stir up our manly instincts so. Charlie got impatient and wandered off to find somebody else to talk to about the war, so I asked Ruth if she'd like to dance.

Durn if she didn't laugh again and say that if we went to dancing and the preacher Mr. Bennet saw us, we were like to get drummed right out of the First Christian Church of Boynton. Besides, since she was the piano player for the evening, it would be mighty hard for her to make the music and dance to it at the same time. So we went off to get something to eat.

Gee Dub stayed where he was, and when I looked back over my shoulder at him he was watching us with one eyebrow raised and a quirk of a smile on his face. For some reason that made me want to make sure my drawers were hitched up and my hat was on straight.

Ruth was in a better mind after that, but I caught her throwing the odd nervous glance Jubal Beldon's way. If he glanced back at her, I didn't notice it.

Alafair Tucker

It had grown hot in the hall, so Alafair and Martha stepped outside for some air and relative quiet. They were hardly alone. There were nearly as many groups of people standing around outside the door as there were milling about inside. The two women took off, arm-in-arm, for a brisk, refreshing stroll around the building.

The Masonic Hall sat on a large lot with a bare dirt field to the south side. The field was rife with vehicles at the moment, buggies, wagons, and automobiles, some still parked, some loaded with tired parishioners who were beginning to move toward the road, raising an irritating dust that just made the heat more uncomfortable. The back of the building was treed and grassy, making it seem cooler and more peaceful. As they passed by the noisy dirt lot, Martha called her mother's attention to two or three groups of men discussing politics over a cigarette and a clandestine sip or two from something that resembled a hip flask. Mother and daughter exchanged a good-natured comment about human folly as they rounded the corner to the back of the hall. It was quieter here. A fresh, damp smell rose up from the ground. Martha squeezed Alafair's arm and nodded discreetly toward a boy and a girl standing head-to-head under an elm at the edge of the lot. The women had almost reached their next turn when Alafair caught sight of another duo sitting next to one another on a tree stump.

Wallace and Randal were both staring quietly into space, not speaking, or even looking at one another. Wallace had propped his hands on his knees, and Randal had crossed one ankle over a knee. One of his hands rested casually on Wallace's thigh.

"Hello, boys," Alafair called. "Taking a break?"

The men leaped to their feet. It was Wallace who replied. "Yes, ma'am. I felt the need to catch my breath after the last round of caterwauling."

"I believe Wallace underestimated the jovial reaction to his attire." Randal gave Alafair a knowing wink.

Martha laughed. "Yes, Wallace, you have provided quite the occasion for comment. How are you finding life in a kilt?"

"To tell the truth, Miss Tucker, it's a mite breezy for my liking. But I think it had the desired result of making my grandmother happy, so I don't mind."

Randal threw an arm across his friend's shoulders. "Yes, ladies, Wallace here may be a scalawag, but I've always known him to do the kind thing, if pressed, even if it does cause a hullabaloo!"

"Especially if it causes a hullabaloo," Wallace responded, "or else what fun is it?"

The gentlemen offered their arms to the ladies, and the four of them made their way back into the Masonic Hall together. None of them noticed Jubal Beldon, standing half-hidden by the shrubbery at the corner, watching them.

◇◇◇

They were met just inside the door by Shaw, trotting toward them with Chase Kemp and Grace in tow. "Alafair, honey!" he called, and they stopped in their tracks, alarmed. "Mr. Bennet says Alice just telephoned his wife and asked them to find us. She's having the baby right now! Doctor Ann is already at her house."

Shaw and Alafair locked eyes, Wallace MacKenzie and his silly outfit suddenly forgotten as they contemplated the pending birth of their second grandchild. Shaw grinned and gave her a little push. "Well, go on then. I'll get the children headed home and be around when I can."

Trenton Calder

When I heard that Alice Kelley's first chick was about to hatch, me and her brother Gee Dub were directing traffic over to the field where everybody was trying to leave for home at once. Those who were on horses or driving teams were losing patience with the automobile folks, who seemed to think that having an internal combustion engine on their buggies just naturally gave them the right-of-way. Scott said he wasn't in the mood to bust up fights, so as soon as he heard raised voices, he sent me over there to keep the peace and Gee Dub came along to help.

Gee Dub's daddy gave us the news at about the time the last rig pulled out. Gee Dub decided that since he had ridden in on his own horse, he'd go on over to Alice's with his ma and his sisters Martha and Ruth and reconnoiter for a bit, instead of riding home right then with his dad and the rest of the youngsters. Seemed like the family was all in a party mood, so when Ruth asked me if I wanted to come to Alice's with her, I figured why not? She said she didn't aim to stay long and I could escort her back to Miz MacKenzie's later, and that sounded like a fine idea to me.

When Miz Tucker and all of us arrived at her daughter's house, Doc Addison's wife, Ann, was already there. Everybody called her Doctor Ann even though she was a midwife and not really a doctor. She had delivered near to every baby in town under the age of twenty-five, including me.

Alice's husband, Walter, was nowhere to be seen.

Now, I liked Walter Kelley. He was the busiest barber in town, with a three-seat shop right on Main Street and a real nice house over on Second. He could tell a good story like nobody I ever knew, and after five minutes in his chair you'd be laughing until you were in tears. But the look that came over Miz Tucker's face when she saw that Walter was missing caused me to figure there were limits to his charm.

Not that he was avoiding the birth of his first child on purpose. Seems he was unaware that the event was imminent when he left his wife alone and went to play cards with his buddies.

I never did see Alice. She was already in the bedroom, and none of us fellows had any desire to go in and say howdy. Miz Tucker and Martha followed Dr. Ann in, though, while Gee Dub and Ruth and me made ourselves to home in the parlor. I was itching to leave, but Ruth decided she wanted to stay for the duration and I had no idea how long that would be. I still had a notion that I could see her back to Miz MacKenzie's house before it got entirely too late.

That's when Miz Tucker came out of the bedroom and waved Gee Dub and me over. Her sour expression could have curdled milk. She told Gee Dub that Walter was on her bad side and she had no particular desire to inform him of what was happening, but Alice had seemed to want him there and we should go get him. When Gee Dub asked where Walter had gotten off to, his ma pulled him close and whispered into his ear. Gee Dub nodded, but I couldn't tell what his opinion of the situation was. That's the way that boy was. He played it close to the vest. All he said was, "Come on, Trent."

Since I was only there because of Ruth, I didn't really want to go, but I wasn't foolish enough to cross Miz Tucker right about then.

"If you run into Daddy, best say nothing about Walter's whereabouts if you can avoid it, son," Miz Tucker said to Gee Dub as we headed out to fetch the prodigal husband. "We don't want Alice's child to be an orphan before it ever sees the light of day."

Wallace MacKenzie

As the church picnic wound down, a childhood friend of Wallace's had invited him and Randal over for a visit and Beckie had urged them to go. "Y'all don't need to accompany me. Marva is at the house," she told them.

So Wallace and his two friends had gone off, looking like a peacock and two wrens walking down the street together, and left Beckie to make her way home on her own.

The young men didn't stay at Wallace's friend's house long. Just enough to fill each other in on what had happened in their lives over the two years that Wallace had been away.

But it had been a long afternoon and a busy day. Randal had met as many strangers as he cared to, and Wallace was hot and itchy in the wool tartan and had had enough sport to satisfy even him.

The sun was well to the west by the time they got back to Beckie's. They could barely see the man who was standing in the deep shade beside the carriage house. A glowing point of orange arced through the air as he removed a cigarette from his mouth and let it hang casually at his side, dangling from his fingers.

Wallace felt goose flesh rise on his arms. He stopped at the bottom of the steps at his grandmother's back porch. "Who is that?"

"He looks familiar," Randal said, loud enough for the stranger to hear. "Like an odd-shaped scarecrow, Wally. Like the man you mortally insulted today at the church potluck. That Beldon fellow."

The shadow man detached himself from the carriage house wall and strolled toward them.

"Looks like he wants to talk to us," Wallace noted.

"So it does, Wall, though I cannot imagine what the likes of him might want to say to the likes of you."

Wallace moved closer to his friend and dropped his voice. "I think we'd better dust off our knuckles, for I fear we may be needing to use them pretty quick."

"He seems to be alone and there are two of us," Randal observed, "so I'd be surprised if he's here to pick a fight,"

The two young men stood their ground and made no attempt to meet Jubal Beldon halfway. Neither did Jubal seem to be in a rush to reveal his purpose when he finally stopped in front of them. He took a long drag on his cigarette, dropped it, and ground it under his heel before he spoke.

"Been waiting for you."

"So it seems, Mr. Beldon. I can't imagine you're here to continue our reasoned exchange of ideas, so what can I do for you?" Wallace's tone was heavy with sarcasm.

Jubal smiled. "Nothing. There ain't nothing you can do for me. There ain't nothing you can do at all."

Had it been anyone else in the world who had uttered these words, Wallace would have asked him what he meant, or laughed, or been annoyed, but the sultry weather, the crooked smile, and the satisfied tone of Jubal's voice combined to cause Wallace a stab of irrational fear.

Randal saved him from the effort it would have taken him to speak. "What do you want?" He barked out the sentence, betraying his own fear.

"I'm on my way to the sheriff's office. Going to let him know that we've got us a couple of perverts in town. Then I'm going to pass the word around town. I reckon y'all will either be on your way to prison or lynched by morning."

There was an instant of stunned silence before the two young men spoke over each other.

"You can't…"

"What are you talking about?"

The snaggle-toothed smile was accompanied by a low chuckle this time. "I knew right away, when you come tripping into the Masonic Hall in your darling little frock there, MacKenzie. Why, I should have figured you out years ago, you pansy. Then you come back to town with your sweetheart in tow. Yes, it hit me like a brick. Then I seen y'all. Right there behind the hall, sitting on a stump with your heads together, canoodling. There ain't no use to deny it. I ain't blind. I stood there for quite a spell. If them ladies hadn't come by there's no telling what you might have got up to."

Wallace MacKenzie may have been a spoiled and self-indulgent man, but he was neither stupid nor a coward. Randal made a noise, and Wallace put his hand on his friend's arm to silence him. "You're insane, Beldon. Yes, you've purely lost your mind, that's how I see it, because you didn't see anything. Do you think for a minute that anybody is going to believe such an outrageous lie? Why, most of the folks in this town have known me since I was knee-high. And there isn't anybody in the county who doesn't love my grandmother. Now, we both know what everybody thinks of you. So who do you think the sheriff is going to believe?"

"Oh, times have changed, fancy boy. There ain't nobody going to take a chance that there's a cancer living among us. They're going to cut it out. Or string it up." Jubal pantomimed the jerk of a noose around his neck and emitted another nasty chuckle. "And don't fool yourself, you filth. Even if there wasn't a war coming, folks love to believe the worst. Nobody likes you that much, anyway."

Wallace felt the tremor that passed through Randal's body. He dropped his hand from his friend's arm and took a step forward. "Why are you here, Beldon? Why come here alone and wait in the shadows, without your posse, to warn us of what you intend to do? If we're such a danger and blight, why not gather all your slimy brothers and thimble-headed friends, grab us up off the street and string us up? Could it be that you want something?"

"I want you to know. I want you to be a-waiting for the law or the lynch mob. I want you to know that you're finished, both of you, you sodomites."

"Are you stupid? Now that you've warned us, we'll be gone before you can bring anybody back for us!"

"Oh, you can run, but I don't expect you'll be able to get too far. Sheriff'll put out wanted bulletins on y'all. No more college for you, or the Army, neither. You are ruined and so are your families. Your rich snooty old grandma ain't going to be able to hold her head up in this town ever again, MacKenzie."

Jubal didn't sound angry or righteous when he delivered his message. He sounded downright pleased, and that was the worst thing of all.

Wallace felt curiously calm. He felt sorrier for Randal than for himself, and more sorry for his grandmother than for either of them. "How much will it take for you to keep your mouth shut?"

Jubal growled. "I don't want no money."

"So you say. But men have been known to change their minds when they're staring at a pile of greenbacks."

A pile of greenbacks. Jubal took a breath, preparing to fling a dusty reply at him.

But nothing was forthcoming, and had his very life not been hanging in the balance, Wallace might have smiled. He seized his opportunity. "I've got our trip money upstairs, almost two hundred dollars. "

Jubal thought for a moment. This was not his plan. He was not a blackmailer. He purely enjoyed knowing things about people, things that they wouldn't be proud for anyone to know, and now he had the power to act upon his knowledge. People were afraid of him, he knew that. His neighbors, people who had always despised him and his brothers, and thought they were better than him, were afraid of what he could do to them. The fact pleased him.

When by sheer accident he had seen Wallace and Randal together, he knew he had hit the jackpot. It didn't matter if it was true or not. The very accusation would mean the end of both of them. This piece of information had given him the power of life or death over two human beings, and for the past hours he had been savoring his knowledge and carefully considering the best way to use it to his own advantage. In the end he had decided it would please him most to see this smart-mouthed, spoiled rotten ponce spend a few years in prison, or maybe even something deliciously worse.

But two hundred dollars. That gave Jubal pause. He could get clean to China with two hundred dollars. Or fix up the farm and buy another quarter-section of land. Folks might look at him with a little respect if he had two hundred dollars.

Wallace and Randal stood together in the eerie light, silent and still as deer watching a panther, while Jubal Beldon thought. What he thought was, *There's no reason I can't see them two swing and have two hundred dollars to boot.*

"Let's see this money," he said at last.

"It's up in my room. I'll have to fetch it."

"Go on then, and make it fast. Not you!" Jubal pointed at Randal as the two turned to head up the steps. "You stay right here till he gets back with the money. If both of you go, I'm heading for the sheriff."

Wallace barged up the steps alone and fumbled across the enclosed porch, through the back door, and into the kitchen. The sky was pale and white as the sun sank toward the horizon, but inside, the house was already eerily dark. Marva was in the kitchen, and Wallace tried to look as normal as possible as he waved at her in passing. He felt his way through the hall, and up the stairs, unwilling to turn on a light lest he alert his grandmother. He closed his bedroom door behind him and pulled the chain on the electric lamp by his bedside. His hands were trembling so much that he could hardly open the drawer that held his leather wallet.

He removed two hundred dollars, folded it, and stuck it into his sporran before turning off the light and slipping down the stairs and out the back door.

Randal and Jubal were standing just as he had left them, eyeing one another suspiciously. Randal's posture was stiff, his fists clinched at his side. Jubal's stance was an insolent slouch. Wallace expected it was a good thing he had hurried because he knew Randal well enough to know that he was almost at the end of his tether.

Both men turned their heads to look at him as he opened the screen and stepped out. He reached into the sporran, and saw Jubal start. *He probably thinks I'm going for a gun*, Wallace thought, and fervently wished he was.

He extended his hand and two hundred dollars unfolded like a fan. Jubal's eyes widened at the sight. He snatched the money, licked his thumb, and began counting. Wallace was unnaturally aware of every detail—the look of concentration on Jubal Beldon's oddly proportioned face and the combination of fear and burning hatred on Randal's.

"It's all there," Wallace said.

Jubal looked up but didn't reply. He stuffed the wad of bills into the back pocket of his trousers and turned to walk toward the horse he had tethered at the side of the carriage house.

"This means you'll leave us alone, right?" Wallace called after him.

Jubal looked back at him over his shoulder. "Might." And that was all he said before he mounted and rode away.

Wallace didn't move. He didn't speak or look at his friend, or even think for a very long time. The sun was low on the horizon now and the wind was picking up. He could see that there were clouds building to the southwest. Not a good sign, he thought, especially at this time of day. Probably a storm coming.

"Do you think he'll keep his mouth shut?"

Randal's question roused Wallace out of his reverie. "What I'm wondering," he said, "is why I just stood here like a fool and let him go? If I'd have knocked him in the head nobody would mind much. I expect my folks would rather I was a murderer than a sodomite, anyway."

Randal was not quite so sanguine. "Are you insane, Wallace? What in God's name are we going to do? He's right. If it gets in people's heads that we're sodomites we'll be lynched, or at least run out of town on a rail! We could go to prison! Oh, Sweet Jesus, what if my father hears of this? He'll never speak to me again."

"Calm down, Randy, and let's think. I reckon we've bought ourselves some time, at least. Even if he has no idea of keeping his end of the bargain, even if he was going straight from here to the sheriff, it'd take him a quarter hour to get into town and another ten minutes or so to get to the jailhouse. If he's aiming to round up a mob, it'll take him even longer. No matter which, I intend for us to be long gone. We'll have to borrow Grandmother's rig. We can leave it at my father's house in Muskogee."

He turned, but Randal grabbed his arm. "Wallace, why run like a pair of scared geese? There's two of us and one of him. We might be able to catch up with him and put the fear of God in him."

"You don't know him, Randy. If we beat him up that'll just make him twice as set on ruining us."

Randal didn't respond. The two young men gazed at one another in silence for a long moment. Finally Randal said, "Do you know where he lives?"

"I know where the farm is, yes." Suddenly Wallace made a decision. His jaw set with determination. "You go hitch up Teacup and I'll throw our things in the cases. I'll leave Gran a note. Now, get on. We may not have much time."

Randal headed for the carriage house as Wallace hurried up the steps. Squares and rectangles of evening light painted the wooden floor and illuminated the side tables, potted plants, and wicker chairs that Beckie had arranged on the big, screened porch in order to create a cool and pleasant place to sit and drink iced tea on a summer day.

Sitting in one of those wicker chairs was Beckie herself, her hands folded in her lap. She was already clad in her quilted dressing gown and crocheted slippers. Her hair hung over her shoulder in a thick, silver-gold braid. The sky blue eyes were staring at Wallace out of a face as still as marble.

Wallace nearly fell over his own feet when he saw her. "Gran!" To his embarrassment, his voice squeaked. "How long have you been sitting there?"

"Get out," she said.

A cold sweat broke out on Wallace's forehead. "You heard." It wasn't a question.

"Get out and never come back."

"Gran, you can't believe…"

"Take your things and your … friend, and never come back here. Don't write to me or telephone me."

Wallace caught his breath. "You don't mean that."

"I do."

Wallace felt his face flush. He was hot, feverish with fear and shame. "Aren't you going to ask me if it's true? And even if it were, don't you love me any more than that?"

Tears started to Beckie's eyes and spilled down her cheeks. "Oh, my boy. Don't you understand? If folks think a thing, it is so. It doesn't matter if it's true or not. Your reputation is ruined. Because of that man, you have no life here anymore, and neither do I. We both must go far away and start anew. Now, grab what you can and go. Go. Take the buggy. There's a train to Muskogee at eight-thirty, but you need to get out of here without delay. Go to your father's like you planned and leave the buggy with him. I'll pack a bag and tell Marva not to come in for a few days. I'll take the train in to Muskogee tonight after y'all are well away. You and Randal can be out of the state by dawn."

Wallace couldn't speak. What was there to say? The earth had suddenly fallen out from under him and there was nothing he could do about it. He turned and went into the house.

Beckie turned her head to stare out into the yard. She was sure her son Junior would take care of selling the place. Still, she loved this house, and was sorry that she would have to leave Boynton forever.

Trenton Calder

It was getting late in the day. It was still hot, but clouds had rolled in on the wind and the sky was overcast. Me and Gee Dub had both left our mounts at the hitching post out front of the Masonic Hall, only about a block from Alice Kelley's house.

"So where are we going?" I asked.

Gee Dub looked over at me. "Walter told Alice he was headed out to the Rusty Horseshoe for an hour or two. Mama said that was just after noon. She's pretty het up about it."

"I'd hate to be in Walter's shoes," I said, and Gee Dub shrugged.

"Mama never did hold a high opinion of the way he does Alice, but I never heard Alice complain about it."

I have to admit I was a mite shocked, but amused, too. Mr. Dills, who owns the Rusty Horseshoe a ways out west of town, calls his place a dance hall, but the rumor was that there was a back room where you could play a game of cards and bend your elbow at the same time, even on a Sunday, which made it doubly illegal. The county sheriff raided the place on occasion, but otherwise let things be unless there was bloodshed. I told Gee Dub that I had ridden by there, but since the roadhouse was out of Scott's bailiwick, I'd never yet darkened the door or even met Mr. Dills.

There was a grin in Gee Dub's voice when he answered me. "I can't say I frequent the place, but I don't expect I'm entirely unknown there, either. Don't tell my folks, but me and my cousins Jimmy Tucker and Joe Cecil have let our curiosity get the better of us on more than one occasion."

We retrieved our mounts and headed out on the farm road that led toward the town of Morris, if two wagon ruts could be called a road. It was near to half-past five of a Sunday afternoon, and the trail was deserted. It took us maybe half an hour to reach the place. From the outside, it looked like an ordinary house sitting all by itself by the side of the road. The front door and all the windows were open and I could hear music and laughing inside. Several horses were hitched at the side of the building and one auto parked in front.

The place was dim, hot, and loud. Several disreputable-looking couples slouched around the dance floor in the center of the room. A piano player was pounding out a ragtime tune, and a country fiddler was scratching along. The cigarette smoke was thick. A game of cards was going on at one of the tables around the edge of the dance floor, and I seen a spirited game of dominoes at another, which tickled me no end.

"I'll be danged," I said to Gee Dub. "There's Mr. Turner who owns the livery over there playing dominoes, and Ed Chandler who works for your uncle James at the cotton gin. Don't see Walter, though." I took off my old Stetson and beat it against my leg. "I see some coffee mugs and a couple of glasses of lemonade. Do you suppose we've stumbled into a Sunday school class?"

Gee Dub laughed. "I reckon Mr. Dills may provide special refreshment for those who swear an undying oath of secrecy." He gestured with his chin toward a closed door to the right of the bar. "Yonder is the place." He shot me a sly look along his shoulder. "So I hear."

"I never suspected you of firsthand knowledge, partner."

"I'm guessing that my lost brother-in-law is in there, so I'll see if I can gain entrance. You being a lawman, you can wait out here for me. Enjoy a hand of dominoes."

"I believe I'm man enough to handle the sight of whatever is behind that door, so if it's all the same to you, I'll go with you."

"Come on ahead, then."

We made our way to the bar and elbowed a space for ourselves. I lifted a boot to the foot rail and draped myself over the bar. "Barkeep, how's a fellow go about obtaining a beer?"

The bartender gave me a long, narrow, once-over. "We don't deal in alcohol here, mister. If a sarsaparilla or a ginger ale don't fit the bill, I suggest you take yourself off to a gin joint."

"Evening, Mr. Dills," Gee Dub said. "I'd like for you to meet my friend Trent from Boynton." His voice sounded like it had bubbles in it since he was trying not to laugh.

The expression on Dills' face changed like magic when he recognized who was talking. "Well, howdy, Gee Dub. I didn't get a good look at you in the dark. I ain't seen you in a while." He turned back toward me and extended his hand. "Always glad to see a friend of the Tuckers'."

Gee Dub got down to business. "Me and Trent are here to find my sister's husband Walter Kelley. Seems he's about to be a daddy."

Dills' eyebrows shot skyward. "Is that so?"

"It is," Gee Dub confirmed. "I don't see him here, Mr. Dills. Is there someplace else around here I might look for him?"

Dills picked up a glass and commenced wiping it out with a bar rag. "Why don't y'all have a seat in the back room? Knock twice and tell Dan I give you the high sign. Say it just like that."

Walter Kelley

Dan let them into an airless room so full of smoke that they could hardly see. Gee Dub's eyes were watering and he wiped away tears with the back of his hand. He had never had any particular inclination toward dissolute living, though when he was at school in Stillwater he enjoyed a night out with his friends as much as the next young man. But this speakeasy was a new experience for him and he was finding it extremely interesting.

They stood by the door for a moment trying to adjust to the atmosphere. There were only eight or ten people scattered about the three tables in the cramped room. A poker game was in progress at the center table. One of the other two tables was peopled with men enjoying both spirits and the company of loose women.

Trent felt his friend stiffen and looked over at him. "What is it?"

Gee Dub's face was still as marble. He nodded toward the second table. When he spoke, Trent could barely hear him. "Yonder is my sister's husband."

Before Trent could react, Gee Dub strode across the room and planted himself in front of the seat of a good-looking man. The fellow had a shot glass in one hand and the other around a tastelessly clad woman who had made herself comfortable on his knee. He looked up at Gee Dub and his black eyes widened in consternation. The woman found herself unceremoniously dumped when Walter Kelley sprang to his feet.

"Gee Dub! What in the world are you doing here? Does your dad know what you're up to?"

"I could ask the same question in regard to your wife. 'Course she's busy at the moment bringing your child into the world." GeeDub seemed relaxed and businesslike, but he took a step forward that put him uncomfortably close to Walter. Trent sighed and geared himself up for trouble. He hated to imagine what Mrs. Tucker would say if her boy came home with a black eye and a split lip. Of course if it was Walter who ended up with a split lip, that might be a different story.

Walter was a tall man, but his young brother-in-law easily matched him in height, he realized. "Now, Gee, it ain't how it looks." His tone was conciliatory. "I was just so worried about Alice that I had to take my mind off things for a bit."

"Well, you'd better get your mind back on her, Walter. Baby's on the way right now, and Alice wants you."

Walter's nervousness disappeared. "The baby's coming?" He grabbed his hat up off the table and glanced at Trent, but was too distracted to register who he was looking at. "I've got my motorcar outside. Come on and we can all ride to the house together."

"We rode out on horseback," Gee Dub said. If he was implying that he didn't want to be around Walter just at the moment, Walter didn't get it.

"All right then. I'll see you later." He waved his hat around at the shadowy figures around the tables. "I'm going to be a daddy!" he cried. And he was gone, all consternation forgotten.

Trent laid a hand on Gee Dub's shoulder. "Take a breath, now. I'm sure that woman made herself to home on his lap without invitation. It didn't mean anything. He more than likely did come here just to relax a spell."

"His timing is mighty bad, is all." Gee Dub sat down in Walter's vacated seat and heaved a sigh. The soiled dove hefted herself off the floor, bruised only in her ego, dusted herself off, and eyed the two young men with interest.

"What can I get y'all to drink?" she asked.

Trent took a step back. He could bust up fights and arrest abusive drunks without breaking a sweat, but speaking to a lady of easy virtue was beyond his ken. "Come on, Gee, let's go."

"Well, now, look who's come to roll around in the mud with us pigs!" Jubal Beldon rose from his solitary seat at a corner table and whooped out a laugh. "If it ain't Mr. College Boy Tucker. I enjoyed the show y'all put on with Kelley. But do you expect Dills knows you've brought the law down on him?" He indicated Trent with a nod.

Gee Dub stood up.

This is not good, Trent thought.

The room fell silent.

Jubal wasn't finished. "I'm surprised you young fellers' mommies let you out on a Sunday. Tired of singing hymns? Since you're here, how about a punch in the gut and a couple of broken ribs?"

Trent stepped between them. "I didn't come here to arrest anybody but I'll reconsider that policy if you don't shut up, Beldon. Come on, Gee Dub."

Over the bar girl's protest, Gee Dub turned without further comment and the two young men headed for the door. But Jubal wasn't about to let the opportunity for mischief pass. "Hey, Tucker, did your sister tell you about our encounter on the road a couple of days ago?"

Trent turned around, his eyebrows rising. Encounter?

"Seems that snot-nose little tree-climber has got ripe all of a sudden. I think she's about ready to pluck, and I may be just the man to do it."

This time it was Trent's reaction that caused the other people in the room to scoot out of the way, but Gee Dub managed to restrain him. "Calm down, Trent, he ain't worth it. Think what Scott would say if Dills has us all arrested for riot and mayhem."

Trent's face was almost as red as his hair as his friend dragged him toward the door. They were halfway back to Boynton before either of them spoke.

"What do you expect he meant about Ruth?" Trent said.

"I don't know, but I mean to ask her."

"You figure the Beldons have taken to harassing her? I don't like that."

"I figure Jubal just said that to rile me," Gee Dub speculated. "He likely didn't know he'd be getting you all hot as well."

"Well, I plan to keep an eye on her," Trent declared.

Gee Dub's mouth quirked up at the corner. "My guess is you planned to do that regardless, Deputy."

Trent couldn't tell whether Gee Dub's tone held approval or disapproval, so he kept quiet. They rode on in silence as their horses picked their way around ruts in the road.

Jubal Beldon

After Gee Dub and Trent left the Rusty Horseshoe, Jubal sat at his table in the dark corner for another twenty minutes, nursing his drink and thinking.

He had always enjoyed having power over people. Especially them who thought they were so superior, who thought the Beldons were low-class, unworthy, ignorant hicks and yokels. *Bedlam Boys indeed.* His chest began to burn with indignation at the very thought. Well, if he couldn't have their respect, he'd have their fear. So he weaseled out their secrets. He watched. He inferred. He put two and two together and came up with four.

And then he let them know what he knew. *No, sir, you are not better than me. In fact, you are worse because you keep your perversions hid. But I know what you are.*

And if what he intimated wasn't so? Well, in a tight little town like Boynton, where everybody knew everybody else, rumor was as damaging as fact.

Fear was all he had ever demanded from anyone. Money hadn't mattered to him so much. But here he sat with almost two hundred dollars in his pocket, and he hadn't even asked for it. Maybe he had been missing a bet. Since his pa had died, the farm was his now. How much he could do with all his carefully amassed information. If he had enough money, enough land, a big house, and nice clothes they'd all respect him then.

He began to review his mental catalog of scandal. Perhaps there was time for one more productive session of extortion this evening.

Marva Welsh

Marva met her husband Coleman at the crossroads and they set off walking out of town together. Coleman's father Marcus had owned the Welsh homestead since before there was a state of Oklahoma. Marcus was one of the many ex-slaves who had left the United States for the Indian Territory several years after the War of the Rebellion. After all, what sort of opportunity was there for a black man in Alabama? Even then the Indian Territory was full of towns that had been founded and built up exclusively by Negroes, mostly on land set aside by the native tribes especially for freed slaves. Marcus had found work in the all-black town of Twine, some ten or twelve miles north of where Boynton was being established. Then he moved south and began sharecropping for a well-to-do Creek farmer, and after a while he was able to buy sixty acres of land on Cane Creek. The old man was still there, nearly seventy years old, but very much the patriarch of his clan. Marva and Coleman lived out in the country, near the brick plant, but like the rest of the Welsh siblings, they made the trek out to Papa and Mama Welsh's place for dinner every Sunday after church.

Marva and Coleman were going to be late today. They had both picked up work in Boynton on Sunday afternoon, so they missed the big family dinner. Heaven forfend they should not see the folks at all on Sunday, though, so the plan was to make it for supper and spend the night.

As they set out on the road, it was that half-light time of day, exactly between day and night, the time that Beckie would call *the gloaming.* While everything on the ground looked gray and smokey, the sky was a lurid variety of orange, fading to an iridescent pink; unnatural colors. Hard to tell what you were seeing, a few moments of illusion before the sunset. It was hot, windy, and muggy, but it was nice to spend the time together, so they enjoyed the walk along the hard-packed dirt farm road that led past fields of cotton, corn, melons, sunflowers as well as cattle, horses, and goats, eventually rejoining the graded road that led toward the town of Morris.

When they reached the turnoff, they were so deep in conversation that they didn't see the rider approaching until it was almost too late to step out of the way.

Trenton Calder

Me and Gee Dub got out of the Rusty Horseshoe without any extra lumps and all our blood on the inside, but when we got back to town we were both still in a bad humor. Gee Dub more for his sister Alice's sake, and me because of what Jubal Beldon said about Ruth. No man worth shooting mentions the name of a respectable woman in a bar. I didn't aim to forget about it, either.

We stopped back by the Kelley place. Walter had made it back in record time, but there was no new arrival to greet him nor like to be for some hours, Miz Tucker told us. So Gee Dub headed home. Ruth allowed as to how it was getting late and she was pretty tired, so I offered to take her back to Miz MacKenzie's for the night. That way she could walk back to Alice's first thing and meet her new nevvy. Her ma thought that was a fine idea, so Ruth accepted.

I figured I'd leave old Brownie back of the Kelleys' and walk Ruth the quarter mile up the road, but she said she didn't fancy stumbling around in the dark. So I mounted up and she swung herself up behind me without a fuss, with her skirt runched up to her knees just like a girl who's ridden double behind her brothers and daddy all her life. Which she was. Truth is, if she'd had her own mount she could have ridden circles around the likes of me, dark or no dark. I know this because she's done it.

It was one of the best fifteen minute rides of my life. We talked all the way up to Miz MacKenzie's, mostly about how excited she was to be going to Muskogee to study music. She said she would be staying with her daddy's aunt, and when her course was over she figured she'd go to teaching piano on her own.

"You expect you'll come back and take over Miz MacKenzie's students?" I asked.

Her voice, coming warm over my shoulder, sounded happy. "I could if I wanted," she told me. "Miz Beckie wants me to. She's already asked me. But I'll have to see how I feel when the course is done. I might like living in the city!"

My heart sank to hear that, but I didn't let on.

We couldn't see any light in the MacKenzie house when we got there, which was no surprise considering the late hour. I rode around to the back and Ruth slid off from behind me. I dismounted to see her to the door in the dark. I went with her up onto the back porch but stopped when she turned around before letting herself into the house. I snatched off my hat and said goodnight, and she put her hand on my arm.

I can still feel it.

"Thanks for the ride, Trent. Come by Alice's in the morning. I should have me a new niece or nephew by then."

She went inside and closed the door, and I stood on the porch for a while, holding my hat to my chest. When I finally decided I'd stood there mooning like an idiot for long enough, I made my way back to Brownie and headed out. As I passed I noticed that the doors to the carriage house were standing open and Miz MacKenzie's yellow-topped shay was gone, but at the time it didn't mean anything to me.

Alafair Tucker

When Alafair and Shaw got home early the next morning, Mary and Kurt were in the kitchen, feeding breakfast to the children. Martha had volunteered to stay in town to look after Alice, Walter, and the newborn, but Gee Dub had found his way home. After the bluster and threatening weather of the night before, the new day was dawning bright and pink and clear. A perfect first day for their new grandchild, Alafair thought.

The offspring crowded around when they came into the house.

"It's a girl," Alafair announced. "A big, bonnie girl with a darling topknot of dark hair."

The young girls began a joyous dance and Charlie's arms flew up. "I knew it!" he whooped. "I win, Gee Dub!"

Gee Dub dug a nickel out of his pocket and handed it to his brother with a wry smile. "Durn, I figured we were about due for a boy around here for a change."

"How's Alice?" Mary asked.

"Happy as a little red heifer in clover," Shaw said. "Seems it was a lot easier on her than she feared. The little babe is healthy and fair, and Walter is over the moon."

"What's her name?" Blanche wondered.

Alafair sat down and Grace climbed into her lap. "Alice is calling her Linda, after my mama, Selinda."

"Glad to hear that Walter is such a family man after all." Gee Dub's tone was bland.

When Alafair answered, her expression left no doubt as to her opinion of Walter Kelley's behavior. "I sure felt like giving him a piece of my mind about leaving Alice alone so near her time, but Alice was happy to see him and I didn't want to upset her. Besides, he was so thrilled to make his little girl's acquaintance that he was about to take off and fly. I doubt he'll be gallivanting around—for a spell, at least."

"Maybe being a daddy will be just the thing to finally get him to change his ways," Mary hoped.

"It will be." Shaw was more optimistic about the prospect than Alafair was. "Baby girls have a way of doing that to a man." He put his hands flat on the table as a signal that he was about to get down to business. "Now, have you boys taken care of the animals this morning? Cows milked and all? Good. Rest of you kids, run on and get ready for your chores, and I will too. Charlie, you can run over to Phoebe's after breakfast to give them the news." He turned in his chair to address Alafair. "Mama, I had me a nap on Alice's sofa last night, so I'm raring to go. But you were up all night. Why don't you get some sleep? Mary can take the young'uns over to her place for a while. It'll be nice and quiet with all of us away, and if you've a mind you can go into town to visit Alice and little Miz Linda this afternoon."

Alafair considered it for a moment, but truth be told she was still going on adrenalin and wasn't sleepy. *I'll probably collapse in a heap later*, she thought, but she said, "No, today's laundry day and if I don't take care of it it'll just be a bigger chore later."

"Now, Ma, I'll do your laundry," Mary chided. "Chase is a dab hand at laundry, aren't you, sport?"

Chase Kemp answered by dashing around the kitchen and whooping, and Grace leaped off her mother's lap and joined in.

Alafair raised her voice to be heard over the din. "Well, all right, honey, I appreciate it. But I'm not up for a sleep right now. I'll separate the clothes for you. These two rowdies can help with that. Maybe later we can all troop into town to see Alice and the baby. Martha said she'd stay over there all day today, so I expect I'll take me a nap after dinner."

DURING

Alafair Tucker

Monday may have dawned sunny and bright, but as the morning progressed, the wind picked up and drizzly rain clouds began to float over. Charlie Dog kept nosing the box of newly hatched chicks Alafair had placed in the kitchen next to the stove, as if he was counting them, and she had to push his head out of the way before she could lay an empty burlap sack over the top of the box for extra warmth. She could have sworn he was worried about the welfare of the infant birds.

Charlie Dog was behaving oddly altogether. He hadn't followed Charlie Boy on his round of chores, as he usually did, but had stayed indoors all morning. In fact, he pretty much stayed under Alafair's feet, so close that she nearly fell over him once or twice. She shooed him out the back door but he didn't go very far, and fifteen minutes later she noticed that he had snuck back inside. He knew he was testing her good nature, so he lurked in a corner by the kitchen door, afraid of attracting her attention and yet still wanting to be within sight of her.

At least he wasn't under her feet anymore, so she took pity and let him stay indoors. The other dogs, Crook, Buttercup, and Bacon, were nowhere to be seen.

It was nearly midday when the sky became overcast and it began to rain in earnest. Mary took in the still-damp laundry and hung it over lines strung across the back porch before rounding up Chase and heading home to feed Kurt. The humidity was heavy and cloying. Shaw and the boys came in for dinner at noon, and the mood around the table was cheerless as the weather. Everyone was foul-tempered and snappish.

"I thought John Lee was going to come over and help you out today," Alafair noted to Shaw as she passed the cornbread. "Did he decide he don't need to eat?"

Shaw snorted. "Fool son-in-law of yours decided he had been away from Phoebe long enough and left me up to my elbows in muck a couple of hours ago." He vehemently spooned mashed potatoes onto his plate. "I declare, Alafair, that fellow is a prime worker when he's of a mind to be, but once he gets it into his head to go gallivanting off to who knows where, he won't be stopped for nothing."

His vitriol shocked Alafair. "No need to bite my head off about it, Shaw. I expect you know why John Lee is chary."

His eyes widened and he gave her a rueful smile. "Sorry, honey. It's this weather, I reckon. Puts my teeth on edge. If it don't storm this evening, I'll eat my hat."

He finished dinner and went back outside, but the boys were slow to follow him. Gee Dub's expression was wry. "I'm glad to hear it's the weather making Daddy short. Up at the stable this morning you'd have thought me and Charlie were the most incompetent two fellows who ever dragged their sorry selves out of bed."

"He acted like we never put an oat in a nosebag before," Charlie agreed. "That's why John Lee decided to go elsewhere, I expect. Daddy's bad temper."

Alafair laughed but didn't commiserate with the boys. It was their duty to put up with their father's peculiarities and not the other way around. "Y'all better get cracking back out there, then, if you don't want him crawling up one side of you and down the other."

After the boys left, she cleared the table and pondered as she drew the dishwater. She was feeling irritable herself, she had to admit. The hot, windy weather of the past several days had tested everyone's patience, but this was different. Something strange was in the air, something oppressive. The afternoon wore on and the wind came up again, whipping dirt about and making it hard to breathe.

Sophronia teased Grace and made her cry, and Grace kicked Sophronia in the shin. Alafair angrily made both of them sit in separate corners and face the wall for half an hour. When she finally let them get up, Grace reported that Charlie Dog had crawled under her bed and wouldn't come out.

Late in the afternoon Alafair went out on the porch to look at the sky. She was watching dark ribbons of cloud sailing northwards overhead when she caught sight of Shaw walking up the path from the barn.

She stepped into the yard to meet him. He removed his hat and wiped his forehead with his sleeve. "I swear I'm about to crawl out of my skin, Alafair," he said without preamble. "Don't have a reason one to be that way either, except for this awful weather. I passed by the chicken coop just now and the chickens have already gone to roost. I'm afraid we're about to get us a right old toad-strangler this evening. Do you see that big black cloud that's coming up in the southwest?"

She peered around the corner of the porch and caught her breath. The advancing wall of thunderstorm loomed huge and black to the southwest. Lightning strobed within the cloud with such frequency that it hurt her eyes. "That's an ugly storm coming, all right."

"Are all the children inside?" Shaw asked her.

"All but the boys. Martha is still with Alice and the baby, and Ruth's staying with Miz Beckie in town tonight."

Shaw nodded. "Probably just as well. Miz Beckie's got her a good sturdy house. I've put the boys to bringing in as much stock as they can and settling the rest in the north pasture. Besides the lean-tos, there are some trees and good low places for shelter out there if they need it."

"My trick knee that got broken is acting up, and Charlie Dog has been hiding under Grace's bed all afternoon."

"That's not a good sign. I haven't seen the other dogs in hours. The stock has been nervous, too."

"Well, we've lived through some bad storms before. I reckon we'll weather this one as well."

Shaw crossed his arms and leaned against the porch rail. "I'll see that the outbuildings are closed up tight. Maybe if we get a good storm, it'll clear the air."

"I hope you're right, honey."

"I was just thinking you'd better not stray far from home today, Alafair. I'm sure Martha's taking good care of Alice, and Alice and the baby will most likely sleep all day anyway." He smiled at the disappointed look on Alafair's face. "I'd just as soon you not be on the road until this weather passes."

◇◇◇

After supper, Alafair couldn't get Grace to go to bed. She was frightened of the lightning and rising wind and clung to her mother's skirt, begging not to be left alone. Grace was not usually disobedient, and Alafair took a moment to figure out how to handle the child's fear.

"Don't be afraid of storms, baby. They have a purpose on God's green earth, just like everything that happens. Here, sugar, let's kneel down beside the bed and pray together tonight. You just tell Jesus how you feel, and he'll see that everything is as it should be."

Grace took to the idea with alacrity and plopped herself down on the floor next to her mother. "Dear Jesus," she prayed aloud, "I'm scared. Please take care of Mama and Daddy and my sisters and brothers, and all the little babies in the world. Amen."

"Amen," Alafair seconded.

Phoebe Day

Phoebe looked up, surprised, when John Lee came in through back door. He had left only minutes earlier to take care of the final chores of the day. Phoebe stopped drying dishes and walked across the kitchen to meet him.

"John Lee?" The way she said his name encompassed her question.

He took off his hat and hung it on the peg by the door. "There's a storm coming, shug. Looks like a bad one. The sky is green and I just saw ball lightning rolling across the barn roof."

"But I just put Zeltha in her crib and I'm in the middle of cleaning up after supper." The instant she said it Phoebe felt ridiculous about voicing her petty concerns, but John Lee was too preoccupied to tease her.

He seized her arm. "Come look."

They stood together at the open door for some minutes and watched as shreds of clouds scudded across the sky, headed north. A smear of molten gold lay low across the horizon. Phoebe would have thought it beautiful if it had not been for the long cloud above, coming up fast, black and roiling, stained with a sickening green. Lightning forked through the black as it rolled toward them, pushing a wall of dirt.

"Mercy!" she managed.

The leaves of the trees in the yard were frothing in the wind. A moment ago, the limbs had been straining to the northeast, but now they were rushing straight up into the sky. Hail began to pound down on the tin roof as loud as artillery fire, and John Lee pulled Phoebe back into the kitchen, alarmed. The rain began pouring down in buckets, obscuring their view through the window. John Lee looked back over his shoulder at Phoebe, whose eyes were wide with fear.

"Fetch the baby and get to the root cellar!" John Lee ordered. "I'm headin' out to the barn to get the mule in."

When Phoebe got to the bedroom, Zeltha was already sitting up on her little cot, roused by the rattle of hail. "Mama!" She held up her arms and Phoebe scooped her up. She ran through the house with the baby on her hip, slamming down the windows on the north side. She was back in the bedroom when the strong wind blowing in from the south shifted to the east. The rain and hail that had been drumming down stopped suddenly and an unnatural calm descended, a moment of dead silence before the end of the world.

The roar came on them like a demon, and the house started to creak. The bedroom window crashed in and the door slammed shut. Zeltha was screaming but Phoebe could hardly hear her over the howl of the wind. Phoebe tried to pull the door open but the pressure of the wind held it closed.

"John Lee, we're trapped!" she called, knowing very well that he couldn't hear her.

Suddenly the wall began heaving and the ceiling was crashing down around her.

Alafair Tucker

When the wind began to roar and the rain to fall sideways, Grace ran into the parlor in her nightdress and grabbed her mother around the knees. Alafair hoisted the terrified child into her arms and gathered Sophronia and Blanche to her with the other arm. "Come on, girls, let's head for the root cellar." She tried to keep her voice as calm as possible as they ran for the door.

"Where's Daddy?" Blanche's voice was shaking.

"I see him coming up the path. Him and the boys will be right behind us."

"Where's the puppy?" Sophronia cried.

"He's with his mama, sugar. She'll take care of him."

"Charlie Dog!" Sophronia called, as Alafair pushed them out the front door. Much to Alafair's surprise the old yellow shepherd came scrabbling out from the girls' bedroom and followed them onto the porch.

The wind hit them like a locomotive. Alafair and the girls barely managed to keep their feet as they strained across the yard toward the root cellar. Charlie Dog wasn't so lucky. The wind caught the dog broadside and swept him off the porch.

Shaw met them in the yard and hustled them down into the cellar as Alafair yelled over the wind. "Where are the boys?"

"They're coming up from the barn now," he hollered, and went back up the cellar steps as soon as his wife and girls were ensconced. The figures of the boys emerged from the wall of rain, heading toward the house at a dead run and clutching their hats to their heads.

Shaw could hardly see through the driving rain. He heard a crack and a crash, but there was no way to tell what had given way. Gee Dub reached him first, and Shaw unceremoniously dumped his son into the cellar.

He was stretching an arm to grab Charlie as Charlie Dog appeared through the blowing dirt, whining pitifully and crawling toward them on his stomach.

Shaw's heart lurched when the boy turned back to get the dog.

"Forget the dog," he screamed. "Forget the dog, son!"

Suddenly the wind exploded, pushing a wall of debris that blew Charlie off his feet. Shaw was yelling at him to let the dog go, to get to the shelter, and Charlie was heartily trying to obey. He was being pelted with shrapnel, and for the first time in this different and exciting day, Charlie felt seriously alarmed. He couldn't stand up. The wind was so strong that he couldn't even close his wide-open eyes and mouth. A straw or pebble could blind him, and if he got in the way of a flying brick or pitchfork, there was not a thing he would be able to do to keep himself from being crushed or impaled.

Charlie wallowed around on the ground and managed to turn himself back toward the shelter, but the wind caught him again and he rolled away, clawing the scoured earth, unable to catch a breath in the gale. He could hear his father's panicked voice, but he was unable to make any sense out of it. He felt strong hands grab him and he was pulled into the cellar like a sack of potatoes, tumbling down the steps and into his mother's arms. He gasped a few times and lay there, momentarily stunned, watching Shaw and Gee Dub struggle to pull the cellar doors closed. Charlie Dog was crouched at Sophronia's feet.

The doors to the root cellar began to rattle and bounce as though something malevolent, a monster, was trying to get to them. The force of the suction was so great that Shaw realized that the two-by-four plank he had used to bar the doors was not going to hold. He grabbed the handles and felt his body being pulled up off the ground. "Boys," he yelled, "help me hold 'er down or we're goners!"

Charlie struggled and broke out of his mother's grasp to help Shaw and Gee Dub hold the doors down, and none too soon. Sophronia grabbed Gee Dub's waist to lend her weight to his. He didn't seem to notice. Alafair was struck by the sudden knowledge that if the doors were pulled off and the men were sucked out into the storm, the girls would go too. "Shaw!" she screamed, but he could not hear her.

She sat down on a potato sack and pulled Grace into her lap as a weeping Blanche snuggled up under her arm. Grace had not cried or said a word since Alafair had scooped her up and run with her across the yard to the root cellar.

Shaw, Charlie, and Gee Dub, Sophronia still clinging to his waist, crowded together in a heap as each seized his piece of the iron door handles. Even in the dim, flickering light from the lantern, Alafair could see them strain to stay on the ground. Charlie's eyes widened and he shot his mother an awestruck glance. The boys both yelped involuntary as they were alternately lifted off their feet and dropped.

Grace put her hand on her mother's cheek, and Alafair leaned down to hear the child over the roar of the wind.

When she spoke into Alafair's ear, her tone was quite calm. "Mama, it's time to die."

Alafair's breath caught, and for an instant she couldn't answer. "Not today, baby. Not if we can help it," she managed.

Alafair shoved Grace at Blanche before she leaped forward to follow Sophronia's example and throw her arms around Shaw's middle.

A strange feeling of dislocation came over her as she pressed her cheek to Shaw's back and hung on for dear life. She was seized with a desire that the last thing her eyes behold on earth be her children, so she turned her head to look at Blanche and Grace huddling together at the back of the cellar. Grace was staring at her, her black eyes huge, still preternaturally calm. Blanche, tears streaming down her face, was hugging her sister and stroking her hair in a desperate attempt to offer comfort. The monster howling outside was so loud that Alafair could barely hear Shaw and the boys yelling. She couldn't tell what they were saying but she expected that was just as well. Sophronia was screeching like a banshee. The ten-year-old hung there, plastered to Gee Dub's back with her arms and legs wrapped around him, monkey-like.

Alafair's eardrums felt as though they were going to be pulled out of her head, so she opened her mouth to relieve the pressure. *Maybe I lied to Grace*, she thought, *and it is time to die*. Resigned, she closed her eyes and pressed her forehead into the straining muscles of Shaw's back. She took a deep breath and filled her lungs with his familiar smell, now acrid with the sweat of fear. She didn't mind dying so much, but she very much resented the fact that there was nothing she could do for her children during their last moments this side of heaven.

The world grew very small then, just the size of the root cellar, dark and painful and noisy, but filled with the ones she loved. She spared a thought for her children who were not there. No use to wonder how they were faring. If they had met their end, she would see them shortly in heaven. If not, she would wait for them, along with these who were with her now. There was no future, only this instant, and she realized that she felt no fear at all. She smiled at Grace, and Grace smiled back, before the wind sucked the light out of the lamp and everything went dark.

Alafair Tucker

Alafair's ears were ringing with silence. Something smelled odd; like wet mud, and the fresh, burnt odor of lightning. At some point she had closed her eyes, but when she opened them again all she saw was blackness. She didn't think she was dead. She didn't think anything at all. Her ear was still pressed against Shaw's back, and she was aware that his heart was pounding so hard that her head was practically bouncing up and down. She never did remember how long they stood there, suspended in that moment. Maybe a minute, maybe an hour. Sophronia slid down Gee Dub's back and the sound of the thump as she hit the floor served to start time moving forward again.

Alafair pried her arms from around Shaw's chest and lunged toward where she had last seen the girls, reaching out like a blind woman in the dark. They were all right. No one was hurt. She clung to the three girls and listened to someone fumble around trying to relight the lantern. The rattle of glass, the scratch of a match, a sudden flash, and the warm glow of light that illuminated Shaw's face.

She wondered if she looked as stunned and haggard as he did.

Gee Dub was still hanging onto the iron door handle with one hand, his face wet with sweat. Charlie was sitting on the dirt floor, right where he had dropped. When the light flared he turned his head, blinked at his mother and barked an incredulous laugh. "We're alive!"

"Let's pray, Mama. I want to pray," Sophronia said. Her voice was weak.

"So do I, sugar," Alafair assured her.

Trenton Calder

The wind blew like the devil and the streets flooded, but the twister missed Boynton. I rode it out in the hotel, but as soon as it let up I high-tailed it over to Miz Beckie's house with a lantern to check on Ruth. Main Street was running ankle deep with water, full of branches and boards and who knew what. I had to wade part of the way up there. I was relieved to see that even though a bunch of shrubs and trees were torn up, the house was still standing.

It was raining pretty good when I got out there and I was soaked to the gills. I ran up onto the front porch and pounded on the door. No one came at first, and I felt a twinge of worry. I backed off the porch and looked up at a lighted window on the second floor, then called her name. Ruth opened the window and leaned out.

"Trent, is that you? Come on in. I'll be right down."

I went in the front door and she came running down the stairs in her bare feet, holding a candle, her chestnut curls loose and streaming behind her. She was in her nightgown. It was a big old thick cotton thing that covered her from neck to toes, but I could feel my cheeks burning. She didn't notice.

"Trent, am I relieved to see you! I'm alone, you see, and the telephone lines are down. Was it a tornado? Did it hit the town?"

"It was quite a storm, Ruth, but if there was a twister it skipped Boynton. I didn't see any more damage than some trees down and some outbuildings blown over. Where's Miz MacKenzie? Are y'all all right here?"

"Miz Beckie isn't here, or Wallace and his friend, either. After you brought me here Sunday night I found a note that she left for me. She said that after church Wallace and his friend decided to go visit Miz Beckie's son in Muskogee and she decided to go with them. I don't know when she's supposed to be back." She put her hands on my chest. "I'm right worried about her, Trent. What if she was on her way home when the storm hit? She could be lying dead in a ditch somewhere between here and Muskogee!"

I shook my head, more to dislodge the picture that her words had conjured than to disagree. But I said, "It's more likely that she's still in Muskogee with her folks, Ruth."

I could tell she wanted to believe me. "You think so?"

"I expect so." *And if she is lying dead in a ditch*, I thought, *there isn't anything we can do about it right now*. "You mean you've been here all by yourself since last night?"

"Well, yes, by the time I found out they were all gone Sunday night, it was too late to go home. And I had lessons to give this morning and a new niece to visit with this afternoon. I figured Miz Beckie would be back by the time I left Alice's this evening, so I came back here. Besides, it was looking bad and I didn't want to walk home in the rain. I had just decided to go on to bed when it started to rain like the dickens. I rode out the storm squatting in the bathroom down here on the first floor. There was big crash, and after the blow was all over I found out a tree had fallen through the window in Miz Beckie's bedroom. There is a bunch of damage to the top story over on that side of the house, and I don't know what to do. I've been upstairs trying to cover the hole as best I can to keep out the rain."

I went upstairs with her and surveyed the damage, which was a lot. A big old cottonwood that had probably been growing in that spot beside the house for a hundred years had broken right in two and a big old limb had crashed through the wall and into Miz MacKenzie's bedroom. The rain was coming in, and that whole end of the room was a mess, the furniture slid all over the place by the wind. But the four-poster bed on the other side sat there neat and made-up like nothing had happened at all. I helped Ruth hang blankets over the hole as best we could. But I told her that I'd come back with a saw when it got light and saw the limb into pieces so we could board up the wall.

"I don't fancy you staying here in this big old beat-up house all by yourself tonight," I told her after we did all we could. "You want me to take you back to Alice's, or to your Aunt Josie's house?"

"I don't fancy it much myself," she said. "Wait in the parlor for a minute until I throw some clothes on, Trent, and I'll ride double with you back to my ma's house."

That was a two-mile trip in the rain over roads that were probably ripped up and strewn with debris. "You sure you want to do that?"

"Yes, I want to make sure that everyone is safe."

"All right, then, but bundle up. It's raining and cold as sin out there, and we'll have to walk back to the hotel stable to get Brownie."

Ruth made off down the stairs toward her little room by the kitchen at the back of the house. "I'll leave a note for Miz Beckie in case she makes it home tonight," she called over her shoulder.

Alafair Tucker

They could only see by the lightning flashes. Alafair listened to the thunder booming overhead, deafeningly loud but moving away quickly. The house was still standing but it was impossible to assess the damage from where they stood in front of the root cellar. All they could see was the underside of the front porch, which had been lifted up and slammed against the front of the house like a wall.

Charlie started forward, but Alafair grabbed his arm. When she spoke it was to Shaw. "Forget about the house right now. We've got to see to the other children!"

Shaw nodded. "Gee, let's you and me get over to Phoebe's. The twister was going that way. Charlie, run over to Mary's. Alafair, you and the girls stay here." Shaw knew she'd never let him go without an argument, but he thought it was worth a try.

"What about the girls in town?" Alafair demanded, hot on Shaw's heels as he and the others turned to rush away. He put his hand on her shoulder, vainly trying to hold her back. Gee Dub was fading into the distance, halfway across the barnyard, and Charlie was already out of sight.

"Alafair, stay here with the young'uns. Light a lamp and go back down into the cellar. You know it's not safe for them to be wandering around amongst all this rubble now that it's dark. We'll see about the house after we know the other children are all well."

"But…"

"I'll send Gee Dub back as soon as we know something. You know I'm right." He made shooing motions with his hands. "Now, git. Go on, get back."

She did know he was right, but it sat very ill with her to be still and wait for word. However, the young girls were hovering around her, frightened and anxious. Their need for her, she admitted to herself, was more immediate. She twisted her neck to its extreme as she walked back toward the cellar with the girls clasped to her sides, and watched Shaw move away into the gloom.

A roll of thunder was followed by a burst of torrential rain and light hail. As unhappy as Blanche, Sophronia, and Grace had been to go down into the dark, dank cellar in the first place, they were eager enough to return to shelter now. The temperature had dropped and a cold rain had begun to fall. Alafair offered to go to the house to check damage and see if she could find some blankets and pillows for them, but this idea was met with a chorus of vetos. Even Sophronia, who would never admit fear, assured her mother that she would rather sleep uncovered on rows of Mason jars than be left alone.

Resigned, Alafair arranged a species of bed for them out of sacks of potatoes and dried beans and created a bedspread from empty burlap bags to cover them as they huddled together for warmth. Alafair knelt beside the bean-sack bed to repeat bedtime prayers with the girls, fervently thanking God for letting them live. After she had decided that all three had fallen into the sleep of exhaustion, she hoisted herself off her knees and raised the lamp to cast its light on her children. Sophronia's face was obscured by a tangle of reddish curls, and Grace was so huddled down between her sisters and under her burlap covers that all Alafair could see of her was the top of her head. Blanche's wide green eyes were staring at her. Alafair gently placed her hand on Blanche's cheek, and the girl sighed and turned over.

Alafair became aware of Charlie's voice calling from a distance. She wasn't going to have to wait much longer to find out if God's mercy had been extended to her other children. She wrapped a gunny sack over her head, pushed open the cellar door and went outside just as Charlie came up the path. Tears of relief flooded Alafair's eyes when she caught sight of Mary and Kurt, with Chase close on their heels.

Mary rushed into her mother's arms. "Oh, Ma! Oh, Ma, look at the house!"

"Never you mind about that. Thank the Lord y'all are all right!"

"We're fine. We were just coming up here to see how y'all are when we met Charlie on the path. We had a bunch of wind damage, outbuildings and tree limbs and the like, and a little damage to the house. Scared us silly, though. When the twister went by, the windows bowed in like they were made of rubber! I had no idea that glass could stretch like that. It was the strangest thing I ever saw. Just blew out an east window in the parlor. We got it boarded up already." Mary gestured toward the upended porch. "Nothing like this. How are Phoebe and John Lee and the Zeltha?"

"I don't know yet. Your daddy and Gee Dub are still over there. Kurt and Charlie, go on over and see if they need some help, then somebody come back right quick and let me know how they are. Then I need one of you fellows to go into town and make sure Alice and Ruth and Martha are all right. I'm about to jump out of my skin with worry."

Mary took charge. "Kurt, you tell Daddy and them to come back to our house for tonight. There's no use Ma and the girls spending the night in the cellar when we have dry beds and plenty of blankets."

Phoebe Day

It took Shaw and Gee Dub a long time to pick their way through the dark and the debris as they made their way east across the field toward the Day farm. It had turned unseasonably cold and it didn't help matters when the rain began to fall again, slowing their progress even more.

When the limbs and odd pieces of board and building began to thin out on the ground, Shaw was briefly heartened. But as they neared the property line, not only was there no debris, there was nothing on the ground at all. No grass, not a weed or a rock.

"Look, Dad."

Gee Dub's voice startled him out of his preoccupation. "What, son?"

"The fence is gone."

The barbed wire fence that divided the Tucker and Day farms now consisted of a couple of broken fence posts sticking out of the ground at crazy angles. There was no barbed wire to be seen.

Shaw's heart fell into his boots with a thud. The landscape was unrecognizable. "Come on," he urged, his voice tense with fear.

If it hadn't been for the creek on the Day side, Shaw expected they wouldn't have been able to find their way at all. The path had been scoured out. The continual lightning threw demonic flashes of light on the collection of leafless, limbless sticks and poles that used to be a stretch of woods. Shaw wondered if hell was similar.

He didn't realize that they had reached the farm until he saw the back of the house. The little white clapboard cottage stood pristine in the middle of a bare yard. Two small saplings that John Lee had recently planted stood straight and fully leafed beside the back door.

"Looks like it's still standing," Gee Dub exclaimed, breathless with relief.

Shaw broke into a run. "Phoebe!" he called.

As they rounded the corner of the house, Shaw stopped so abruptly that Gee Dub ran into him. The back of the house was untouched, but the front of the house was gone.

It had been sheared in half as neatly as if by a giant buzz saw.

Even the floor was gone. There was no parlor or kitchen, though Phoebe's heavy iron cookstove stood on the ground in its usual place. The recently added bedroom at the back of the house was neat as a pin. Three walls stood undamaged but the fourth had disappeared, along with half the roof. The bed was made up with a colorful quilt and white eyelet curtains hung at the window. A rocking chair sat on top of a rag rug next to the bed, opposite a chifforobe upon which lay a comb and mirror, a shaving cup with brush, and a crocheted doily. All in all it was like looking into a giant doll house, complete with a doll.

Zeltha was sitting on the floor with one leg of the chifforobe sitting on the tail of her nightgown, her face wet with tears and purple with fear. She shrieked when she saw her grandfather and lifted her arms to him.

Shaw scrambled up onto the foundation and hauled the child free as Gee Dub lifted the heavy dresser off of her gown. Her little body was shaking with cold and terror. Shaw snuggled her up to his chest and wrapped his coat around her.

"Do you think they're blown away?" Gee Dub had one arm around his father's shoulders and was patting Zeltha's back with his other hand.

"Phoebe put the leg of that chest on Zeltha's shirttail." Shaw raised his voice to be heard over the girl's wails. "Your mama used to do that to keep little ones from straying when she had to do a quick task. Maybe they've run to check the animals. Zeltha, baby, where's Mama, honey? Where's Mama?"

"Mamaaaa!" Zeltha howled, but offered no other enlightenment.

Shaw walked over to the gaping hole that was once the bedroom wall and yelled into the night. "Phoebe! John Lee! Holler if you can hear me, young'uns!"

Shaw heard no answering call, but Gee Dub had younger ears. He stiffened. "Listen, Dad."

Shaw cocked his head and strained to hear over Zeltha's sobs and the receding crackle of thunder as the storm moved farther away from them. His first thought was that he was hearing a wounded calf bawling, but he realized with a jolt that whatever it was, it was speaking English.

"Daddy, Daddy, Daddy…" A high-pitched voice that he didn't recognize, a woman's voice.

But Gee Dub did. He started out into the muddy yard. "It's Phoebe, Daddy. Come on, come on!"

They rushed toward the voice as fast as they could in the dark. They didn't have to worry about debris since the yard had been scoured right down to the bare ground, but the landscape was so changed that they had no way of recognizing where they were. Zeltha was snuffling quietly against Shaw's chest, now, clinging to him.

If it weren't for the near-constant lightning, they'd have never been able to see Phoebe, barefoot and clad in a cotton housedress and apron, so pregnant that she could hardly bend over. She was frantically digging in a pile of what seemed to be muddy firewood. When she saw them approach she stopped calling for her father, but she didn't stop flinging sticks and pieces of wood off the pile. Her auburn hair was wet and hanging in strings over her face and shoulders.

Shaw handed the two-year-old to Gee Dub and scrambled up onto the woodpile to grab Phoebe's hands. "Honey, what in the world are you doing? You'll hurt yourself! Come on down with me. We found Zeltha right where you left her. Where's John Lee?"

Phoebe shook him off and grabbed another stick of wood to throw aside. "He's here, Daddy, help me! He went to see that the barn was closed up when the storm hit."

"The barn?"

"This is the barn. It collapsed and John Lee is under here somewhere!"

Shaw felt like he'd been hit in the chest by a fist. He picked Phoebe up bodily and carried her kicking and protesting off of the hill of splintered wood.

"Hush, honey, hush." He spoke right into Phoebe's ear as she squirmed in his arms. "Look, here's Zeltha! Hold her while me and Gee Dub dig John Lee out. Look, honey. Zeltha needs you."

Gee Dub thrust Zeltha into her mother's arms, and Phoebe squatted down on the ground with her, freezing and bruised, but refusing to go any further. She had no idea how long she hunkered there, with her skirt tucked around her bare feet and Zeltha pressed against her breast, watching her father and brother dig through the rubble. At intervals, Shaw or Gee Dub would call John Lee's name, then stand still for a few seconds, listening. Thus far there had been no response.

Phoebe caught sight of a dim spot of light coming up the path. Kurt, carrying a lantern, and Charlie. She could tell who it was by the lightning illumination.

She ran to meet them and was in the midst of explaining the situation when Shaw yelled, "He's here!"

Phoebe tried to follow Kurt and Charlie up the woodpile that had once been the barn but Shaw grabbed her arm. "Stay out of the way, honey."

"Is he alive, Daddy?"

Shaw would not keep the situation from her. "I can't tell yet, darlin'. But you can't help. Think of Zeltha and this other little one who need their mother right now."

◇◇◇

They began to dig with fingers and sticks. Miraculously, Kurt found a shovel and a hoe, both of which worked well as prying instruments and speeded things along considerably. They worked by the light of Kurt's kerosene lamp. Shaw insisted they dig slowly to avoid a disastrous shift of the rubble, but inch by agonizing inch, John Lee was disinterred.

The rescuers took turns standing over John Lee's head, shielding his face from the rain with their coats and bodies.

It took all of them to lift a beam from the barn roof which had fallen across one leg, and then he was free. Shaw knelt down and ran his hands over the limp figure, briefly assessing the damage before attempting to move him. It didn't take much of an examination to feel several raw, pulpy wounds and a couple of broken bones. John Lee's right leg was bent at an odd angle. Shaw could feel breath on the back of his neck as his other boys anxiously huddled close, trying to see what was happening.

John Lee's eyes fluttered open briefly. "Water," he croaked.

If his tears hadn't been warmer than the rain, Shaw might not have known he was weeping with relief.

Phoebe appeared at his side, desperate to get to John Lee. Shaw blinked at the bedraggled figure in the sodden housedress, not quite sure how she had gotten past him. She was so agitated that Shaw feared she would go into labor then and there.

He looked up at Gee Dub, standing behind her. "Gee Dub, get Phoebe and Zeltha out of here. Take them back to the house. See if you can find her some shoes and a coat and get them to Mary's house. Your ma is over there now. "

"No, Daddy!" Phoebe protested, but Shaw cut her off.

"Phoebe, you're making it harder for us. Me and Kurt will get him out and rig up a stretcher. Honey, we'll bring him to you as fast as we can. You're going to hurt the baby and Zeltha's going to end up with pneumonia. Get back to the house and take care of that child before she freezes clean to death. Gee Dub, go on. Hurry up, now. Charlie, go with them and bring me back some drinking water and see if you can find another lamp."

Gee Dub Tucker

Gee Dub dragged Phoebe most of the way back to the half-a-house, but as soon as they were out of sight of what was left of the barn, she stopped struggling and allowed Gee Dub to lead her, docile as a lamb.

Since the kitchen had disappeared Charlie couldn't find any water, so he left with a glass of sweet tea that was still standing on the bedside table and a couple of sodden candles that would be useless in the rain.

Zeltha had fallen into an exhausted sleep against Gee Dub's shoulder. He laid her down, still asleep, on her parents' bed, and wrapped the quilts around her. He sat Phoebe in the corner rocker and threw a quilt over her while he rummaged through the clothes press, hunting for something warm for her to wear over her housedress. It was downright cold, now, and three walls were no adequate shelter against the drizzly rain.

No coats. They had probably kept their coat tree in the parlor, the contents of which were more than likely in Missouri by now. Gee Dub cast a glance over his shoulder at the bedraggled figure huddled in the chair. He could hear her teeth chattering from across the room, whether from cold or shock he couldn't tell. He pulled out one of John Lee's flannel work shirts and a woolen shawl and seized a pair of Phoebe's shoes and some stockings. She limply allowed him to slip the shirt and shawl over her dress. He knelt down and slid her feet into the stockings and shoes, talking gently to her all the while. Her feet were bloody. He knelt there on the floor for a moment, overcome with a feeling of unreality as he looked out at night where the wall had been an hour earlier.

Why am I so calm, he wondered? He stood and took Phoebe's hands to pull her up. They were black with mud and blood, her fingers shredded. If they were hurting, she didn't show it. Gee Dub briefly considered first aid, but where was he going to get water to wash her wounds or clean bandages to wrap them?

He picked up the sleeping child and arranged her against his shoulder, then tucked his free arm around his sister. "Come on, now," he urged. "Let's go to Mama."

"Is John Lee dead?" Phoebe's voice was small.

Gee Dub was firm. "No. Daddy and Kurt and Charlie are pulling him out of the mud right now." He fervently hoped it was so. He led her out through the gaping hole, across the yard and toward the path that led to the Lukenbach farm.

Phoebe straightened in Gee Dub's grasp. "Let me hold my girl. Soon as I get her to Mama and get some proper clothes on, I've got to get back here to John Lee."

The tenor of her voice had changed in the blink of an eye. Gee Dub was not surprised. He knew his sisters. Phoebe didn't have time to be weak right now when there was work to be done.

The rain had let up but a fine mist was in the air, so fine that it barely wet their hair. Gee Dub handed Zeltha to her mother, hoping that Phoebe had enough strength left to manage the girl's leaden weight. When they reached the path, he moved ahead of her in order to remove any impediments.

Behind him as they walked, Phoebe began to talk. "Me and Zeltha were alone in the house, Gee. When the ceiling started to cave in I knew we were in for it, so I stuffed her under the dresser. I'd have got under there with her but there's too much of me right now, so I just scrunched down as close to her as I could and held on. I swear, Gee Dub, the walls moved in and out like they were breathing! Then the roof lifted off like a lid and then sat right back down again. Then…I swan! There was a noise like I never heard in all my born days, and half the house was just gone! I couldn't even believe what I was seeing, all hunkered down there just staring at the front yard instead of the wall like I should have been. Jesus was watching over us sure, Gee, 'cause if we hadn't been in the bedroom we'd be gone, too!"

Trenton Calder

It didn't take me and Ruth long to realize that we weren't going to get very far on the road to her folks' farm. Truth is, there wasn't hardly any road anymore. The wind had scrubbed it right off the face of the earth and laid the ground over with broken trees and pieces of barns and furniture and dead animals. We didn't see any dead people, thank the Lord, but that's just because we didn't go far.

I had to talk faster than a carney in order to persuade her that this was a bad idea. "Better wait until light so we can see where we're going. Otherwise we'll end up riding around in circles all night and that won't do your folks any good. Besides, they've all got root cellars, so even if they've got storm damage, they're all right."

I didn't think she was going to listen until I suggested that we go back to Alice's and see what the Kelleys had to say about the situation. Walter let us in when we got there. Alice was sitting in an armchair with the new baby, and the oldest Tucker sister, Martha, was pacing up and down the floor just as concerned about her family as Ruth was. I was glad to see that Martha's betrothed, Streeter McCoy, was there, too. I admired Streeter McCoy a bunch. If anybody was going to figure this thing out, it was him. He was Boynton's town treasurer, which means that he had a good head for figuring.

He didn't waste time. "It's cold, raining, and black as sin out there," he said to the women. "Trent couldn't even find the road a bit ago. Now, I'm as worried as you all are, so I suggest that Trent and I take a couple of good lanterns, some tools, and maybe some quilts, if you've got some to spare, Alice, and we'll see if we can pick our way through the mess on horseback. Walter needs to stay here with Alice, and, besides, I'll feel better if you all have a man around tonight."

That plan went down with the Tucker girls all right, so me and Streeter loaded up and walked over to the livery to saddle him a horse. While he was busy getting ready, I stopped in at Scott's house. I reckon him and his wife Hattie didn't know where I was until I showed up at their door, so Hattie fussed over me and Scott acted put out until I told them what I had been up to. Scott had already walked around town to look at the damage and had sent a couple volunteers out north and west of town to check on the farms. I told him what we were planning and left to meet Streeter in front of Mr. Turner's livery.

The streetlights were out and a steady rain was falling when we set out. We could barely see five feet in front of ourselves.

"This is a fool's errand. You know we're not going to get out there tonight," I said after taking fifteen minutes to get a hundred yards. We still couldn't find the junction for the road to the Tucker farm. "It'd be a whole lot smarter to wait until daylight."

I couldn't even see Streeter's face when he spoke up. "Why'd you come, then?" I figured he was chiding me for my faintheartedness, but he didn't sound angry.

"Well, if I hadn't made the effort, Ruth would have gone haring off in the dark by herself."

He chuckled at that. "She'd have had to knock Martha out of the way. We may not get anywhere till morning, but at least if we try, the ladies will stay put for a while."

Alafair Tucker

Shaw and his sons managed to rig a stretcher out of coats and boards and they carried John Lee the half mile over the bare field and across the road to the Lukenbach farm. Mary had already brought her mother and sisters back to her barely damaged house, where the children were piled together like puppies, sound asleep on a heap of blankets in one corner of the extra bedroom. Alafair and Mary were fussing over Phoebe with hot bricks wrapped in flannel, salve and bandages for ravaged feet and hands, and cups of warming tea. But the kitchen table was cleared in a trice when the rescuers arrived with the wounded man. John Lee was in and out of consciousness. He roused himself when Phoebe bent over him.

"Zeltha…" he managed.

"She's fine, darlin'," Phoebe said. "And so am I. And you're going to be fine, too."

Shaw drew Alafair and Mary aside. "His right leg is broken," he murmured. "He might have a broken jaw. I know he's got some busted teeth. Y'all can see to his cuts, and I can set that leg. It looks like a clean break. But I can't tell about his innards. Or worse, his head. He needs a doctor."

"Kurt can fetch one." Mary volunteered her husband.

But Gee Dub was close enough to hear the conversation. "I'll go, Dad. Kurt and Charlie can come with me back home and check on the livestock. They can take care of the animals while I ride in for Doc Addison. "

Shaw and Alafair glanced at one another. The likelihood was that at least a few animals had been killed or wounded by the storm. It was cruel to let them suffer any longer than need be.

Shaw nodded. "All right. Kurt, you have some firearms handy?"

"I do, sir." Kurt looked grim, and Charlie, uncharacteristically, had nothing to say.

"Mary and me will help Daddy with John Lee," Alafair said, "so you fellows get on. Judging by the direction of the wind, the worst of the storm probably missed Boynton, but Gee Dub, you be sure to check on the other girls while you're in town."

The boys had barely walked out of the house when a commotion in the yard caused Alafair's heart to jump into her mouth. What fresh disaster could possibly have befallen them now? She hurried out the back door with Shaw and Mary, leaving Phoebe to tend John Lee.

In the dark it was hard to see what the dust-up was, at least until Alafair raised her kerosene lamp high enough to cast some light into the yard.

Kurt, Gee Dub, and Charlie were trying to catch a horse.

The horse was fully saddled, a tall roan with a light-colored mane and tail. He was probably a handsome animal, though it was hard to tell, what with the dark night and the coat of mud on him. How he had managed to survive the storm all in one piece was a wonder. All four of his limbs were certainly in working order, the front two currently flailing at his would-be rescuers, his eyes white-rimmed with panic. The men had encircled the terrified animal and were trying to calm him with soft words and soothing noises, but he was having none of it. His agenda consisted of nothing more than escape, and he reared and whirled himself in a counterclockwise circle, looking for a gap between the outstretched arms of his tormenters big enough to bolt through.

Once he reared and whirled, and twice, and three times, before Shaw managed to catch the whipping reins and expertly calm him into a standstill. As Shaw stroked the heaving horse's muzzle and murmured into his ear, Charlie checked him quickly for injuries.

"He's full of splinters and he's got a bad-looking puncture wound on his thigh," Charlie exclaimed, "but nothing's broken that I can find. Looks like somebody was riding him when the storm hit, Daddy." Charlie was running his hand over the tooled leather saddle. "Maybe we'd better go out and see if we can find the rider. He might be off in a ditch hurt."

"I'm afraid whoever was riding that horse is dead."

Shaw turned his head to look at Alafair, who was still standing in the door with Mary. Her comment surprised him. "What makes you say that, hon?"

A flash of lightning in the distance illuminated her face just enough for Shaw to see her grim expression. "Yonder beast just turned three times widdershins. Someone has died, sure enough."

He handed the reins to Kurt. "Take this animal to shelter, son, then you and the boys set to your task."

The young man's wide blue eyes regarded his father-in-law with confusion. "What does she mean, sir, *widdershins*?" Having been born and raised in Germany, Kurt often required an explanation for some term or another.

Shaw glanced at Alafair, and when he answered, he kept his voice low. "The horse circled three times to the left, contrary to the path of the sun. It's the sign of the unnatural. Alafair's likely right about the rider. Women know these things, Kurt, that's been my observation. Now, get on."

Gee Dub Tucker

The horse was docile enough as Kurt led him to the barn, but when the boys tried to get him into a stall, all bets were off. He shied and skittered, reared and tried to bite. Kurt was barely able to keep hold of the reins and avoid having his head staved in by a hoof, but it wasn't until Gee Dub managed to throw a feed sack over the animal's eyes that they were able to get him into a stall and unsaddled. Charlie pumped a measured amount of water into a bucket and threw some oats into the feed box, and the horse drank thirstily while Kurt examined the wound on his hip.

Odd. It was a narrow puncture wound, maybe an inch wide. It wasn't bleeding and the edges were clean, but swollen. Whatever had pierced him wasn't still in the wound. Kurt hastily washed the wound and covered it with a clean cloth. That was all he had time for at the moment.

They left the unlucky beast blindfolded and tied in the stall and the three young men set out down the path back to the Tucker farm. The stable where Shaw kept his riding stock had lost a corner of its tin roof, but was otherwise intact. The horses in their stalls were restless but unhurt, so Kurt and Charlie took lanterns and headed for the pasture where the mules and draft horses had ridden out the storm. They left Gee Dub to saddle his own chestnut mare, Penny, for his trek into Boynton.

Penny had been Gee Dub's mount since she was a long-legged filly and he was a scrawny lad, and they had grown into one another comfortably. He had never found another horse he liked better. She was curious and oddly playful, for a horse, which had always appealed to Gee Dub's wry sense of humor.

He hung an unlit lantern on the saddle horn and swung himself up onto her back. The lightning was sporadic now as the storm receded into the distance, and the night was black as a bucket of pitch. A light, gritty snow was blowing about, a strange phenomenon that sometimes happened in the wake of a twister, even in the middle of summer. Gee Dub was sure it wouldn't last long, but it added to the general misery of the situation. He buttoned the top button of his coat and pulled his hat down low on his forehead as he made the turn out of the drive and onto the road that led to town.

He let the mare pick her own way through the rubble strewn across the road, and he could tell by her gait that the normally well-packed dirt road had become a sucking, muddy bog. The trip to Boynton from the farm normally took no more than twenty or thirty minutes on horseback, but forty minutes after he left, Gee Dub didn't seem to be any closer to town than when he started.

In fact, he didn't rightly know where he was. Was he even still on the road? He didn't think so. There was vegetation on the ground, and it was rutted, as though it had once been plowed. A fallow field. He couldn't see worth a darn. It was so black that he couldn't get his night eyes, and he wondered if the horse was as blind as he was. He swallowed a momentary pang of unreasonable fear. Even if he got hopelessly lost, the sun would come up eventually and he'd find his way home.

Something was moving ahead of him. He tugged on the reins and squinted at the apparition, not sure he had actually seen anything. But there it was—a pale, man-shaped figure weaving toward him through the darkness. His first thought was that someone had been killed by the storm and his haint hadn't yet figured out that he was dead. Gee Dub smiled, amused at himself, and felt oddly better.

"Is somebody there?" he called.

The figure stopped, but no reply was forthcoming. He clucked at Penny and she walked a few steps forward. He was near enough now to see it was a man, strangely white from tip to toe. He unhooked the lantern from his saddle horn, fished a match out of his breast pocket, struck it on his thigh, and lit the wick. He held the lamp up and its weak yellow light illuminated the figure of a man standing exactly in front of him, bruised eyes staring at him out of a white face, stark naked, his bare skin tattooed with dirt and splinters.

Gee Dub nearly dropped the lantern. "Mr. Eichelberger? What in the name of Pete…are you all right?" As soon as the words left his mouth, he felt like a fool. Mr. Eichelberger obviously was not all right. Gee Dub flung down out of the saddle and seized the man by the arm.

Eichelberger stared and blinked at him. He slowly lifted one skinny arm and pointed off in the direction from which he had come. "There's a dead man over there."

Gee Dub was removing his coat to cover the man's nakedness, barely aware of what he had said. "Mr. Eichelberger, you're hurt! Get up behind me, now, and I'll take you to Doc Addison."

The suggestion roused Eichelberger to action, and he shook Gee Dub off. "No! I can't go! I'm all right! I found him over there." He dropped Gee Dub's coat into the mud and ran off into the darkness, bare as the day he was born.

Gee Dub didn't call after him. It was just one more bizarre incident in a night full of them. With the lantern in one hand and Penny's reins in the other, he walked ahead slowly, gingerly casting his eyes about for a body. He had only walked a few steps when Penny snorted and shied, and his heart jumped into his mouth. Mr. Eichelberger wasn't delusional after all.

He said a few soothing words to the horse before he wrapped her reins around the stubby stick of a ravaged sapling and made his way forward through the weedy ruts, lantern high.

At first he thought he was seeing a dismembered leg, and he paused, nauseated by the idea. When he took a step closer he saw the shape of the rest of the man, half-buried in mud. He put the lantern on the ground, fell to his knees, and proceeded to dig the body out of the muck with his bare hands. He moved quickly at first but slowed when it became obvious that the man was quite dead. He scooped mud off the face, out of the hollows of the eyes, and reached for his lamp in hopes of identifying whomever it was he had just disinterred.

The eyes were wide open. The mouth was open, too, and full of mud, as were the nostrils. Gee Dub stood up. Something about him was familiar, but he couldn't put a name to him. The skin on the face had been practically flayed off, and the cheek and jaw on the right side were crushed in. The man had either been flung face-first into something hard, or skinned by the shrapnel of dirt and rocks and exploded buildings.

Somebody has died, sure enough, his mother had said. Was this the lost horse's rider? Gee Dub lost track of how long he stood and looked down at the body. He had seen death before. He had even seen violent death before. Though death had always horrified him, it had never seemed personal to him, even when the one who had died was known to him, even loved.

Gee Dub gazed down at the dead stranger and wondered why this was different. The possibility of war, probably. Would he grow inured to sights like this? A tornado, a bomb, what was the difference? Something comes out of the sky and you're dead in the blink of an eye.

The corpse had been a man. That was all Gee Dub could tell for sure. Only a few sprigs of hair remained on the scoured scalp. They looked dark. The man was oddly unreal, like he had never been alive at all. The odd, staring eyes might as well have been painted marbles. Whatever it was that animated a man was long gone.

Early this morning, Gee Dub thought, *this fellow got up out of bed, put on his clothes, ate breakfast, and it never crossed his mind that he'd never do any of those things ever again. A storm came and killed him without so much as a by-your-leave.*

Gee Dub felt bad. The guy was all skint and muddy, with his mouth hanging open. It was undignified, and Gee Dub felt bad for him. Whoever he had been, he wouldn't have liked to be seen this way. Gee Dub was seized by an urge to re-bury him, just to give the man a little privacy. He closed the corpse's staring eyes.

"I wish I could do something for you, Mister," he said aloud, and felt foolish. There was no help for the dead man now, and he shouldn't be wasting time like this.

Since Gee Dub wasn't really sure where he was, he looked around for a way to mark the location of the unfortunate soul, but found nothing that could differentiate the spot from the ruination around it. He thought of breaking the branch off of a bush and sticking one of the man's boots onto one end and planting the other end in the ground next to the dead man's head. But the body was only clad in the remnants of trousers.

He was going to have to take the body with him or risk never finding it again. He glanced at his horse, who twitched an ear and snorted.

Penny wasn't going to like this.

Gee Dub didn't relish the idea of riding around in the dark with a mutilated corpse slung behind his saddle. He untied his blanket roll and rolled the body up in it like a cocoon. He knotted his rope around the man's feet, then remounted and moved on slowly, dragging his ghoulish burden behind. He held the lantern high as he rode, but the road to Boynton was not to be found. Finally he gave Penny her head to pick a route south across the open field, and hoped she could make her own way toward town.

Dr. Ann Addison

Gee Dub had no idea how long he had been wandering around. He had hoped that he would eventually be able to navigate by the glow of the street lamps in Boynton, but there was no glow. He wasn't surprised. The wind and rain had surely blown the street lamps out. But he was disappointed, nonetheless.

He did the best he could by holding the lit kerosene lantern up high for as long as his arm would allow. He was pretty sure he was still headed southeast, and when he suddenly found himself riding under the broken branches of his grandfather's apple orchard, he knew he was on the right track.

He came up on his grandparents' house from the rear and was relieved to see that it was largely untouched, apart from a missing section of fence and the loss of some roof shingles. He considered stopping for a welfare check, but since they seemed to have suffered little damage and he was eager to get the dead man into town, he pushed on into Boynton.

Tree limbs were down all over town, some outbuildings blown over and windows blown out, but the tornado seemed to have largely missed the town. Still, nothing alive was stirring and every window on Main Street was dark. He dug his heels into Penny's side.

He turned up Second Street past Alice and Walter's place and saw the dim glow of oil lamps through the window, but he didn't stop until he reached Doc Addison's house further down the lane. He slid off the horse's back and left her in the middle of the road while he pounded on the front door.

Doctor Ann opened it at once.

Once he had blurted out his story, Doctor Ann told him that her husband was not at home. "Joey Bond from over your way came and got him just a few minutes ago. He said that the twister had blown their house to pieces, and the fireplace had fallen on his ma."

Gee Dub cursed under his breath. He shouldn't have lingered over the body of a man who was beyond help. "John Lee is hurt bad, ma'am. We've taken him over to my sister Mary's house since there's no other place. And I'm afraid he's not the only one who's hurt. Mr. Eichelberger is injured for sure, and I've been dragging the dead man behind my horse for near to an hour. I don't know what to do with him this time of night. I passed more than one farmhouse that isn't there anymore. My guess is there are a lot of folks out that direction needing the services of a doctor."

Doctor Ann listened with growing concern before inviting Gee Dub into the house. The other two doctors in town were likely tending to the wounded as well, but she tried to telephone them anyway. It was a futile effort. Even if Mrs. Smith was trying to operate the switchboard after-hours because of the storm, the lines were down.

"I'll go out to the Lukenbach place myself, son, being as there's no other option."

Gee Dub watched the tall, dignified, midwife grab her bag and throw a shawl over her shoulders. "You won't be able to get out there in a buggy, ma'am," he warned. "You'll have to go on horseback, and it's next to impossible to see where you're going."

Doctor Ann paused long enough to give him a thin smile. "We Cherokees have no trouble finding our way in the dark, my boy. I'll borrow a horse from Mr. Turner."

"Yes, ma'am. I've got to do something with my sad burden out there. I reckon I'll go by Scott's. Maybe he'll tell me where to take it. I told my ma I'd check on my sisters while I'm here, as well."

Doctor Ann was already heading for the door. "As you wish, Gee Dub, but if you're not at the livery by the time I'm saddled, I'm leaving without you."

Trenton Calder

That was one strange night. I didn't recognize where we were. There was no road, no houses, nothing left to where we could get our bearings. Me and Streeter kept going northwest, but we couldn't recognize where we were by the landmarks because all the landmarks had been blown away. We found a turnoff that we thought was probably the right one, so we set off down that way. About a mile down, a big old uprooted persimmon tree lay right across our path. We were going to have to leave the road, such as it was, and go around it.

I turned Brownie to the left and there, looming up out of the dark, was the gate to the Ross Dairy, broken but still upright. I hollered at Streeter, who was riding in front of me. "We're heading toward Muskogee!"

It was the right road. Wrong direction. I could see Streeter slump in the saddle before he turned his horse. "Come on, then, we'll have to go back."

We made our way back toward the road, but we didn't get there before I heard a shrill cry. "Help! Oh, help!"

At first I thought I was hearing a child, but then I recognized the voice. "It's Miz MacKenzie!"

Streeter straightened up in the saddle and hollered back. "We hear you! Where are you?"

Her voice was squeaky with panic. "I'm just on the other side of this fallen tree! I can't get around it. Please help me."

Streeter gave me a look that said, *What in the world is she doing out here?* "Mrs. MacKenzie," he yelled, "it's Streeter McCoy. Trent Calder is here with me. Are you hurt? Did the tree fall on you?"

"Oh, boys, I'm so glad you've come along! No, I'm not hurt. I'm on my way home from Muskogee, but this tree is blocking my path. I'm in my shay and I can't get around."

"Hang on, we're coming…"

We recommenced our trip around the barrier, picking our way real slow in the dark through the debris. It took us near to fifteen minutes to go twenty feet, but we got around. And there we found Miz Beckie MacKenzie sitting in her one-horse conveyance with the top up against the rain, holding the reins in her gloved hands and wearing a fluffy hat just like a queen. Her little saddlebred mare was patiently standing with its nose to the roadblock, enjoying a snack of persimmon leaves, which according to my ma, was real good for her.

We surveyed the situation for a minute. "Whatever possessed you to be out on a night like this, Miz MacKenzie?" I asked. "Ruth told me you've been at your son's house. Couldn't you have stayed over another night?" What I was thinking was, *Whatever possessed your son to let you out on a night like this?*

Her hand went up to her throat. "Then Ruth is all right?"

"Yes, ma'am. I went by your place to check on y'all as soon as the storm went by. She's fine, but I'm afraid a tree about as big as this one took out a corner of your upstairs."

That didn't seem to bother her much. I could plainly hear her relief. "Oh, thank the Lord! When I left Muskogee late this afternoon I figured I could beat the weather, but when it started storming bad I stopped over in Crecola with my friend Letty Allen. There is no telephone in Crecola and the telegraph office is closed, so I just had to try and get home and make sure dear Ruth is safe. The road is a mess, and it keeps getting worse the closer to Boynton I get!"

"How long have you been sitting here, ma'am? You should have turned around and gone back to Crecola!" Streeter lifted up his hat far enough to run his fingers through his sand-colored hair and make it stand up on end.

Miz Beckie looked abashed. "Well, yes, Streeter, I know you're right. I just drove up not ten minutes before I heard you. I was pondering whether I could guide Teacup around, but it's so dark that I was afraid to try."

Me and Streeter were both dismounting as she talked. "It's

a good thing you didn't try," I said. "You'd have got stuck for sure in this buggy."

"What shall I do, boys?"

Miz Beckie stayed put while we reconnoitered for a spell and calculated our options. "I think the safest thing would be to unhitch the horse and guide it around. Leave the buggy here and retrieve it later," I said to Streeter.

He nodded. "Mrs. MacKenzie, can you ride astride?"

We were standing beside the shay and couldn't see her face, but when she answered she sounded the littlest bit affronted. "Of course I can, dear. I'm not entirely helpless, you know."

Streeter chuckled and walked over to give her a hand down. "I apologize for implying otherwise, ma'am."

Ruth Tucker

Streeter and Trent managed to wend their way back through the ruination and the intermittent rain and deliver Beckie to her house. Since her house had sustained damage, the men offered to take Beckie to Sheriff Scott Tucker's house for the night, but she wouldn't hear of it. "If the house is still standing," she insisted, "I will go back to it."

The compromise solution was that they would take Beckie home and then Trent would go back to Alice Kelly's house and fetch Ruth, if she was willing, to stay with her mentor until morning. To their surprise, Ruth was already at the MacKenzie house when they arrived. She took Beckie's sodden coat and droopy hat and ensconced the older woman in her armchair by the fire. She took her a cup of strong tea, then returned to the kitchen to pour steaming mugs for the men and exchange information. She was disappointed that they had not made it to the farm, but marveled that they had come across Beckie the way they did.

Ruth had news of her own.

"Gee Dub came by Alice's a while ago and told us that Mama and Daddy had some damage to the house and Mary and Kurt are more or less unscathed. But the twister came down on John

Lee and Phoebe's place. They're all alive, but their house is about gone and the barn fell in on John Lee and broke his leg. Everybody is at Mary's tonight, since it's the only house that's big enough and all in one piece. Gee told me he found a dead man and brought the body into town with him and Scott had him take it to the Masonic Hall."

"A dead man!" Trent was shocked. "Who is it, did Gee Dub know?"

Ruth shook her head. "He says the body was so damaged by the twister that he couldn't tell." She shuddered at the thought. "I talked Gee Dub into bringing me back here. I was here during the storm so I knew that the house isn't busted up that bad. Besides, I know where Miz Beckie's pistol is if I need it. Gee stayed long enough to help me move the rest of Miz Beckie's bedroom furniture away from the hole in the wall, and then he wanted me to come home with him."

"Why didn't you go?" Streeter wondered.

"I was set on being here in case Miz Beckie showed up and needed me, and it looks like I was right. Gee Dub left not an hour ago. He said he aims to go back out to Mary's and let them know all of us are all right before Mama takes a notion to walk to town herself."

Streeter leaned back in his chair and sighed. "Ruth, honey, I don't like the idea of you two ladies staying out here in this damaged house all by yourselves tonight. What if there comes another storm before morning?"

"I'd be glad to sleep on Miz Beckie's parlor couch tonight," Trent volunteered.

"Now, you fellows don't need to fret so. Me and Miz Beckie will be just fine. Besides, I'm sure Alice and Martha are anxious to know what has become of you two. So drink up and ride on back to town. If it'll set your minds to ease, drop back by in the morning on your way out to Mama and Daddy's and see how we fare."

The men sat in weary silence for a moment after Ruth left them to tend her charge. Trent found himself mesmerized by the steam in his mug, and he jerked as his head dropped toward the table. He was suddenly aware of the amused look on Streeter McCoy's face.

Streeter chuckled. "You'd be well advised to go home and get some sleep. I'll go back to Alice's and fill them in."

Trent scrubbed his face with both hands. "Naw, I figure I ought to stop by Scott's real quick and let him know what it's like west of town. If you don't mind, I'll go with you out to the Tuckers' in the morning."

Streeter nodded. "I'll meet you in front of the hotel at dawn."

Beckie MacKenzie

Ruth returned to the parlor to find Beckie holding her cup and saucer in her lap, staring out the window into the darkness, gray with exhaustion.

Ruth sat down on the ottoman beside the fireplace. "I'm so glad to see you're all right, Miz Beckie. I was worried that you got blown clean away on your way home! Did Trent tell you that a tree fell into your bedroom? The rest of the upstairs is intact, though."

"Yes, he did, dear, but that's no matter. It can be fixed. I'll sleep in Wallace Junior's old room for a while, or down here by the fire if I must. All I care is that you are unhurt."

"What possessed you to try and drive all the way back here from Muskogee tonight?"

"It wasn't so bad when I left late this afternoon, just windy and threatening rain. But the sky looked so bad at sunset that I considered turning back. By that time I was much closer to my friend's house in Crecola than to Muskogee. Once it started hailing I thought it would be the better part of valor to find shelter immediately. It was quite a storm, a great deal of thunder and lightning, Ruth dear, but Letty and I had supper and a nice chat. By that time it had blown over enough that I thought I could make it home with little trouble. I didn't get but half a mile before I realized it was much worse than I imagined, and then I grew so *fashed* at the thought you might be hurt and alone that

I just had to get home. Thank heavens those young men came along when they did."

"Oh, Miz Beckie, now I have to scold you!" Ruth said. "It was foolish of you to come all that way by yourself, even if there hadn't been a tornado. Didn't your son offer to drive you home?"

"He did. But as I told Junior, I may be naught but a silly little old woman but I'm still capable of driving a buggy. I knew it was a bad storm but I had no idea that there had been a twister. Oh, Ruth dear, when I neared Boynton, it looked as though the end of the world had come. Why, some of the farms that were just northeast of town don't exist anymore! The road was hardly there, either. I dodged many a roadblock between here and Crecola, let me tell you!"

"All's well that ends well, I suppose. What about Wallace and Randal? Have they resumed their trip to Colorado or are they still at your son's house?"

Beckie paled and her blue eyes filled with tears. Concerned, Ruth placed her hand on Beckie's knee. "I know you miss him."

It was some moments before Beckie was able to answer. "They were still at Junior's when I left. Wallace seems to be making a great effort to get along with his father."

"Perhaps his time at Vanderbilt has matured him," Ruth offered, though she hadn't noticed much of a change in his maturity level herself.

"Perhaps," Beckie agreed. "But now, Ruth dear, I must take myself off to bed before I succumb to sleep right in this chair. We can talk more in the morning."

John Lee Day

Shaw set John Lee's leg and splinted it with one of Mary's broom handles. Kurt and Charlie lifted John Lee off of the kitchen table and got him propped upright in a chair, where Phoebe tenderly brushed out her husband's snarled hair, careful to avoid the raw, bare patches where it had been jerked out by the roots. Gravel and splinters fell out onto the floor, so much that when Mary swept it up, she had nearly enough to fill a half-pint jar. John

Lee managed a smile for Phoebe's sake. "You ought to save them rocks and wood for me to rebuild the house with," he mumbled through his smashed jaw.

Alafair would have laughed if she had any laughter left in her.

"Listen," Shaw said. "Someone's calling the house!"

The two of them went to the door to see Doctor Ann in front of the house, dismounting a horse so black he was hard to see in the night. "Gee Dub must have got through." Alafair was breathless with relief.

Doctor Ann pronounced the bone-setting job well done, for the moment at least, until an actual doctor could make his way out and do a more thorough evaluation. Alafair steadied John Lee's head as Doctor Ann carefully unwrapped the linen strips holding his broken jaw in place. "Can you open your mouth and let me see?"

He managed a finger-width, enough for Doctor Ann to see the bloody gaps where several teeth had been. She looked at Alafair.

"He's already spat out the teeth," Alafair assured her. "I counted to make sure he didn't swallow any."

Ann rummaged around in her carpetbag and withdrew a small glass jar containing what appeared to be a single amber stone. She tipped the stone into her palm and began kneading it between her hands until it started to soften. "This here is mostly pine resin with a few herbs in it to stave off infection. Here, let me work this in between your teeth. Clamp down. Gently, now. That'll set hard as cement in a bit and hold everything together real good."

The pain of the procedure caused gritty tears to run down John Lee's cheeks, but he did not make a sound. Ann bent down for a closer inspection. His normally luminous black eyes were red and swollen. "Looks like you have gravel in this eye, son. Can you see out of it?"

"Some," John Lee croaked from between clenched jaws. "It's cloudy-like."

"Well, all those little pieces will have to work themselves out over time. I'll give your wife some eye medicine to help ease things along. I expect your eye will get better directly."

However, it was to Alafair that Ann handed a stoppered vial from her bag. "Put ten drops of this wine of opium in two tablespoonfuls of cool, well-boiled water. Put two or three drops of the solution in that eye several times a day. It'll help the pain considerably."

"I'll make it up for him," Alafair promised.

Ann was satisfied. "Then I'll leave the patient to you and Mary, but before I leave I want to look over the expectant mother."

"I can't leave John Lee's side now." Phoebe didn't look up from her husband's face. His eyes narrowed and he pushed her away as her mother took her by the arm.

"John Lee won't thank you for your concern if after all this shock and upset you miscarry of your child." Alafair was firm.

Phoebe was convinced. She let Doctor Ann lead her back into the spare bedroom but she could barely hold still for the exam, so anxious was she to get back to her wounded darling. Her lacerated feet and hands had been cleaned and wrapped, her clothing changed and hair toweled dry. Her chilled arms and legs had been well chaffed to bring the blood to the surface. A quart of hot tea had been poured down her throat. All in all, Phoebe was in good hands. The baby's heartbeat was strong and its little feet kicked when Doctor Ann prodded its mother's belly. Satisfied that all was well enough for the moment, Ann didn't linger, but headed back to town in case she was needed elsewhere.

Gee Dub showed up shortly thereafter with a report on the welfare of his sisters in town and the story of the dead man in the field. "Scott had me take the body over to the hall. They're making a field hospital and morgue out of it," he told them. "Doc Perry was already there. Looks like several people out northwest of town were killed or hurt." Then he curled himself up on the settee in the parlor and dropped off.

Mary turned her bed over to the invalid couple, who were both wrapped in warmed quilts and left to their exhausted sleep. Kurt and Mary made a pallet for themselves on the parlor floor, leaving the bed in the second bedroom for her parents.

But Alafair and Shaw never went to bed at all. They sat out the last hours of darkness at the kitchen table with bleary eyes, and fortified themselves with coffee so strong it nearly ate through their cups. Charlie prowled up and down the floor, impatient to get on with it, whatever *it* may be. He didn't need coffee to combat sleep. His youth coupled with adrenaline worked quite nicely.

Trenton Calder

This time when we set out for the Tucker place, me and Streeter went better prepared. When I met him out in front of the hotel before dawn, he showed me that he had brought a compass and an electric flashlight, which helped a lot. We managed to make our way out to the farm just as the sky began to show a little light. I'd just as soon it stayed dark. The ruination north of town was unbelievable. It was like hell with the lid blown off. I seen things that I never did before and hope to never see again. A two-by-four rammed right through an iron gatepost like a cross. Fifty-foot trees pulled out by the roots. Saplings with every inch of bark and leaf stripped right off them. I seen a three-hundred pound pig completely rolled up in barbed wire like he was wrapped for Christmas. I seen naked chickens running around with all their feathers gone. A hunk of board full of nails had nailed itself right onto a horse's neck. We stopped long enough to shoot the poor critter and put it out of its misery.

"I don't know how anybody could have survived this." Streeter sounded spooked. "I pray to God that they all made it to shelter."

So did I.

We finally reached the Tuckers' front gate, a long, barbed wire thing that was standing just like nothing had happened. The fence it had been attached to was nowhere to be seen. I opened the gate for us to ride through, though now that I think back on it, we could just as easily have ridden right around the side.

The early morning light was still dim enough that we had to get pretty close before we could tell that the house looked to be in pretty good shape. The roof was still on and I could see that the barn and the outhouses were where they were supposed to be. The trees had been stripped of most of their leaves and there were a lot of big branches down. We got right up to what was left of the picket fence around the house before we saw that the porch had been lifted and smashed up against the front door. The brick pillars that had held the porch up were still right where they ought to be.

We had both started hollering at the house as soon as we turned up the drive, and when we saw the damage, we just hollered louder. But nobody answered. We dismounted and started hunting around, but all we found were several mighty bedraggled chickens, Mr. Tucker's two filthy, spooked, hunting dogs, and little Grace's puppy Bacon, who came crawling out from under the house covered with mud and his whole hindquarters wagging with joy at the sight of us.

I picked up the pup just as Streeter came back around to the front of the house. "Looks like they're not here," he said. "There're a couple broken windows and some wind damage in the bedrooms, but they missed the worst of it."

"They're probably still at Kurt's." It was hard for me to talk what with little old Bacon trying to lick my face off.

Streeter was about to agree with me when we heard a gunshot and fell to listening. About a minute later there was another. I looked down at my feet so Streeter wouldn't see my expression. I didn't wonder what the shooting was about. I'd lived through bad storms before and knew what they could do to animals in the field. We'd just had to do our duty to a couple of suffering beasts ourselves.

"Can you tell where it's coming from?" I said to my feet.

"Sounds like over toward the creek. Toward the Day farm."

I stuffed Bacon into my saddle bag and we took off toward John Lee's place with the hounds trotting behind us, but we didn't get very far before we met Mr. Tucker and his sons coming up the path with their old yellow dog by their side. Charlie was overjoyed to see the puppy's head sticking out of my saddlebag and fetched him out. The hounds near to knocked Mr. Tucker over, they were so glad of the reunion.

Mr. Tucker looked relieved to see us. "Glad you made it out, boys," he said. "I reckon you heard what happened to Phoebe and John Lee. We've just been over there trying to round up his calves."

"Yes, sir, we heard the shooting." Streeter sounded grim when he said it.

Mr. Tucker smiled but there wasn't any humor behind it. "We managed to save most of them. Lost a few of my mules, but the horses are all right. Can't see well enough yet to go out to inspect the cattle in the back pasture. Right now we're on our way to the house to see what we can do there. You saw the porch? We could use a hand."

Alafair Tucker

The sun was well up by the time Alafair and her two younger girls finally made their way back to their house to assess the damage. She had left Chase and three-year-old Grace with Mary, fearful that dangerous debris lurked in the muddy yard. The overcast sky and murky light made it eerily difficult to see detail. But at eleven and ten years of age, Blanche and Sophronia were old enough to be cautious. Alafair was relieved and happy to see Trent and Streeter and exchange updates.

Shaw didn't allow much time for visiting. He shooed the females off to the side and deployed his work crew with ropes, crowbars, hammers, and nails to pull down and secure the porch. When the men eased the intact floorboards down from vertical to horizontal again, the porch looked like nothing had happened.

Shaw wasn't going to let anyone climb onto it until he had made very sure it was safe, so Alafair and the girls went around to enter the house through the back door. One of the parlor windows was broken, but the fact that the porch had closed like a lid on the front of the house had kept the parlor and kitchen from being damaged at all. Everything stood neat and untouched, as though the rest of the world had not just been visited by disaster. The back of the house was a different story. All the east windows had been shattered, and the furniture in both bedrooms was piled into corners as though some recalcitrant child giant had tossed everything awry.

The chifforobe and the clothes press in the girls' room were lying in a splintered heap against the north wall, doors and drawers open, their contents nowhere to be seen, sucked by the winds into the night. "Oh, Ma!" Blanche moaned. "All our clothes!"

Alafair gave the children the once-over. Both were still dressed in the summertime clothing they had on when the storm struck, as were the boys, and Alafair herself. They were all grimy, wrinkled, and slept-in—the girls wrapped in a couple of Mary's old blankets in lieu of jackets. Grace had been wearing nothing more than her cotton nightgown and shoes. Alafair hugged Blanche briefly to her side. "Never mind, shug. Now you'll be getting all new clothes."

Sophronia was intrigued by the notion. "Can Alice make our new dresses for us?" Alice was a particularly talented seamstress.

"Alice is going to be busy with her new baby for a quite a spell," Alafair told her. "We'll have to make them ourselves." She sighed as she eyed the cabinet of her pedal sewing machine, lying on its side in two pieces. "Maybe Alice will let us borrow her machine, though."

Trenton Calder

As soon as there was enough daylight, Mr. Tucker put Streeter McCoy in charge of shoring up the porch, since he had studied engineering back in Ohio. He detailed Charlie Boy to be Streeter's assistant and sent Gee Dub to the field to inventory the cattle and have a look at the damage to the feed crops and the cotton. I started to follow Gee Dub, but Mr. Tucker put out his hand to stop me.

"I aim to go see how the Eichelbergers have fared," he said to me. "Gee Dub met the old man on the road last night, and from what he told me I fear the worst. I don't want to take the young'uns, but I'd appreciate it if you'd come with me."

I said I would be proud to, but I was halfway between pleased that he had so much confidence in me and dread of what we were like to find. As we rode up the road to the entrance to his neighbor's farm, Mr. Tucker told me all about how Gee had run into Mr. Eichelberger and found the body in the field.

Eichelberger's gate and fence were clean gone. Things looked entirely different out that way. I doubt if we could have found the place if it hadn't been for the fact that the trees that had shaded the house were bare stumps now, so from the main road there was nothing to keep us from seeing clear across the field to the smashed remains of the house. Neither of us said a word as we rode up what used to be the drive.

Mr. Eichelberger was sitting on an upside-down washtub in front of the woodpile that had been his house. He didn't look up at us or act like he knew we were there. He was buck naked. There was an ugly gash over his eye and he was covered with a coat of white dust from top to toe. He looked like a ghost. It made my skin crawl.

Mr. Tucker stepped down out of the saddle and got down on one knee, eye-to-eye with the poor dickens. "Mr. Eichelberger…" His voice was real gentle. "Mr. Eichelberger, look at me, now."

Eichelberger didn't move but his eyes shifted toward Mr. Tucker, so I reckon he knew we were there. Mr. Tucker put his hand on the man's shoulder. "Mr. Eichelberger, can you tell me where your wife is?"

Eichelberger's voice was creaky as a rusty hinge when he spoke. "All gone. I can't find Maisy. I tried to hang on to her, but the devil sucked her out of my arms."

Mr. Tucker looked up at me, and I nodded and made for the rubble pile to hunt for Mrs. Eichelberger.

I found her.

Mr. Tucker only had enough time to throw a coat over Eichelberger's shoulders before I got back to him. He must have read my face, because he turned kind of pale. I just shook my head. Mr. Tucker stood up and drew me aside.

"Dead, is she?" he murmured, and all I could do was nod.

It took me a minute to get my voice back. "She's around back of the house, lying in the yard plain as day. She's busted up. Looks like she has a broken neck, at least. I expect he found her right off."

Mr. Tucker heaved a sigh and glanced back at Eichelberger, who was still sitting on his washtub, muttering to himself. "Well, we've got to get him out of here. You ride on back to Kurt's and see if you can rustle up a pair of britches for him and maybe a blanket to cover her with. I'll hang around here and keep an eye on him till you get back."

"Where are we going to take him?" I wondered. "Back to your place?"

Mr. Tucker shook his head. "I'd rather not. The children are disquieted enough as it is. I don't want to bring a deranged man home on top of everything. I'll try to figure it out while you're gone."

"I'll be back directly," I promised, and mounted up. I left Mr. Tucker on his knees in the mud, murmuring soothing words to his broken neighbor. I skipped the drive and cut out directly across Mr. Eichelberger's fallow field for a shortcut.

Alafair Tucker

When Trent returned to the Eichelberger farm, he brought more than a pair of britches. He brought Alafair, riding her gray filly and hauling a load of first-aid supplies. The sky was still overcast, though it wasn't raining at the moment. More worrying was the fact that the wind was up and the temperature was rising again, making it muggy and uncomfortable and presaging another storm.

Trent looked abashed when he explained that Alafair had insisted on coming back with him, but Shaw didn't give him any grief over it. He was quite aware that a twenty-two-year-old deputy sheriff didn't stand a chance against Alafair. He passed Mr. Eichelberger into Trent's care and helped Alafair take down the pack from behind the saddle. His unnecessary aid gave him a chance to talk privately with his wife for a moment.

"You didn't need to come," he said to her, though he was glad she did. He knew from experience that Alafair's quiet, competent presence was calming and would do Mr. Eichelberger good. Not to mention Shaw himself.

"Trent told me what happened." Her eyes brimmed, but she blinked back the tears. "I loved Miz Eichelberger."

Shaw put an arm around her. "I tidied her up best I could. I found a quilt in the rubble and covered her up. She's beyond trouble now."

"Amen. How is he?"

Shaw glanced at the man on the washtub. "He's a little better. He's making sense when he talks. He knows she's gone. He wanted to look at her, so I took him around back. He cried a mite. I think he'll do, but he'll have a hard row to hoe."

"We'll do the best we can for him." Alafair handed Shaw the drawstring bag containing a pair of Kurt Lukenbach's overalls and a shirt—far too big for the diminutive Mr. Eichelberger. "I took the girls back to Mary's. She's fixing dinner for them. Streeter and the boys are all still at our house. The porch is fixed. When I left they were boarding up the broken windows and salvaging what furniture they can out of the bedrooms. There are a couple of leaks in the roof that'll have to be dealt with right quick. Still, I think we can sleep in our own house tonight. Phoebe and her bunch aren't up to going anywhere, even if they had somewhere to go. So Mary and Kurt will be having company for a while yet. They'll be glad to get the rest of us out of there, even if we all have to sleep on pallets at home for a spell."

"I think I'd better round up my helpers and set them to clearing the road from here to town. We can't leave Miz Eichelberger here in the yard. We have to get her back to town as soon as we can. If this weather keeps up, the road will be impassible tonight, even without the downed trees."

"I surely would like to get into Boynton long enough to check on my girls and my new granddaughter."

"We will, sugar, one way or the other."

"What are we going to do with him in the meantime?" She nodded at Eichelberger.

He shook his head, unsure. "If the young'uns are at Mary's, then we better take him to our place for a bit."

Alafair approved of that idea. "Maybe I can get him cleaned up and fed, let him rest a while before he has to face his plight."

Trent stood up from Mr. Eichelberger's side as they approached. He had heard the end of their conversation. "The mud on the road is already sucking at the horses' feet," he warned.

The previous winter had been one of the wettest of Shaw Tucker's lifetime, and the road to town had often been too boggy to travel easily. Bringing supplies home had been difficult, to say the least. He had learned a few tricks then, though he had hoped he would never have to put them into practice again. "Trent, when we get back to the farm, you and the boys get to clearing the road. Don't worry about moving every stick and branch. Just do a good enough job for us to get the buckboard through. Tell Gee Dub to bring along a couple of good saws. While you're doing that, me and Streeter will fetch Miz Eichelberger's body and load up the buckboard with sand and boards. We'll carry our dead to town this afternoon. If we can't get there by road, we'll go cross-country."

Mary Lukenbach

After Mary Lukenbach had fed dinner to her charges, she packed an enormous basket of food for the repair crew and set out for her parents' house. She filled a little pail with biscuits and a small basket with the fresh summer squash she had managed to pick before the storm, then loaded down her littlest sister, Grace, and her newfound cousin Chase Kemp and took them with her. She left her husband, Kurt, at home to look after Phoebe, Zeltha, and John Lee. Blanche and Sophronia were competent helpers, so she left them with Kurt. But Mary wouldn't think of expecting him to handle two overstimulated little whirlwinds on top of everything. Being a former grammar school teacher as well as the second-oldest of ten had already given Mary expert child skills. She gave the children a task.

They were more than halfway to her parents' farm, walking across the middle of a muddy, branch-strewn field, when it started to rain again. Chase wasn't bothered, but Grace began to whine. Mary removed her own floppy, big-brimmed felt hat and plopped it on the little girl's head, which amused Grace for the moment. Mary took her hand and quickened the pace. The path was muddy already. More rain would turn it to glue. Mary's honey-gold hair was coming loose from its coil and plastering long, uncomfortably wet tendrils to her neck. Chase was fifty feet ahead of them by now, flitting hither and yon and swinging the basket of squash about alarmingly.

"Chase," Mary called. "Slow down!"

As the words left her mouth, he disappeared over the top of a little hill that abutted the path, and she huffed impatiently.

"Where'd he go?" Grace wondered.

Mary picked her up, pail and all, ready to go after Chase, but he reappeared on top of the hill and waved at them.

"Chase, quit your fooling and get down here!"

"Quit your fooling!" Grace echoed.

"There's a baby doll over here," he hollered back. "It's all muddy. The wind must have blowed it in!"

"Never you mind. It's raining and we need to get dinner to your auntie's house before we drown."

"I want to see the baby doll," Grace protested.

"It's crying," Chase yelled.

Mary hesitated and her eyebrows knit. She put Grace and her picnic basket down and with a stern warning to the children to stay put, she clambered up the hill. Sure enough, leaning against a pile of branches and half buried in wet grass and muck at the bottom, she saw a round-headed little baby doll.

Mary let out a breath, relieved. Until it moved.

Her heart leaped into her throat. Without a thought she half slid down the slippery rill, unaware and unconcerned that she was covering the seat of her dress with mud. She touched the little hand, and it moved again. Mary dropped to her knees and frantically dug the baby out of the mire, then scooped a handful of black mud off of its face. It was a little girl, maybe six months old, dressed in a white cotton shift and nothing else. She was barely breathing.

Mary scrambled back up the hill with the baby in her arms. She grabbed Grace by one hand and rushed to her mother's house as fast as she could go, dragging the startled girl behind her and leaving Chase to keep up as best he could.

Alafair Tucker

Once Alafair got Mr. Eichelberger home, she managed to sponge the filth off of him and get him decently dressed. She had just ensconced him at her kitchen table with a mug of hot coffee, a bowl of warmed-over bean soup, and a piece of leftover cornbread when Mary burst through the back door with her muddy bundle and two small children in her wake.

"Mama!" Mary yelled, so loudly that Alafair leaped to her feet, knocking over her chair. "We found a baby! It must have gotten picked up by the wind and blown all the way out to your pasture."

"My stars! Is it alive?"

"Yes, I think so."

Alafair took over. "Grace, bring me that tub yonder. Mary, put the little'un on the cabinet while I get some rags. Chase, take this bucket and pump some water for me. Scoot, now!"

Everyone rushed to his or her task, eager to assist.

The baby's eyes were closed and her chilly limbs were limp. Alafair could feel a heartbeat, but the child's breath was undetectable. Still—she was pale, not blue. Alafair gave Mary a hopeful glance.

Mary and her mother cleaned off the baby as best they could with kitchen rags until Chase lugged in a half-full pail of cloudy water from the well pump outside the back door. Alafair would normally have warmed the water in the reservoir of her cast iron stove, but time was at a premium. Mary removed the baby's sodden shift and sat the child in the tub of cool water. The tiny body shuddered under Mary's gentle touch, and surprised blue eyes opened wide. The baby's pink bottom lip pooched out and she started to cry.

"Oh, thank you, Jesus!" Alafair exclaimed. Mary said nothing. She was weeping as well.

Grace was hovering around, worried. Alafair had her fetch a clean towel from the pantry to wrap around the infant, then sent her to stand by the stove until she dried. Since she had lost most of her clothes in the storm, Grace was clad in one of Chase's shirts, which made a perfectly adequate dress for her, tied around the middle with twine for a belt.

Mary sat down in a chair with the baby in her arms and began to croon to her, and Grace leaned on Mary's lap and joined in the familiar lullaby.

Alafair stood watching for a moment as the baby sucked eagerly on Mary's knuckle. She was sure the little girl badly needed sustenance but unsure how to provide it quickly. She was the mother of many children, but she had never before had need of a baby bottle. She decided to make a knot in a dishtowel and soak it in water so the child would at least have something to suck until she could make up some gruel. She was turning to take another towel out of a drawer in her baker's cabinet when she noticed that poor addled Mr. Eichelberger was no longer in his chair at the table.

Blast! she thought, though she never would have uttered such a shocking epithet aloud. *What next?*

She quickly assembled her wet dishtowel pacifier and handed it to Mary, then headed outside to look for Mr. Eichelberger. Surely he had gotten out the back door while they were distracted. She circled the house, but he was nowhere to be found. She stopped in the front yard, and put her hands on her hips, thinking. The boys were out clearing the road. Shaw and Streeter were in the barn preparing the buckboard to carry the dead. There was no one to spare to hunt for a befuddled old man who was probably trying to find his way to a home that no longer existed.

It was going to have to be her. She walked up the newly repaired front porch steps and into the house to tell Mary where she was going, but as she passed into the parlor, she found Eichelberger sitting demurely in one of her armchairs. Chase Kemp was standing beside him, cheerfully relating how he had discovered the living baby doll. Eichelberger looked at her when she came in. His eyes were full of sadness, but aware. He gave her a hint of a smile, and she smiled back, weak with relief.

Chase had taken charge of the old man. Alafair had not even noticed when Chase led him into the parlor and seated him in the armchair with his blanket around him and his mug of coffee on the side table. Alafair paused, touched. Chase was not generally so thoughtful. Perhaps he had never before had the opportunity to be.

Alafair Tucker

The day after the storm was one of the longest days Alafair could remember living through. She had planned to survey the damage to her large truck garden in the afternoon, but the weather kicked up again with heavy intermittent rain, wind, and a couple of brief hailstorms. During a lull, she scribbled a note to let Kurt know what had happened to his wife and sent Chase running with it. Chase didn't come back, but Blanche and Sophronia did. They said they were eager to see the baby, but Alafair suspected that after living through the tornado, the girls were too spooked to be away from their mother for long. When she did propose leaving them alone while she made a foray to her garden, they objected strenuously.

So for a few hours Alafair was stuck in a dark, leaky house with boarded-up windows, three nervous young girls, a shattered old man, a fretful yellow dog, and a stupefied infant that the wind had blown in. And Mary.

Mary heaped plates with the food she had brought for them from her own house and firmly insisted Alafair and the girls take their dinner into the parlor to eat and keep Mr. Eichelberger company. Then she busily shuttled around Alafair's kitchen with the foundling on her hip, stirring up a pot of stew for their supper.

Alafair found herself looking at Mary with new eyes. Martha had always been her mother's lieutenant, and Mary was her older sister's laughing, easygoing shadow. But Martha was stuck in town, and circumstances had thrust Mary to the fore. She stepped up heroically.

Married less than two months, she had taken in her suddenly homeless sister's stricken family without a second thought, and for who knew how long? She had provided shelter and sustenance to her parents and siblings as well, and had opened her home to her little cousin as though he was her own.

What a heart she has, Alafair thought, on the verge of tears. And Kurt as well. No wonder they fell in love. They were made for each other.

Shaw Tucker

Shaw and Streeter McCoy came back to the house a little after noon in the middle of a downpour. The men pulled off their sodden boots and hung their limp hats on the back porch before they entered, but they were both so wet that they couldn't avoid dripping all over the kitchen floor. Not that it mattered.

Shaw entered first and found himself eye-to-eye with Mary, who was standing at the stove with a wooden spoon in one hand and an unknown, round-eyed infant on the other arm.

"Who's this?" It wasn't the first thing Shaw had planned to say, but this was a day full of surprises.

"We don't know, Daddy. Chase found her out beside the path that crosses the pasture between my place and here. We figure she got picked up by the tornado and blown in from who-knows-how-far. She's shook up, but we can't find anything else wrong with her. It's a miracle she wasn't killed."

The little pink fingers clutched Shaw's big brown finger and her wide blue eyes gazed into his kind hazel ones. His wet black hair was sticking out every which way and his bristly mustache was floppier than usual. It occurred to him that she must be wondering what manner of creatures inhabited this place to which she had been delivered. He straightened. "If that don't beat all," he said. One more odd thing to add to the list.

"Her folks must be frantic. If they're alive," Streeter said.

Alafair had heard their voices and came into the kitchen in time to hear the end of their exchange. "That's why we've got to let Scott know we have her. You fellows stand over by the stove with Grace and dry off. I'll dish you up some of this stew Mary made and pour you a hot drink."

"I don't think we'll be dry anytime in the near future," Streeter observed.

Shaw smiled because it felt so true. "We'll have a quick bite, Alafair, but the buckboard is ready and we're going to try for town right quick before the weather gets any worse. The boys haven't come back yet so I don't know if the road is cleared enough or not. Even if it is we may not be able to get through because of the mud. I can't say how long the trip will take. We're bound and determined, though. Streeter's hankering to get home and I'm hankering to deliver the remains of the departed to the undertaker. We've already put Miz Eichelberger in the wagon and pulled a tarp pulled over the bed."

"I want to come with you," Alafair said.

"I know you do, honey. But you can't. Not now."

Alafair drew herself up, desperate to make her case. But she had long ago learned to judge by the look in Shaw's eyes when it would be productive to argue and when it was better to keep her peace. She didn't argue.

Trenton Calder

Me and Gee Dub and Charlie had the worst dadblamed time clearing that road. I swear the mud was ankle deep and our horses didn't like that one little bit. We had better luck when we got down on our feet and dragged stuff off to the side with might and main and our own six hands. Mostly the road was blocked with tree limbs and the like. There were a fair number of entire trees, though, and we had to do some sawing. One big old loblolly pine near to got the best of us. We ended up sawing a chunk out of the middle and using the horses and some ropes to lug it out of the way.

After we had been at the task for a few hours, we were all covered with enough sap and mud and muck and gunk head-to-toe that it was hard to tell which of us was which. The more dirty and miserable we got, the more we took to joshing about it. Gee remarked that when the wet slop on us finally dried out, it'd be hard as cement and we'd be found later in various statue-like attitudes, unable to move one way or the other. We all got tickled at that and laughed and hooted a lot more than the joke was funny. What else can you do?

We found more than just trees that we had to move. There was a piece of somebody's wall with the unbroken window still in it. Charlie found a perfectly good mop in a bush. We could more or less track the path of the twister by the line of trees standing up with no leaves or branches and the steel windmills that were twisted like corkscrews. The bridge across Cane Creek was partly torn up. We pondered on that for a spell, then decided to re-lay as many sound boards as we could find. When we got done, you could walk across if you watched your feet. We reckoned a wagon might stand a chance. We came across a number of trees that had been decorated with odd objects; a tin bathtub, clothes, dead animals. No more dead people, thank goodness.

As we got fairly close to the turnoff toward town, one of Mr. Tucker's brothers, Howard McBride, met us on the road. His dad, Mr. Tucker's stepdaddy, had asked him to see if he could get to the farm. Howard already knew what had happened to Phoebe and John Lee Day because of Gee Dub's trek into Boynton the night of the storm. Word gets around fast. Anyway, Howard fell to helping us, but it was nigh to a hopeless task. It kept raining off and on, and eventually the road could have been clean as a whistle and it still would have been too boggy for any wheeled conveyance to navigate—and maybe any animal as well.

Early in the afternoon Mr. Tucker and Streeter caught up to us in the buckboard. We had only cleared the road about halfway to town. Mr. Tucker had poor Miz Eichelberger in the bed of his wagon and he wasn't about to admit defeat. He got down off the bench and took his team by the head and led them off the road and into the field, where the grass made better footing for the horses. All us fellows went along ahead of him and hauled debris out of the way and, foot by foot, we made progress. Of course, we couldn't get all the way into Boynton like that. Every few hundred yards, Mr. Tucker would have to take the wagon back to the road to avoid trampling what was left of somebody's crop or fence. Then we'd have to scatter sand or put boards down in front of the wheels every time the wagon sunk in the mud. Which was a lot.

It was late afternoon before we made it.

Shaw Tucker

The streets of Boynton were littered with greenery, shingles, and pieces of fence. It was a mess, but the houses and buildings had only suffered minor damage. Shaw's shoulders finally relaxed and he let out a breath when his small caravan finally turned due south onto the brick-paved main street and began to move at a normal pace rather than a slog. The spate of water that had rushed down the street had receded, leaving leaf- and grass-filled puddles and runnels.

Howard McBride veered off toward his parents' house and Trent headed to the sheriff's office to deliver their reports. Shaw sent Charlie to Alice's house to do the same. He kept Streeter and Gee Dub with him to help unload the body.

They had just pulled up in front of Mr. Lee's funeral parlor when Trent returned and informed them that neither Mr. Lee nor Scott was in his accustomed place. They were both still at the makeshift morgue in the Masonic Hall.

Shaw didn't like the sound of that. He exchanged a distressed glance with Streeter before climbing back up onto the buckboard. "Well, come on then, boys. May as well get it done."

Scott met them in front of the building. His normally jolly demeanor wasn't jolly anymore. The blue eyes were heavy with concern. He shot a sour look at Trent. "Where have you been?" he barked. Trent wasn't offended. He could tell Scott had been worried.

"Trying to get the road northwest of town cleared. Not having much luck at it, either, as you can tell by the sight of us."

"I hate to ask," Shaw said, "but how many folks have been killed that you had to bring them to the hall?"

Scott turned to his cousin. "We've got six killed thus far, all from outlying farms. We've got us a clinic in here, too. Maybe two dozen hurt. Every doctor in town is here. I've sent my boys and whoever else I could find to check as many places as they can. I hear John Lee's got a broke leg. How are y'all faring?"

"Me and Alafair have some damage to the house but nothing we can't fix. Lost most of our clothes and bedding, though. John Lee is banged up good. They've lost most everything. They're at Mary's right now. I'm afraid I've got another casualty for you. Miz Eichelberger was killed…" The expression of dismay on Scott's face caused Shaw to hesitate for an instant. "Mr. Eichelberger made it through, but their house is gone. We've got him out to our place. Also, Mary found a little baby girl alive and unhurt out in the back pasture. Is there anybody missing a youngster?"

Scott's eyebrows shot up. "I'll be switched! A baby? Nobody's come looking for a baby yet. I do have the bodies of a young couple that got found over southwest next to what was left of a conestoga. Nobody has been able to identify them yet. I figure they were traveling and got caught in the storm. Maybe the little gal Mary found was theirs."

"May *be*." Shaw thought this as likely an explanation as any. "Well, I guess we'd better deliver this dear soul inside, then. By the by, did you ever discover who it was that Gee Dub dragged in last night?"

One of Scott's eyes twitched. "He's not a pretty sight, but there's no doubt it's Jubal Beldon."

"Ah. Tore up bad, is he?"

"Real bad."

"You know, Scott, a white-maned bay showed up in Kurt Lukenbach's yard last night, saddled and wild-eyed, with a wound in his side. My guess is that the twister sucked Beldon right off his horse."

Scott thought about this for a minute. "You sure it's Beldon's mount?"

"It looks like his, for certain."

"Well, that's interesting. When I come over here to the hall early this morning, the undertaker was waiting for me. He informed me that Jubal is a lot deader than the others."

"What did he mean by that?" Shaw asked.

"Mr. Lee said it looks to him like Jubal has been dead too long to have been killed by the storm. 'Course he can't say for sure, but by the state of the body he guesses that Jubal died a day or two before the storm picked him up and tossed him around."

"But he's not sure? What did Doc Addison say about Jubal when Gee Dub brought him in?"

"It was Doc Perry who checked him over. Said he had a broken neck and a punctured artery in the leg and he was probably slammed about in the wind. Said the sand and debris had scoured the skin right off him."

"So last night he didn't think Jubal's death was suspicious?"

"Shaw, with all the hullaballoo that night none of the doctors had a lot of time to spare for the dead. They were too busy with the living. They turned those who had passed on over to the undertaker. But Mr. Lee noticed right away that rigor was advanced and Beldon's backside was livid. So it seems likely that Jubal didn't die in the tornado after all. He was already dead when the tornado skinned him. He broke his neck, all right, but that puncture wound in his thigh would have been lethal. Now, that could have been done by debris turned into a missile by the tornado, or it could be somebody slipped a blade into his leg. Mr. Lee said there was nothing left sticking in the wound. I looked at the wound myself, and it was a mighty even-edged little slice."

"I'll be whipped! You think somebody may have murdered him?"

"I don't know, Shaw, but I need to find out. I hope it'll turn out that his horse threw him on his head and he fell on something sharp to boot. But if it's murder…"

"Do you suspect anyone in particular?"

Scott shrugged. "Considering that it's Jubal Beldon, I got about a hundred suspects."

The conversation was interrupted by Dr. Jasper Addison, who loomed up in the door of the hall, his shirtsleeves rolled up and his long white beard frazzled and on end. "Scott, we're out of disinfectant. Find out if anyone has whiskey. Don't give me that look. I don't care if it's legal or not, and don't you go arresting anyone who comes forth."

Scott laughed, relieved to have something to laugh about. "Don't kick up a row, Doc. We have a bunch of carbolic soap at the mercantile, and it's all yours."

AFTER

Trenton Calder

In the end, there were about a dozen people who lost their lives to that storm, if you count Mr. Warner and Nanny Jensen who were both banged up so much that they died by and by. The first funeral was held three days after the tornado in the midst of a rain. The cemetery was so boggy that Mr. Lee's motorized hearse had to be pulled to the grave sites by horses. I hated that. I hated the idea of being laid to rest in the mud.

There were two bodies that didn't get claimed right away, and one that Scott kept hold of. It was the middle of summer so we couldn't wait too long before doing something with them. Mr. Khouri had a refrigerator in the back of his store. No, we didn't store the bodies alongside the slabs of pork, but Mr. Khouri did supply us with ice. After a day or two, though, Mr. Lee the undertaker had to go ahead and embalm the unclaimed deceased.

Anyhow, it was going to take a while to identify the young couple that nobody knew. Scott sent me out to where they were found, and I set about searching all around for something that would help us figure out who they were. They had been driving a wagon packed with household goods, which the storm had scattered over half the county. I found their mule dead in a field, lying halfway in a farm pond. I trekked up to the farmer's house to tell him about it so he could haul the animal out and bury it before it fouled his water. Eventually I picked up a piece of a book with "E.J. Mitchell, Mina, Ark." written in pencil on the inside cover. Now, that book could have belonged to somebody else, but I didn't know of any Mitchells and I knew most everybody who lived around Boynton. So I figured that would give us someplace to start looking.

The other strange thing was that nobody came looking for Jubal the next day. It's true that the Beldon farm was just about as close to Morris as it was to Boynton, and given the state of the roads it was likely that the Beldons were hunting for their kin off in that direction. But finally Scott figured that he'd better make the trip out there and let them know that Jubal had been called to his reward in a manner that called for investigation.

Ruth Tucker

Beckie MacKenzie was not herself. That was Ruth's assessment. She supposed that she shouldn't be surprised by the older woman's somber mood. After all, Beckie's beloved Wallace had left and her house was partially staved in.

Beckie had always been an energetic person whether she was in a good mood or not, but since she had come home from Muskogee she seemed so listless and uninterested in the normal things of life that Ruth wondered if she was ill. Ruth tried to question her about it, but Beckie had nothing to say on the subject.

And then Wallace came home. He came into the house through the kitchen, where Ruth was cleaning up after dinner. She was actually relieved to see him.

"Wallace MacKenzie, I do declare! I figured you and Randal would be all the way to Denver by now."

He plopped himself down on a kitchen chair with a sigh and took off his flop-brimmed hat. He looked tired. "No, Randal and I have delayed our trip indefinitely. In fact, while we were in Muskogee, we both enlisted in the Army. We're supposed to report to Fort Riley, Kansas in two weeks."

For a moment Ruth doubted her own ears. "The Army…" she repeated.

A familiar flash of irony appeared in the blue eyes. "Try not to look so surprised, Ruth. Yes, the Army. We came to the conclusion that war is probably inevitable so why not volunteer before we're drafted?"

"So you've come to take leave of your grandmother?"

He looked away. "More or less. We spoke about it before she left Muskogee, so she won't be surprised. Grandmother sent a note to Father yesterday and told him that a twister had come through here while she was away, and she has damage to the house. Father was going to come and arrange repairs for her, but I said I'd do it. I just arrived on the train a few minutes ago."

"I don't know if you could see it when you came up from the station," Ruth told him, "but the cottonwood over to the side of the house was broken right in the middle and the top crashed through her bedroom window. Streeter McCoy had a look at it and said the upstairs is still structurally sound, but she had a lot of water damage in that room and water leaked down into the music room, as well. Trent Calder and my brother helped board everything up. It hasn't rained today so I don't know if it's still leaking, but that wall needs rebuilding and the window will have to be reframed."

Wallace nodded. "I can do that, if I can get my hands on the materials."

"Streeter said that all in all it could have been a lot worse. Well, Wallace, I have to say that I'm mighty glad you're here. Your grandmother has been in the dumps since she got back. She'll be elated that you've come."

Wallace stood up. "I hope so. Would you do me the favor of letting her know I'm here?"

It was a strange request, but it was his tone that gave Ruth pause. He sounded unsure, which was not like Wallace at all. She dried her hands and hung the towel over the washbasin without questioning him. "Certainly. Go on upstairs and have a look at the damage."

Ruth found Beckie sitting in her armchair in front of the parlor fireplace, as she had been for much of the day. "Miz Beckie, guess what? Wallace is here. He's come to repair your storm damage. Ain't that nice?"

Beckie didn't look up at her. "Has he indeed?"

Ruth blinked, surprised at Beckie's lack of enthusiasm. "He has. He's gone upstairs to survey the damage. You want to say hello to him?"

"...Grandmother." Before Beckie could give Ruth an answer, Wallace spoke from the parlor door.

Ruth stepped back and Wallace took her place beside Beckie's chair. It occurred to Ruth that she ought to leave them alone, but she was too intrigued by this unexpected situation not to listen.

For a long moment the two simply looked at one another, Beckie from her chair and Wallace standing at her side. It was Wallace who spoke first. "Father got your note. He was going to come himself, but I volunteered to come instead."

Beckie's tone was subdued. "You didn't need to do that."

"I wanted to, Granny. Who knows when we'll see one another again?"

When Beckie responded there was a quaver in her voice. "Did Mr. Wakefield come with you?"

Wallace paused. "He did. He's staying at the hotel in town, though. I'll stay here while I'm doing the repairs, if you don't mind."

"Does Mr. Wakefield intend to assist you?"

"No, Grandmother, he does not wish to impose."

Beckie stood. "That will be acceptable," she said. She left the room, but Ruth noticed that she affectionately placed her hand on Wallace's arm as she brushed past him.

Neither Wallace nor Ruth moved until the sound of a mournful piano etude drifted in from the music room.

Ruth couldn't contain her curiosity. "Whatever has happened?"

Wallace shook his head. "She's conceived a dislike for my friend." He headed for the stairs and Ruth followed him.

"Did they have a row?" Ruth asked his back as they trooped up the stairs. "Randal is such a nice fellow that I can hardly credit the idea."

Wallace didn't answer until they reached the landing on the second floor. He slid Ruth a sarcastic look out of the corner of his eye. "Let's just say she doesn't approve of his politics. That's as good a reason as any."

"Well, that seems unfair. My daddy says everybody's entitled to his own feelings."

Wallace turned to go into his grandmother's bedroom. "Gram has her own ideas about what a person is entitled to feel."

Alafair Tucker

It was going to take weeks to clean up and repair the damage done to the farm by the storm. Fortunately, Alafair and Shaw had more help than they knew what to do with. As soon as the road to town was cleared enough to travel on, Alafair slogged to Boynton on the back of her gray mare to spend a couple of hours with Alice and the new grandbaby. When she returned home, her sister-in-law Josie Cecil came with her.

When Shaw returned to the house at suppertime, he was amused to find that his eldest sister was on her hands and knees in the girls' bedroom, scrubbing the floor with hot lye water. Alafair had been relegated to a chair in the parlor along with Mr. Eichelberger. She didn't look all that happy about it.

She looked up at Shaw with an expression of exasperation mingled with relief. "Sure glad you're home." She kept her voice low. "Your sister is going to 'help' me right out of my mind."

Shaw laughed and gave her a sympathetic pat. But he knew better than to gainsay Josie. He greeted Mr. Eichelberger and sat down next to Alafair. "What are you writing, sugar?"

She handed him the list she had been making on a piece of butcher paper. "I took inventory of the garden. This is what we've lost altogether, and this is what I figure will come back. The potatoes, carrots, and turnips will be all right, but I don't know about the squash and pumpkins. The greens are gone but they'll likely come back. The sweet corn is in bad shape and the tomatoes are ruined. I can probably save some of the bean plants. I'll salvage what I can. I've already canned enough early vegetables to get us through the winter, I think. But we'll have to make do with less."

"I thought I heard you, Shaw." Josie appeared at the bedroom door with a bucket in one hand and a scrub brush in the other. "Alafair, you won't have to do without anything. Between all us Tuckers and the ladies at church, we'll round you up enough canned goods to last through next year."

Shaw winked at Alafair. "See, honey?" Alafair's sour look prompted him to change the subject. "How are Alice and little Linda doing?"

Alafair's mood improved instantly at the thought of her new granddaughter. "They're just fine as cream gravy. That is one beautiful little baby, if I do say so myself."

Josie placed her bucket against the wall and sat down on the sofa next to the silent Mr. Eichelberger. "Alafair told us about how all y'all's clothes got ruined. Me and Martha are going to collect togs enough to tide you over till you can get some more made. Martha offered to do some sewing, and Alice, too, when she gets to feeling better. Walter says you all are not to worry about money. Him and Alice have plenty to share. After I fix y'all some supper I'm going back to town and betwixt me and Martha we'll take care of Alice, so Alafair doesn't have to make that trip into Boynton every day unless she wants to. Oh, by the way, Shaw, my boy Joe went on the train to Okmulgee yesterday and talked to Charles. His lumber yard didn't suffer any storm damage. He will sell you the lumber y'all need for repairs at a discount."

One corner of Shaw's mouth twisted up in his signature quirky smile. "Charles may be family, but what say we let him speak for himself on that matter?"

"Charles will sell you the lumber at a discount." Josie was firm on that point.

Shaw spared a moment of pity for his brother.

Trenton Calder

Me and Scott rode to the Beldon farm early the next morning. We started before dawn, because those folks lived way to the heck and gone and we didn't know what state the road was in out that far. As it turned out, once we got past the storm path about three miles west of Boynton, the road was boggy but clear enough. The Beldon farm was pretty big—near to half a section the old man had bought off of Sarah Fishinghawk when he came to the state back in '07. They raised cotton, mainly, but he had a nice little herd of whiteface cattle, too. We rode by the cotton field on the way to the house. The cotton had taken some damage from hail, but the twister had skipped them over and the crop was still standing. The house stood pretty close to the road so Scott started hollering to let them know we were coming as soon as we turned up the drive. Miz Beldon hollered right back that she was in the kitchen and we ought to come on through.

We found Mildrey Beldon sitting in the corner of her kitchen, brushing Lovelle's long, yellow hair. The little gal was standing between her mother's knees, hanging on to a doll and doing her best to endure the grooming session. It was probably seven o'clock in the morning by the time we got out there, but two of those Beldon boys were still at the kitchen table wolfing down biscuits and gravy and giving us the stink eye. Hosea was not one of them.

When me and Scott came into the kitchen, Miz Beldon stood up. Lovelle went to squirming. "You about done, Mama? I want to go play."

"All right, honey, there you go." She gave Lovelle a little push, and the child dashed out of the room. Neither of the boys at the table moved.

"Welcome, Sheriff, Deputy Calder." Miz Beldon said. "Y'all have a seat and I'll fry you up some eggs."

I'd have taken her up on it, since at the time I was newly grown and had a hollow leg, but Scott shook his head. "Thank you, Miz Beldon, but we cannot avail ourselves of your hospitality. I'm afraid we have come to deliver some bad news about your boy Jubal." The two at the table stopped stuffing their faces and fell to listening.

Mildrey eyed Scott warily for an instant, then nodded and sank back into her chair. "I was wondering where he was. He get caught in the tornado?"

"Well, ma'am, it looks like he died the day before the twister hit. Near as I can tell right now he fell off his horse and broke his neck. I'm dreadful sorry."

Mildrey looked thoughtful. She picked up a peck basket full of green apples from the sideboard and positioned it in her lap. I had noticed an apple tree beside the house when we rode up, loaded down with unripe apples. "I wondered. He pretty much comes and goes as he pleases. But he ain't usually gone this long."

I just stood behind Scott and didn't say anything, but I could feel my eyes bugging out. You never can tell how folks are going to react when you tell them that somebody in the family has died. Sometimes those who you'd never suspect of caring will fall clean to pieces, or someone who you know loved their kin will have no reaction at all. But I didn't have much experience with delivering bad news back then. I was flabbergasted that a mother didn't have a tear to spare for her dead son.

"I'd have not expected him to fall off his horse, though," Mildrey went on in a conversational tone. "Jubal always was a good rider and that horse of his was his pride and joy. He spent many an hour training that beast."

Scott crossed his arms. "Maybe the horse got spooked. One of the Tucker boys found Jubal's body in a field right after the twister went through. His horse turned up later that night. You have any idea where he was going Sunday night?"

Mildrey commenced to peeling an apple with a little paring knife. "I don't know. Maybe he was coming home. I haven't set eyes on him since he brought me back here after the church picnic last Sunday."

"He wasn't home Sunday night?"

"No," Mildrey said. "Nor Monday neither." She gestured toward the table with the half-peeled apple. "Likely Hezikiah knows where he got to."

Scott turned his attention to the fellows at the table. "Did Jubal talk to you before he left, Hezikiah?"

By this time both the younger Beldon boys were standing up. They looked like they wanted to fight with us…who knows why?

That was just their natural way, I expect. The taller one, Hezikiah, couldn't think of a good reason not to answer. "Not to me, but I heard him tell Hosea that he had some business he wanted to take care of and I did see him ride off toward Boynton."

"What time was that?"

Hezikiah's face screwed up while he thought about this. "Sunday afternoon. Before dark, anyway."

"Either of you see him after that?"

Hezikiah shook his head, and the fair-colored one, Caleb, said, "Never no more."

Scott looked the boys up and down, then told them to be on about their business while he talked to their mama. When they were gone, I kept standing in the corner but Scott pulled up a chair so he could talk to Miz Beldon face to face.

"Miz Beldon, we've got your son's body at the undertaker in Boynton." His voice was real gentle. "It's been a couple days so Mr. Lee had to go ahead and embalm him. If that goes against your beliefs, I'm sorry, but we had no choice. I would like for you to come into town at your earliest convenience and claim the body for burial. Now, I've got to tell you that the twister picked him up and battered him about, but Mr. Lee did his best. Do you have a place for Jubal to rest? Mr. Lee can help you with all that, funeral arrangements and the like, if you need it. Is there anybody else you'd like for me to contact?"

Mildrey watched Scott's face while he talked, but her hands kept peeling those green apples. "No, I reckon not. As for a funeral, I reckon we don't need one of those, either. Jubal wasn't exactly religious. We'll just bring him back here and bury him next to his daddy out on the hill next to the grove."

Scott nodded. I couldn't tell what he was thinking. "I know that your late husband left the farm to Jubal, but do you know what will happen to the place now? Did your husband make an alternative disposition, or do you know if Jubal had a will?"

I doubt if Mildrey knew what an "alternative disposition" was, but she got the drift. "D.J.'s will said that I could stay here until I die, but otherwise everything went to Jubal. If Jubal has a will I'll be mighty surprised."

"Well, then, you'll probably have to go through probate. I'll talk to Lawyer Meriwether on your behalf. But don't worry. Likely the property will go equally to you and your children."

Scott clapped his hands onto his knees and stood up. "Well, that's all, then. You have one of the boys bring you into town as soon as you can. I'm sorry you lost your son. We're doing our best to figure out how he come to break his neck."

Miz Beldon looked up at us. "Me and Jubal never did have much to do with one another, and I won't much miss him now he's gone."

Scott didn't ask her any more questions. I was shocked that Miz Beldon didn't love her own young'uns any better than she did, but Scott told me that he'd seen a lot worse in his time and not to fret myself about it.

We left Miz Beldon peeling her apples and went out the back door. We were leading our horses away from the house when Hosea Beldon come running up from the barn. When he got up to us he slid to a halt so fast he raised dust. "You found Jubal? He's dead?"

Scott gave him a narrow gaze. "When was the last time you saw Jubal, Hosea?"

"Sunday evening. He brought Ma and the brat back from that church do and then turned around and went back to town."

"Do you know what he was aiming to do when he got there?"

"Said he had some business is all. I figured it was some gal since he didn't come home that night." He gave me a spiteful look. "Maybe that Tucker gal who lives with the old MacKenzie woman. He has a yen for her."

I would have liked to fling myself at him and rip his arm off, but I didn't want to give him the satisfaction of knowing he'd got to me.

But he didn't care about me. He had other things on his mind. "You told Ma that Jubal's dead?"

"Yes."

I swear that a look of triumph passed over Hosea's face before he could school his expression to be properly somber. "Does that mean the farm is mine?"

Scott gave him a suspicious squint. "Ain't you going to ask how your brother died?"

Hosea shrugged. "It was just a matter of time till somebody shot him, but since there was a twister on Monday I figure that's what got him."

"The twister picked him up and blew him into a field after he was already dead. What killed him was a fall from his horse the day before the storm."

"Is that a fact? So do I get the farm?"

"I was just talking to your mama about that. Y'all will have to take it up with a lawyer, but I expect you will all get a cut." Scott's tone made it plain that he disapproved of this line of discourse.

"I'm next in line," Hosea blurted. His cheeks were getting red. "I should get it fair and square."

"Y'all will have to hammer that out amongst yourselves, but the law will have something to say about it if y'all can't agree. Now, if you'll excuse us…" We mounted up and Hosea went scuttling into the house, more than likely to badger his mother about it.

"Well, that was unseemly," I said to Scott, once we got out of earshot.

He looked to be mulling the incident over. "It was peculiar," he decided.

By the time we turned out onto the road, I was almost feeling sorry for Jubal Beldon. Then suddenly I remembered the last encounter I had with him and got over that feeling real quick. "Scott," I said, "if Miz Beldon and them haven't seen Jubal since Sunday evening, then I believe I saw him after that."

He shot me a look. "You don't say? And when was that?"

"You remember how I told you that after the church picnic on Sunday, when Alice Kelley's baby was coming, Miz Tucker sent me and Gee Dub out to the Rusty Horseshoe to fetch Walter back home?"

He cocked an eyebrow. "So you did."

"Jubal was there. We exchanged words. That must have been, oh, at least a couple or three hours after Miz Beldon said he took out from home. It was after dark when we got back to town, anyway."

"I presume he didn't tell y'all where he was headed?"

"You presume right. We flung a few barbed remarks at one another and then Gee Dub and me left."

"Well, Trent, that gives us a place to start. Head on over to the Rusty Horseshoe right now and see if Dills knows anything. I'm going to stop over at Cousin Shaw's."

Alafair Tucker

Alafair sat on the porch with Mr. Eichelberger beside her, shelling the few beans she had been able to save from the garden. She was supervising Grace, Zeltha, and Chase Kemp as they picked up twigs and branches from the front yard and stacked them in a pile beside the gate. The little children were doing a surprisingly good job, even Zeltha. At least until she decided to create a fence around herself with sticks upended in the soft earth. Alafair left her to it. There was only so much solid work you could expect from a two-year-old. The other two were intent on their task. Chase was eager to help and Grace was determined to do anything her older cousin was doing.

Alafair had sent Sophronia, Blanche, and Charlie into the woods behind the house in order to retrieve anything useful that the twister may have deposited there. Alafair could see from the backyard that the broken trees were decorated with clothing and bedding, flapping in the breeze like Fourth of July flags. Mr. Eichelberger was much as he had been when Shaw had first brought him to the house after the storm—docile and silent. He sat in his chair, wrapped in a quilt in spite of the heavy heat, and watched the children scurry about. Alafair talked to him continually, gentle and kind, saying nothing of any consequence. But the sound of her voice seemed to soothe him.

She stood up when she heard Scott holler to announce his presence as he rode up to the house. The sight of him coming up the drive on his roan made her heart skip a beat. Now what? She handed the basket of beans to Mr. Eichelberger and walked down the path to meet Scott at the gate. The children clustered around her skirt like a flock of ducklings.

"Hey, Scott," she greeted. "What brings you back so soon?"

"Hey, Alafair." He dismounted, tipped his hat, and nodded at Eichelberger. "How's he doing?"

Alafair didn't look back. "He doesn't have much to say, that's for sure. But he knows what's going on around him and he's eating all right. I think he's just nearly too sad to live." Unbidden tears sprang to her eyes. The thought of losing your spouse after so many years, and in such a violent manner, was almost too awful to contemplate.

"The telegraph lines are back up as of last night. I sent a wire to his daughter in El Reno. She wired back this morning that she'll be here as soon as she can." Scott reached over the fence to pick up Zeltha before he addressed the real reason he had come. "I need to talk to Gee Dub about…" He hesitated and glanced at the eager youngsters who were hanging on his every word.

Alafair got the message. "All right, you scalawags, are you done with your work? I don't think so. Off you go."

When the little ones were out of earshot, Scott got down to business. "I need to talk to Gee Dub about Jubal Beldon."

"Jubal? What has happened? What could Gee Dub tell you that he hasn't already?"

"A couple of things. I want to see where he ran across the body, if he can find the place again. And Trent told me that him and Gee saw Jubal Sunday night at the roadhouse when they went to fetch Walter. I want to have a look at that horse y'all found on Sunday night, too. We waited a while for kinfolks to claim Jubal, but we couldn't wait longer and Mr. Lee embalmed the body. Trent and me made our way out to the Beldon farm this morning to tell Miz Beldon that Jubal is no more—"

Alafair interrupted him. "You made it to the Beldons? How are they? Still standing? How is Mildrey?"

Scott's mouth quirked. "They didn't suffer much damage, as far as I could see. As for Mildrey, she wasn't exactly broke up about her son's untimely demise."

"Oh, I'm sorry to hear that. That is a strange family, to my way of thinking." She paused. "Shaw tells me there's some question about whether he died in the storm or was already dead when the storm hit."

"That is so."

"Does his death look suspicious?"

"It looks like he got thrown by his horse. But there's one or two things about his death that don't fit, and I aim to look into it. That's why I need to trace Jubal's movements on Sunday."

"Well, I hope Gee Dub can tell you something helpful. He's over to Kurt's right now. They're building onto the corral so they can keep John Lee's wounded livestock over there for a while. Kurt has Jubal's horse in his barn, too, so you can kill both your birds with one stone."

When he rode away, Alafair turned toward the porch and her eyes fell on Mr. Eichelberger. She suddenly realized that he had probably heard every word they said. He had not moved, but he was gazing at her with a startling look in his eye. If she had not known better, she might have called it satisfaction.

Alafair resumed her seat and relieved Mr. Eichelberger of the basket of beans. The old man's demeanor had changed so much in the space of five minutes that Alafair knew something significant had happened. She took a guess. "Did you hear Scott say that your daughter Abra Jane will be here directly? What a blessing that will be."

"I heard. I heard it all. Abra Jane is coming. And now Rollo can come home, too."

Alafair caught her breath. This was the first really sensible thing she had heard Mr. Eichelberger utter in three days. "Yes, I'm sure Rollo will come home, as well." Rollo was Eichelberger's simple-minded son. "I declare, I haven't seen Rollo since Noah built an ark. Where is he now?"

"He's been living with my daughter Abra Jane in El Reno for a couple years. We sure have missed having him at home. Maisie would be so happy." He paused to choke back a sob and wipe his eyes, and Alafair squeezed his hand.

"Why did Rollo go to live with Abra Jane in El Reno in the first place? I remember Rollo as a good, simple soul, but he wasn't so feeble he needed tending, and he was a good worker and a great help to y'all on the farm. Did he get worse, or have an accident? If I remember right, he left awful sudden. Miz Eichelberger was mighty sad about it."

Eichelberger shrugged. He didn't answer for a moment, and Alafair thought he was probably considering how much he could say. "Oh, we just figured it'd be better all around if he lived with Abra Jane. Rollo will need looking after all his life and me and Maisie aren't getting any younger. It near to broke his mama's heart to lose him, though."

"Could it have had something to do with Jubal Beldon?" Alafair asked.

He blinked at her. "What makes you ask that?"

Alafair could tell by the old man's reaction that she was on the right track. "Just a hunch. Jubal Beldon was known around here for starting dark rumors about folks whether or not they were true. It looks to me that you've decided that now Jubal is dead, it's safe for Rollo to come back. Like I said, I don't know anything. But I think it would be a good thing if Rollo came back home. I surely do."

Eichelberger withdrew an enormous handkerchief from the pocket of his borrowed overalls and wiped his nose. "Rollo wants so bad to come home," he admitted. "He never did understand why we sent him away."

Scott Tucker

There was so much news to hear that Scott spent more time at the Lukenbach farm than he had intended. If he went back to town without a full report on the state of every member of the extended Tucker family, his wife, Hattie, would never let him hear the end of it.

He listened to John Lee's horrifying tale of being trapped in the rubble of the barn and Phoebe's account of watching the side of her house peel away. He informed Mary that he had telegraphed the sheriff of Polk County, Arkansas, in hopes of finding out if the name in the book Trent had found by the wreckage of the dead couple's wagon, "E.J. Mitchell, Mina, Ark.," was a clue to the identity of the foundling. No reply yet.

Scott felt a small pang when he saw how relieved Mary was to hear that. He glanced at Kurt, whose expression told him that what he feared was true: Mary was becoming attached to her little guest. She had even given her a name. "I'm calling her Judy," she told Scott. "She just looks like a Judy to me."

"Now, Mary, honey, you know we're going to find her folks."

Mary didn't look at him. "I know it. Don't worry. Kurt keeps reminding me."

Eventually Scott managed to extricate himself from family duties and walked out to the corral to find Gee Dub.

Gee Dub saw him coming and met him in the yard. Scott liked his cousin's son, a tall, laconic young man with his mother's dark eyes and curly hair and his father's dry wit. Gee Dub had never been one to raise a fuss, but Scott had always thought there was a deep well there that nobody had yet plumbed.

"Hey, Scott," he greeted. "What's up?"

"Gee, do you think you could lead me to the spot where you found Jubal Beldon's body the other night? It would help me to figure out where he died."

Before he answered, Gee Dub wiped his sweaty forehead on his sleeve, removed his gauntlets and stuffed them down the waistband of his chaps. "Dad says Mr. Lee thinks Beldon died before the twister got him."

"Maybe a whole day before," Scott conceded. "Broke neck. Horse may have tossed him."

Gee Dub nodded. "I hate to admit it, but I could no more find my way back to that spot than I could fly. I was so turned around in the dark that I was lucky I didn't end up in Texas. Out in the middle of a fallow field somewhere. There were old furrows on the ground. 'Course, whether he was already dead or not when the storm hit, I don't know that it matters where I found him. He's just as dead either way."

"It matters if somebody killed him."

If Gee Dub was taken aback, he didn't show it. "You think that?"

Scott shrugged. "I don't know, but something about this rubs me the wrong way. I've been asking around if anybody saw Jubal right after the church picnic on Sunday, and Trent says you and him ran into him at the Rusty Horseshoe."

"That's right. Must have been six or so. Around suppertime, anyway. Didn't say anything of consequence to one another, though. I can only vouch for the fact that he was alive at the time."

"All right, then. You ponder on it for a while and if you think of anything helpful, you let me know. Now, show me where that wounded horse y'all found that night is stabled. I want a look at him."

Gee Dub led him to the barn and pushed open the barn door, but before going in he said, "The horse is crazy, you know. Lost his mind. I wanted to shoot him, but Mary said, 'I am not letting you kill that horse. After what he has been through, he deserves to live.' So I didn't. Kurt and me got him cleaned up, but be careful, Scott. He will kill you if he can."

"I declare, the wind surely blew a peck of trouble in on Kurt and Mary the other night," Scott commented.

Gee Dub cast him a knowing glance. "Every wounded and lost thing knows it can find welcome here with Mary."

The gelding was in an open stall at the back of the barn, blindfolded and haltered with a lead rope tied to the wall. He was a handsome animal, well cared for, his cream-colored mane and tail carefully trimmed. He was standing four-square with his head lowered and his ears back. One ear twitched in their direction as they neared. He snorted. It didn't sound like a welcome. The two men stopped well back from the slats.

"He likes Daddy better than most," Gee Dub said. "At least he can get within a mile of the critter without getting bit or trampled."

"He got a brand?" Scott asked.

"Oh, yes, it's the Beldon lazy B, all right. The saddle has 'J. Beldon' written on the underside, too."

"I'll let the Beldons know he's here. I imagine one of the Beldon boys will take him off your hands directly. What kind of wounds did he have when he come in?"

"Splinters, mostly. Only one bad hurt place, on this side, there, see?

Through the slats on the side of the stall Scott could make out a large white dressing on the animal's left side, fairly high, close to the hip. "Looks like somebody was able to get close enough to tend to the wound," Scott observed.

Gee Dub nodded. "Dad did that. Had to blindfold the beast, though. He does better blindfolded, as you see. Dad said it's a narrow, deep, wound, and a lucky thing the horse's innards weren't punctured. Just the muscle."

Scott folded his arms and looked at the horse in silence while he thought, gazing at the white square of bandage on the horse's flank. "I'd like to get a closer look at that puncture wound," he said finally. "I'm not keen to get my head kicked in, though."

Gee Dub didn't question his motives. "That covering is just stuck on there with a little mastic. I can lean over the fence and pull it off easy. It wouldn't hurt him none."

Scott was remembering the condition of Jubal Beldon's body, flayed by the tornado, bones broken, and one narrow, deep, puncture wound on his left thigh. Then he thought about the condition of the storm-maddened horse. Not flayed, not broken, no bodily injury worse than splinters, and one narrow, deep, puncture wound on its left hip. He nodded. "I'd be beholden if you'd do that, son."

Trenton Calder

The Rusty Horseshoe dance hall was about a mile due south and southwest of the Beldon farm, and there was no direct road betwixt the two. I could either have gone three or four miles back into Boynton and picked up the road to Morris, or I could go cross-country as the crow flies. Since most of the fences in the area were still down and there was a footpath or two that I knew of in that direction, I chose the last one. I had to ride across some private property on the way, but I didn't get caught. And if I had, I doubt if anybody would have objected much.

There was still an awful lot of wrack and ruin to see as I rode that first mile south, then the damage thinned out and for another mile it didn't look too bad. Then I turned west. The closer I came to Morris, the worse things got. I could make out the path of the tornado plain as day.

I reined old Brownie in and scouted the terrain for a minute. The storm track ran almost like a graded road about a hundred yards wide, directly southwest to northeast. I started thinking about Jubal Beldon's body, deposited by the twister in the middle of a field. If he was dead before the wind picked him up, then he had to have died somewhere to the southwest of where he was found.

Now, I hadn't seen the spot where Gee Dub found Jubal, but from what I had been told, it was in a fallow field somewhere between the Tucker place and Boynton. But the Tucker place was northwest of Boynton. What was southwest? I consulted the map in my head.

The Beldon farm was southwest of town, but it was west of the storm path, and I had seen with my own eyes that they had sustained little damage. It had to have been somewhere east of Beldons'.

Well, I wasn't going to figure it out right then. But I could tell that if the storm path stayed true, I wasn't going to find much left of the Rusty Horseshoe, either.

I was right about that.

At first I wasn't sure I had the right place, being as it had been dark when I was there last. But if I had been there a hundred times, I still might not have recognized it. There wasn't much left of the little house by the side of the road. No roof, the front wall gone, two walls caved in, and one wall standing bright and chipper like it had no idea what had happened to its mates. Mr. Dills and several other men were going through the rubble, which was strewn across the yard and into the trees, separating out usable bits of building material. There wasn't much.

I reined in at the edge of the biggest heap of kindling, where Dills was picking out bricks and stacking them into a neat pile. "By durn, Mr. Dills!" I said. "I'm sorry to see this."

Dills gave me a narrow squint. "Who the hell are you?"

"Name's Trenton Calder. I was in to your place the other night with Gee Dub Tucker. We come looking for Walter Kelley."

"I remember. Well, as you can see, I am currently not in business, so if you're in the market for a snort, I suggest you go elsewhere."

I dismounted and walked over to him, picking my way through the damage. Dills straightened up when I stopped in front of him, annoyed at the interruption but curious, too.

"That ain't why I'm here, sir. I come on behalf of Scott Tucker, law in Boynton. I want to ask you about Sunday last."

Now Dills really did look put out. "I know Scott. I ain't in his jurisdiction and he never has set about trying to change that fact. If he aims to persecute me for violation of the blue laws, he has picked a blamed bad time to start."

I couldn't help but grin. "No, sir, Scott has no such notion. I'm trying to track the whereabouts of Jubal Beldon last Sunday night. When I was here with Gee Dub, Jubal Beldon was here, too. In fact we exchanged some pleasant conversation. Was he a regular customer of yours?"

Dills removed his leather gauntlets and sat down on his brick pile, resigned to the fact that he was going to have to deal with me. "Yes, I saw all them Beldons right regular. Good customers, but I sure had to keep an eye on them. What roguery has Jubal got up to now?"

"He's got himself killed, is what he's got. The last time his ma saw him was late Sunday afternoon and the next thing anybody knows it's Monday night and Jubal is dead. We're trying to retrace his movements between the two events."

"Well, I'll be switched! Killed, you say. I can't say I'm much taken aback by the news. Jubal was here for a spell that evening, it's true. He was in the back room most of the time, so I didn't see what he was up to. But Dan may know. He keeps a good eye on what goes on back there." Dills turned on his seat. "Dan," he hollered, and the big galoot who had let us into the secret den of iniquity that night put down the ceiling beam he was hauling across his shoulder and came over.

"Yes, sir, Mr. Dills?"

"Dan, this feller is asking after Jubal Beldon. Him and Gee Dub Tucker seen him here on Sunday night and he's wondering if any of us know what became of Beldon after they left I said that you'd know if anybody did. Did you talk to him any?"

Dan rolled his muscle-bound shoulders while he conjured up the memory. Finally he pooched out his bottom lip. "He just sat by himself in the corner and had a drink or two, like he was thinking something over real hard. I didn't engage him in conversation, but I did notice that he counted some cash while he was sitting there. He didn't make a fuss over it, but it looked to be quite a wad. That was before y'all come in. I remember you." Dan nodded at me and cracked his knuckles. "I thought for a while I was going to have to bust some heads."

Dills shot me an ironic glance, and I said, "Yes, well, good sense prevailed and we left in peace. What time was it when he come in, and how long was he here after we left?"

Dan shrugged. "He wasn't here long after you'uns left. Less than an hour."

"Did he say where he was going?"

"He did not. He just stood up and put two whole bits on the table and left. I was surprised. Jubal never was a good tipper before that."

I turned back to Mr. Dills. "Did you see which way he went when he left?"

"No. I had no interest in the matter. You think he met his killer after he left us?"

"Jubal got killed?" Dan's hat practically flew off. "Well, knock me over!"

"Now, I never said he was murdered," I cautioned. "But he did get killed somehow. Sometime that night, we reckon. Before the twister, anyway. I'm trying to figure out where he went and who he met."

Dan started to say something, but hesitated and looked at Dills for guidance. I wasn't surprised. I figure a place like a roadhouse relies on its reputation for discretion.

"It's all right, Dan," Dills said, then answered the question himself. "I don't know where Jubal went after he left, but an hour or two later, his brother Hosea come in. I told him he had just missed Jubal. Hosea stayed long enough to have a drink, then he left, too."

Well, well, I thought. *Hosea didn't mention that, did he?*

"Now, mind," Mr. Dills added, "them Beldon boys may be trouble and I got no use for them generally, but they're good customers, and the truth is I doubt if Hosea killed his own brother."

"Mr. Dills, I tend to agree with you. But Hosea could know something that'll help, so I'll ask him. Thank you for the information." I waved my hand at what was left of the roadhouse. "You intend to rebuild?"

"I do, indeed, young feller. You can tell Scott I'll continue providing the local farmhands with ice tea and a place to play dominoes for as long as I'm on this side of the ground."

Trenton Calder

I wasn't entirely convinced that looking into Beldon's oddly timed death was the best use of my time. It looked to me that he got tossed off his horse and nobody noticed he wasn't around until after the storm. But Scott had a bee in his bonnet about it, so I didn't argue with him. I just figured that Jubal had been such a low-down dog that Scott naturally assumed somebody killed him.

I went directly to the jail to report to Scott, but his son Butch, who sometimes watched the office, told me that he hadn't shown up yet. So I went around to his house.

"As far as I know, Trent, he's still out to Shaw and Alafair's," Hattie said.

Well, there wasn't much I could do until he got back, so I dropped in on Miz Beckie to pay my respects and ask how she was doing since Streeter McCoy and me had rescued her. Of course the real reason was to see Ruth. I didn't want to dally, so after a tip of the hat and a solicitous inquiry I took my leave of Miz Beckie, but Ruth followed me out and asked me if I'd accompany her home now that the roads were cleared up enough for horses. She said she hadn't left town since before the storm, and she was missing her family and feeling homesick.

I felt like I had won the jackpot. And to boot, if Scott was still there and jumped to the conclusion when he saw me that I had gone all the way to Tuckers' to tell him what I found, I figured he'd give me credit for zealous application of duty. So Ruth and me rode out of town together, me on old Brownie and her on Miz MacKenzie's mare Teacup. The day had advanced considerably. The cold aftermath of the tornado had moved on, and it had gotten hot and humid and windy. But the sun was shining, for once. We talked a lot on the way out there.

She said that as much as she loved Miz Beckie, the atmosphere in that house was mighty gloomy, especially since Wallace had come back, and she didn't know what to do to make it better. She told me that the two of them had fallen out over his friend Randal Wakefield, which I thought peculiar. Of course, I liked Wakefield a lot better than Wallace. I told Ruth that I expected that Miz Beckie, for all her going on about what a good soldier Wallace would make, was not happy that he had joined up. And now that she was faced with the idea of him going to war and getting killed, she blamed Randal for either talking him into it or going along with it.

Ruth said that sounded reasonable. She kindly thought Miz Beckie was a mite jealous of Randal.

I told her that Scott was determined to look into Jubal Beldon's demise in case the death was not an accident. "Scott said that Jubal was such a nasty creature, always digging up dirt and making up evil stories about folks, that he'd be surprised if it turned out somebody *didn't* kill him."

Her expression changed in a blink. She was wearing a blue-green scarf around her neck, which caused her eyes to turn the color of the turquoise stone in the bracelet my sister had brought my mother from her trip to New Mexico. The color amazed me so that I had to concentrate real hard in order to understand what she was saying. "Does Scott think Jubal slandered the wrong person and got killed for it?" she asked me.

"It wouldn't surprise me if that's just what he thinks, Ruthie. All these years I've known Jubal and his brothers, they're always looking for a dog to kick. Makes them feel like big men, I reckon. Do you know of somebody in particular who Jubal might have had something bad on?"

"Who doesn't have secrets they'd rather keep hid, Trent, whether it's their own or a loved one's? He threatened to spread a calumny about me, for one."

The idea that a disgusting piece of work like Jubal Beldon could have something to threaten Ruth Tucker with was so ludicrous that my first reaction was to laugh. My second reaction was a red-hazed rage. "What did he say to you?"

A corner of her mouth twitched, which usually meant that she was amused. Not this time. "He implied that if I didn't give him my favors, he'd just tell everyone I had anyway." Then she did smile. "No surprise, I guess."

That's when I knew in my bones that Scott was right. Somebody murdered Jubal Beldon. If I'd of had him there at that moment I'd have killed him myself. A man would do anything to protect the ones he loves.

My cheeks were hot. It galled me to know that I had flushed red and that she could see my feelings written plain on my face. I realized that I hadn't breathed in a while, and I let my breath out in a gush. I came within a gnat's eyebrow of saying something unfit for her ears, but I caught myself in time and said, "That's low."

"But how on earth could Scott possibly tell for sure if Jubal was murdered, Trent? After what the wind did to Jubal's body, there's no way he could be certain it wasn't just an accident."

"Well, you know Scott. He'll want to make sure if he can," I said. "He don't countenance murder under any circumstance."

She guided Teacup over toward me till she was close enough to put her hand on my arm. It was soft and warm and nearly burned a hole in my skin. "Trent, maybe someone did kill Jubal, and that's a bad thing. It's a sin. But I wish y'all could just leave it to God, and not go to digging up the sad secrets of all them that Jubal tormented."

Now, I knew Ruth Tucker for one of the kindest girls on earth, and it didn't surprise me one bit that she wouldn't want innocent folks' family secrets exposed to public ridicule. But, dang me, I suddenly got it in my head that she was keeping something from me. "Miss Tucker, do you know something about the death of Jubal Beldon that you're not telling me?"

If my tone disturbed her, she didn't show it. "Certainly not. I'm just thinking aloud, Trent. If he tried to get something from me by making up stories, I'm sure he must have done the same to others."

"If you know who might have had cause to kill him, Ruth, you need to tell me. We can't be making judgments about whether he deserved it or not. The law has to judge without prejudice. That's why they say that justice is blind. If you know who all Beldon threatened, whether for a good reason or not, you've got to trust the law to do the right thing. We won't be spreading tales."

She may have been younger than me, but she recognized a pompous ass when she saw one. Fortunately, she forgave me for it. "Oh, I trust you and Scott. I'm just asking you to be careful, and to consider the consequences."

I opened my mouth to spout more arrogant claptrap, but she glanced up at me with her turquoise eyes, full of perfect confidence in my honesty and good will, and I suddenly realized that I was going to do whatever she wanted.

"Well, I'm pretty sure Scott aims to do a little poking around on the quiet before bringing the county sheriff in on it," I said. "Maybe we can discover who Beldon had dirt on without making a fuss. Nobody needs to know right yet."

She didn't take notice of my collapse. She never doubted that I'd see the rightness of her position. "Well, I can only guess, but I'm sure there's quite a list." She pondered what she had just said. "I suppose it's too much to hope for that there actually is a list written down somewhere."

I snorted at the idea. "I doubt if Jubal ever held a pencil in his fist more than to write his name. And even if there was, it's been blown clean to the Atlantic Ocean by now."

"Who might he have taken into his confidence?"

"Those knucklehead brothers of his, if anybody."

She shook her head. "They're not likely to tell us anything. More likely they'd use any information Jubal gave them to their own advantage. What about their mother?"

"Heavens! Him and his ma barely spoke two words to one another. Jubal wouldn't have told Miz Beldon if he was up to no good."

"She might know more than you think. In my experience, your mother knows a lot more about you than you wish she did."

We both laughed at that, an uncomfortable laugh, since it was so true.

"Yes, well, in my experience, Ruth, your ma may know all your dark and evil thoughts but she's the one person you can count on not to betray you with them."

Alafair Tucker

Mr. Eichelberger was in his usual place on the porch, but he had undergone an amazing transformation since Trent had seen him last. No longer catatonic with shock and grief, he greeted the young people and solemnly accepted their condolences before directing them into the house. Ruth found her mother in the parlor with her sewing basket and a pile of children's clothing that the youngsters had retrieved from the woods. Alafair had washed the clothes by hand in a tub on the back porch and was now mending rips and patching tears in the pieces that weren't so badly damaged that they couldn't be salvaged. Grace was at her feet, playing with the puppy, which had also been washed in a tub before being allowed into the scrubbed and disinfected house.

Alafair and Grace both hugged Ruth until she feared she'd pass out from lack of air, even though it wasn't as though they hadn't seen one another for days. Alafair had already been to town several times to monitor the well being of all her town-dwelling children. After hearing that Scott had gone on to the Lukenbach farm, Trent took his leave and continued on his errand. Ruth was directed to the settee and given several ripped shirts to match with patch-sized scraps from the rag basket.

Alafair told Ruth that Chase Kemp had gone back to Mary's, intrigued by all the action there. Mary was glad to have him, believe it or not. Mary had her hands full with the injured John Lee, very expectant Phoebe, and the foundling baby, so Chase had become Zeltha's enthusiastic and surprisingly competent babysitter. Grace, though, was still traumatized enough that she was unwilling to leave her mother's side unless she was forced.

"The bedrooms are still too tore up to use," Alafair said, "so the boys have been sleeping in the old farmhand's room off the toolshed and the rest of us have been finding whatever spots we can. We're all still spooked after the twister. Every time the wind picks up, the young'uns all get distrait. It's been hot, so the girls have been bunking on the porch along with Mr. Eichelberger. All but Grace. She's been sleeping with me and Daddy." She nodded toward the big double bed that Ruth had last seen in her parents' room, now dominating the parlor. "I had your daddy move the bed under the front window so that if the wind shifts, I'll know it right quick." She smiled. "I'm a mite distrait myself."

Ruth caught her mother up on news from town, including the fact that Wallace had come back to help repair his grandmother's house. And that, wonder of wonders, he and his friend had joined the Army.

"I'm glad Wallace is able to say good-bye to his grandmother before he has to go off to Fort Riley," Alafair said.

"I'd have thought that Miz Beckie would be so glad to see him one more time, Ma. But she's hardly spoken two words to him since he came back. She doesn't want to tell me what is wrong, but Wallace believes that she's taken a dislike to Mr. Wakefield."

"Did he tell you why he thinks so?"

Ruth shrugged. "He told me that she doesn't like Randal's politics, but I wonder if that's not a stretch. It's true that Miz Beckie is mighty conservative. Randal may have said he admires Mr. Wilson or some such. But she's such a lady that I can't imagine her being so ungracious about it."

"Unless it's Mr. Wakefield who is being ungracious," Alafair offered.

Ruth looked skeptical. "You've met Mr. Wakefield. He's the furthest thing from ungracious. More than likely it's Wallace who is at fault somehow. Whatever it is, I know it hurts her deeply. I hope they make up soon, because she's going to be heartbroken when he finally has to go for good. I wonder if it might not have been better if he hadn't come."

"Oh, I don't doubt she'll forgive him. She dotes on that boy even if he is an imp. Is his friend Mr. Wakefield helping fix the house?"

"No, he's lying low at the American Hotel until him and Wallace have to leave. They aim to travel together on the train up to Kansas and report for duty at Fort Riley in a couple of weeks. I haven't seen him at all. I imagine he doesn't want to inflict himself on Wallace's grandma and make things worse between them."

Alafair rocked in silence for a time, intent on her sewing. She bit off her stitch, reached for a spool of thread, and held it next to the material, critically comparing the colors. Satisfied, she threaded her needle and resumed sewing. "I wonder if Wallace has taken his friend's side in a manner that his grandmother thought was insolent and disrespectful?"

Ruth didn't take her eyes off the rag basket. "Now, that wouldn't surprise me at all. Wallace loves his friend."

The memory of Wallace and Randal sitting together in quiet harmony on the stump behind the Masonic Hall leaped into Alafair's mind. She looked up from her stitching. "What did you say, sugar?"

"I said that Wallace loves his friend Mr. Wakefield."

Alafair lowered the frock into her lap. "Loves him? What do you mean, 'loves him'?"

"I can feel it in the air between them, Mama, the way they look at each other, like one knows what the other is thinking. Wallace is different with Randal than he is with anybody else. I know love when I see it."

"Are you saying you think that they are sodomites, honey?" Alafair blurted out the sentence before she had quite thought about it.

"What's that?"

Alafair felt the heat of her furious embarrassment spread right up to the roots of her hair. She could hardly believe that she had actually uttered the word aloud, and to her daughter, of all people. "Well…well, people who love each other improperly."

Ruth lifted her eyebrows and smiled. Alafair realized that Ruth had no idea what she was talking about. "How can two people love each other improperly? There are all kinds of love. I love my friends and family very much. Don't you have friends you love, Ma?"

Now it was Alafair's turn to smile, desperately relieved that her daughter had lived such a sheltered life. "Yes, puddin', I do. I guess Wallace is lucky to have such a good friend."

"Yes, it'll be much easier on him to go into the Army with a friend to support him."

Ruth fell silent again, engrossed in matching patches to holes, but Alafair didn't lift the sewing from her lap. Ruth's innocent remark had given her too much to think about.

Trenton Calder

I missed Scott, of course. Kurt Lukenbach told me that he had already headed back to Boynton by the time I got there. I should have rushed right back to let Scott know what I found out, but I had told Ruth that I'd ride back into town with her after her visit, so I stayed at the Luckenbachs' for a spell and helped Gee Dub and Kurt finish working on the corral. After we finished, we went inside to say howdy to Phoebe and John Lee. I was dismayed to see how beat up John Lee was, even though Phoebe told me he looked way better than he had when they pulled him out from under his barn.

His head was all wrapped up, his eyes were so bloodshot that they didn't look human, and his jaws were clinched shut. His right leg was splinted with two boards and stuck straight out in front of him. He could hardly move around but to hobble with a crutch somebody had carved for him out of a crooked branch. Considering that they had lost near to everything they owned in the storm, John Lee was in a pretty good mood, though. Cheating death will do that to you.

The little cousin of theirs that Miz Tucker had brought back with her from Arizona, Chase Kemp, was babysitting Phoebe's girl Zeltha, which consisted of him hauling her around like a sack of potatoes. She didn't seem to mind.

Mary Lukenbach fed us pie, and while we visited I got to bounce the little orphan baby on my knee. The baby was a pretty, white-blond, big eyed girl, surprised to find herself where she was, I reckon, and wondering how on earth she got there.

It was the middle of summer so daylight lasted long, but by the time I got back to the Tuckers', the shadows had stretched out. Miz Tucker sat me down at her table and plied me with more pie. Not that I complained any. I told them about what I had discovered at the Rusty Horseshoe.

"Are you suspecting Hosea, now?" Ruth asked me.

"I don't know," I told her, "but I figure Scott will want to press him further. I'll tell y'all, I got to thinking about it on the ride back to town, and it could very well be that Jubal died somewhere close to the Rusty Horseshoe." I pushed my empty plate away and took a pencil stub out of my breast pocket. "Miz Tucker, may I trouble you for a piece of paper?"

She looked at me like I'd lost my mind, but she brought me one of the young'uns' composition books. I tore out one of the blank pages and began to sketch out a map. "Now, here's Boynton, and if I remember right, here is how the roads go out of town and here is where everybody's farm is situated." I drew a bunch of X's next to my lines then sat back and studied my handiwork. It wasn't pretty but it would do.

"Y'all get the idea, I hope. Anyway, here's the path the twister carved out." I drew a broken line. "It ain't due northwest but mighty close. The twister set down close enough to the roadhouse to knock it down, then traveled right along this way, across the Morris road, right past y'all's place here, and through the Day place and on toward the northwest. I don't know where Gee Dub found Jubal's body, but it had to be on the storm track between your place and Boynton. Around here, most likely. So if Jubal was heading home from the Rusty Horseshoe that night and met somebody on the footpath between the two, he could have fell off his horse dead and lain there unseen in the tall grass all day. This is close enough to where the tornado set down that it ain't impossible for him to have got caught up by the wind and carried clear to here." I tapped the paper with an index finger.

"That's nearly three miles, Trent," Ruth said.

I shrugged. "That's nothing. That little baby your sister found is like to have been blown at least that far."

◇◇◇

Ruth decided she'd better get on back to Miz MacKenzie's for the night. Her mama wanted her to stay, but she said she'd rather go back than have to find some corner to curl up in at her folks' battered house. I fetched Teacup for her and we headed out back to Boynton.

We carried on chattering like a couple of happy jaybirds almost all the way back, and I was feeling like I could take off and fly then and there. Until she asked me a question that I never in my life expected to hear from a gently brought up girl. In fact, I couldn't believe my ears. So she repeated herself.

"I said, what exactly is a sodomite, Trent?"

I don't need to tell you that I near to fell off my horse. It took me a minute to recover. "Why do you ask?"

She looked puzzled by my reaction, which meant that I had probably turned red as a beet. The realization made me turn even redder. "Something my ma said. It occurred to me to wonder," she said. "I always heard of it in the Bible, but I never rightly knew what that meant."

"Well, Ruth, you don't want to know. You oughtn't be inquiring about such a thing."

"I wouldn't ask if I didn't want to know." She sounded annoyed. "And I don't appreciate being told what I think."

That put me in my place. I swallowed and did my best. "Well, I believe a sodomite is a person who indulges in filthy and perverted behavior."

"What does that mean? You mean like torture and murder? Mama said it had to do with improper love, whatever that is."

I blinked at her, then turned my head to stare at the road while I considered how to answer without getting my face slapped. "Not so much improper love as unnatural behavior, Ruth. Think of the Bible story of Sodom and Gomorrah."

"Like when Lot offered his daughters to the crowd so they wouldn't beat up the angels? Oh, now that is bad. I always thought that was a particularly horrible thing for Lot to do to those innocent girls."

Oh, Lordy, this wasn't going to be easy. "Not exactly. It's more like when a man uses another man like…" I was desperate to come up with a comparison that didn't make her faint dead away. My voice went up about an octave. "…like a bull uses a cow."

Ruth had grown up on a farm. She didn't look a bit scandalized at my explanation. I was the one who was like to faint. "You mean a man who loves another man like a wife?" she asked.

I was relieved that she saw it like that. "That's a good way to put it."

She pondered the implications of this for some time before she said, "That's not possible, is it?"

I wasn't about to educate her on the matter. "I don't see how they manage it, myself, but I hear some do."

After another moment of puzzling over the problem, she shrugged. "Well, if a fellow never finds the right girl to marry, it's nice to have somebody to care about, ain't it?" Her tone was chipper.

Now that made me laugh. "That's a good Christian attitude, Ruth."

It didn't occur to me to ask why she was thinking about such a thing. Not right then.

Alafair Tucker

After Trent and Ruth left for town Alafair began making cornbread for supper. Blanche and Sophronia decided they would rather be elsewhere and had disappeared long before their mother could put them to work peeling something.

Alafair was left with her ever-present shadow, Grace, who was sitting at the kitchen table with Trent's pencil and a fresh scrap of paper from the notebook, industriously drawing a picture.

"That's pretty good, cookie," Alafair said, as she passed by on her way to the oven. "What is it?"

"It's Bacon, Mama." Grace sounded a bit put out that her mother didn't recognize the dog. "He's going under the house to get away from the twister."

Alafair grimaced. It was going to take the children a long time to get over the trauma of the storm. "He's a smart pup, sweetie pie. No twister will get him." She stood behind Grace's chair for a moment, wiping her hands on a dishcloth and watching the girl draw, when Trent's hand-drawn map caught her eye, still lying on the table where he had left it.

Where did Jubal Beldon die? Alafair sat down and pulled the sketch over toward her.

"Are you going to draw, too?" Grace asked.

"Mmm-hm," Alafair murmured absently.

How far could a twister carry a body? She ran her finger along the broken line that represented the storm track. The tornado had traveled past the Rusty Horseshoe and blown it down. It passed the Beldon farm, but far enough to the east of it not to do much damage. It came near her own house, but not near enough to destroy it. Instead it rolled like a juggernaut directly over John Lee and Phoebe's little house, then headed northeast, out of her ken.

Jubal's body had been…where? Like Trent she had not seen the place where he came to rest, somewhere between Boynton and this farm on the path of the tornado. She was trying to triangulate the location on the map with her fingers when Grace cried, "Gee! Ma and me are drawing."

Alafair looked up, startled, to see Gee Dub standing in the kitchen door. Was it that late? "Why, there you are, son. My, I've lost track of time! Are your daddy and Charlie coming in?"

Gee Dub's eyes crinkled with amusement. "They'll be right along, but I'd rather supper was late than stop y'all from finishing your works of art."

Alafair leaped to her feet and hollered out the back door for the girls to put away their playthings and come set the table, while Gee Dub admired Grace's masterpiece. When she came back inside, Grace was on her brother's lap and Gee Dub was studying Trent's map. "What is this?"

Alafair told him. "Trent was thinking that Jubal Beldon could have died anywhere along this storm track and then got picked up by the wind and deposited where you found him. But Jubal had to have lain dead somewhere all day Monday, somewhere off the beaten path or somebody would have found him."

Gee Dub nodded and looked back at the drawing. "Not exactly to scale, is it?"

"You were the one who found Jubal's body, son. Where exactly was it?"

"Well, I can't say for sure, Mama. It was dark as sin and I was lost. But I did run into Mr. Eichelberger right beforehand. And when us boys were clearing the road the next day, I did notice that there is a fallow field not too far back of his house. So upon reflection, if I had to guess I'd say right about…here."

"Out in this field here, halfway between our house and town as the crow flies? Behind the Eichelberger place?"

"That's right." Something about her tone gave him pause. He shifted Grace on his knee. "What are you thinking, Ma?"

Her countenance was the picture of innocence when she looked up at him. "Nothing. What do you mean?"

"Mama, you know what Dad would say." He put on a stern expression and came out with a fair approximation of his father's voice. "Alafair, I do wish that just one time you'd leave the work of the law to the lawmen."

Alafair laughed at that. "Oh, honey, I'm just ruminating out loud. Jubal Beldon's death, whether it was murder or just an accident, has nothing to do with me or mine. So I don't intend to involve myself."

Gee Dub smiled. He had heard that declaration before. "Just in case, I won't mention your rumination to Dad." He and Grace went out onto the back porch to wash up for dinner and Alafair turned to clear the table, but her eye returned to Trent's map and she found her finger moving over Jubal Beldon's known route on Sunday.

Late Sunday afternoon he had left the Masonic Hall in Boynton and chauffeured his mother and sister home. Then a couple of hours later he appeared at the Rusty Horseshoe with a wad of cash. He left an hour or so later and was not seen again that night. Then twenty-four hours later, his storm-violated body was found in the middle of a field three miles from his last known location.

Where did he get that money? It only made sense to Alafair that he had extorted hush money from one of the many people whose secrets he had threatened to expose. Someone with a very, very bad secret. Not like what he had threatened to say about Ruth—that was schoolyard bully stuff that no one who knew Ruth would believe. Ruth had told her mother that one of Marva Welsh's relatives had been a victim of Jubal's evil tongue. That was a frightening idea, for rumor and innuendo could do a colored family real harm. But as far as she knew, the Welshes didn't have that kind of money. No, it had to involve someone who could pay. A really horrendous piece of information, something that would ruin a person's life. Maybe even send him to prison.

Her conversation with Ruth about the love between Wallace and his friend popped into her mind. Could Jubal have gotten the money from Wallace in exchange for silence about an illicit relationship between the two young men? After all, Randal and Wallace and Miz Beckie had all left town without warning that very night.

But Jubal was seen alive at the Rusty Horseshoe after he got the money. And Randal and Wallace had come back to town after the storm. Not the action of killers on the run.

Suppose that Jubal had shaken down Wallace and in the process discovered that blackmail was a lot more satisfying—and lucrative—than simple bullying. It was so easy to make them pay and run them out of town to boot. Why not capitalize on the rest of his cache of secrets?

She conjured the scene in her mind. Jubal sitting in the dark at the Rusty Horseshoe, counting his immoral gains, making a plan to squeeze someone else. Someone who, as it turned out, was not so easily intimidated.

Her finger moved on the map. From the roadhouse back to town, east. Or from the roadhouse northeast, to the crossroads. To Eichelberger's, right in path of the storm.

She heard Shaw and Charlie clattering and laughing as they came up the back porch steps and she swept the papers off the table with a mutter of self-reproach. Supper was going to be a makeshift meal tonight.

Trenton Calder

I went over to Scott's as soon as I got back to town and told him what I had found out from Mr. Dills. He was real interested in Dan's story about Jubal waving around a wad of money at the roadhouse that night, because his trouser pockets were empty when Gee Dub brought his body in on Monday night. Scott wondered where he had got hold of so much money, and what had happened to it. I pointed out that except for the pants, the wind had carried away every stitch of Jubal's clothes, so folks around the area might be digging dollar bills out of the bushes for a long while to come.

Then Scott's eyebrows about crawled up to the top of his head when I got to the part about Hosea showing up at the roadhouse right after Jubal left.

"And Dills told Hosea that Jubal had been there?"

"That's what Dills told me," I said.

"Well, then I figure you and me had better make another trip out to Beldons' tomorrow and have a further word with Hosea."

That suited me. Then Hattie said I might as well stay for supper, which suited me even better.

Spike, the only one of Scott and Hattie's four boys who still lived at home, talked up a blue streak all the way through the meal, about how he'd been helping folks in town clean up their yards and mend their fences and outbuildings. He said that Mr. and Miz Ogle had lost all their guinea hens and that Jerome Reiger's little dog had got crushed by a tree branch. Hattie told me about how her and all the church ladies had been gathering clothes and home-canned goods for them who had lost so much in the twister. She said that they had about run out of soap and candles and bedding at the mercantile, and she didn't know when they'd be able to get more in.

I related everything I had found out at the Tucker and Lukenbach farms, and Hattie peppered me with all kinds of questions about that little lost baby and John Lee Day's broken leg. Scott hardly said a word. He was acting real quiet and occupied all evening and I knew he was working things out in his mind, but none of us questioned him about it. I knew he was tired and discomposed by all the destruction and misery of late.

When I went to walk back to the hotel, though, he hollered at Hattie that he needed to stretch his legs. Then he grabbed his hat and followed me out of the house.

We strolled down the street in silence for a spell, until we were almost to the turn off onto Main. "Trent, I wonder if you'd help me with something?" he asked, which surprised me. He never did usually ask, but just told me what he wanted me to do. Of course I would, I told him, which is when he commenced to telling me about the wound on Jubal Beldon's horse. I listened, though I didn't get the point and he didn't bother to explain it to me. What he did say was, "I want you to come with me to the stable and help me figure something out."

So we walked on through the hotel foyer and out into the back where the stable for the guests was. Old Brownie was munching away on his oats and didn't look too happy when Scott backed him out of the stall and threw his saddle on. I just stood there and watched.

Scott handed me the reins. "Go ahead and mount up."

I did. "Where am I going?" I asked.

"Nowhere. Just sit there." Scott came up on my left side and stood there for the longest time peering at my leg like he had never seen one before. He put his left index finger on the middle of my thigh and the right one on Brownie's flank just behind the saddle skirt, like he was measuring.

I was pretty bewildered by then. "All right, Scott, what are you doing?"

He let out a big breath and stepped back before he looked up at me. "I reckon I know what happened to Jubal Beldon," he said.

Scott Tucker

Trent looked down on Scott with pricked ears as Scott theorized about Jubal Beldon's demise. "Jubal had a stab wound in his left thigh, Trent. Now, considering how busted up he was, it just makes sense to figure that the puncture came from some flying debris. But Mr. Lee told me it was a neat wound with clean edges, an inch wide, and whatever made it sliced the big blood vessel in the thigh. He'd of bled to death within a couple of minutes. No way to prove it was a knife that cut him, though. Except that his horse had an identical wound on the hip; clean edges, about an inch wide." He put his hands on his hips and started wandering around the stable, thinking aloud as he walked. "I figure Jubal was on horseback, just like you are, maybe talking to somebody standing on the ground. And that somebody plunged a blade into his thigh…"

Without warning, Scott ran at Trent and whacked him in the thigh with his fist. Trent yelped, and the horse, startled, shied away. Scott looked satisfied. "…and then he tried to stab him again, but the horse shied and he ended up stabbing the horse instead. So I reckon that if Jubal hadn't of died of the broken neck he got when his horse reared and throwed him on his head, he'd of died of a knife wound in the leg." He looked up at Trent, who was patting Brownie's neck to calm him down.

"It makes sense," Trent admitted. "The thing is, though, that how Jubal died is one thing and who made him die is another."

Scott agreed. "I'd give a bunch to know who he was going to see that night. 'Cause whoever it was is my main suspect. After what you told him about Hosea showing up at the Rusty Horseshoe, I have a picture in my mind of the two brothers meeting on a dark road late Sunday night. So early tomorrow morning we're riding back to the Beldon farm."

Mildrey Beldon

When Scott and his deputy arrived at the Beldon place, only Mildrey was in the house, so Scott took the opportunity to let her know what was happening before they sought out Hosea. She had planned to go into Boynton and claim Jubal's body for burial that day, but Scott told her that under the circumstances, she would do well to wait a day or so. All the other boys were out causing trouble somewhere, so Scott, Trent, and Mildrey were the only three occupying her warm, fragrant kitchen. Lovelle was in the parlor, playing with her doll. Mildrey served her guests coffee and biscuits, but as soon as she sat down Scott dispensed with the pleasantries and got right to the nib of the matter.

"Miz Beldon," he said, "I have some disturbing news. I know how it was that your son died."

Mildrey didn't seem surprised. It was more like she was exasperated that her dead boy was still causing her trouble. "You know how he was murdered?"

"I believe I have figured out the malicious act that led to his death, yes, ma'am. But whether it was meant to be murder is another question. So I have to ask you again to think back on the last time you saw Jubal alive. Think hard, now. Do you have any idea where he was going that Sunday night or who he was planning to see? Even a guess would help."

She shrugged before she answered. Scott noted that she didn't bother to ask about the manner of Jubal's murder. "I don't, Sheriff. I'm sorry. Like I told you before, all them boys come and go as they please and don't feel the need to tell me about it."

Now it was Scott's turn to look exasperated. "Tell me everything that happened on Sunday as best as you can remember it. I don't care if you think it's important or not."

Mildrey sat back in her chair and thought about it for a while before she began. It started out like a usual Sunday, she said. She told Scott about fixing breakfast and cleaning it up, then getting herself and Lovelle prettied up for church. She hunted around for Jubal and talked him into ferrying her and Lovelle into town. Same thing every week, she sighed. He usually grumbled at the bother. But he always ended up driving them there, dropping them off, then coming back to pick them up. She told them every picayune detail of the church service and the picnic and how nice everybody was to her. Scott could tell that Trent was becoming impatient with Mildrey's endless recitation, but the sheriff let her ramble. He figured that she had little enough opportunity to reminisce about something in her life that was actually pleasant. He sat quietly, sipping coffee and listening as though every word was of grave consequence.

Scott and Trent had both been at the picnic and had witnessed the altercation between Jubal and Wallace MacKenzie, such as it was, so that tale didn't surprise them. Mildrey told them that Jubal brought her and Lovelle home at maybe four or five o'clock. "When we got back he grabbed Caleb by the collar and made him take the buggy to the barn. Then him and Hosea argued a while out in the barnyard, and after a while he saddled up his roan and lit out again before supper."

"What did Jubal and Hosea argue about?" Scott asked.

"I didn't pay no mind, but I think it was the usual scrape about how Hosea didn't want to do something Jubal told him to. Them two argue all the time. There wasn't anything unusual about it, Sheriff."

She stopped talking then, but Scott said, "Is that all that happened that day?"

Mildrey shrugged again. "That's the last I ever saw Jubal. I fixed supper like I always do. Hezikiah, Hosea, and Caleb showed up to eat it. Zadok and Ephraim went fishing so they didn't. They came home later with a mess of catfish for me to clean. Right about dark that MacKenzie boy and his friend drove by looking for Jubal. But he wasn't here so they talked to Hosea a minute and left. Right after that Hosea went off somewhere. I heard him come back into the house sometime in the middle of the night."

The minute she mentioned "that MacKenzie boy" Scott jerked up straight in his chair so fast that his coffee slopped out of his cup and all over his hand. "Wallace MacKenzie came by here that night?"

He asked the question a little too loudly and Mildrey's eyes widened. "Yes, sir, him and that dark-haired boy who was with him at the picnic. They were driving Miz MacKenzie's yellow-topped shay. But like I said, Jubal was gone already so they only stayed but a minute."

Scott was thinking, *Why in the name of all that's holy didn't you mention this in the first place, woman?* But he didn't say it. He said, "What did they want with Jubal?"

Mildrey looked nervous, now. "I don't know. Once I told them Jubal wasn't to home and I didn't know where he went, they drove up to the barn to talk to Hosea. I saw them head out back toward town not ten minutes after that."

"And you didn't ask Hosea what it was all about?"

"Well, like I said, Hosea saddled up and took off not long after that and I didn't see him again until the next morning. By that time I had forgot the whole thing. I'm sorry I don't know no more, Mr. Tucker. Do you think the MacKenzie lad killed Jubal?"

Scott took a breath before he answered. It was no use to get aggravated at the poor woman. She had trouble enough.

"I don't know, Miz Beldon, but because of the way Jubal died, my conjecture is that he met somebody on the road that night. Until you told me about MacKenzie, I had no idea that he was anywhere around here that night. Now, how long after Jubal left did MacKenzie show up here?"

"It was a quite a while. Two, three hours?"

"And how long after that before Hosea left?"

"Not long. I saw him ride by the house maybe a quarter hour later."

Scott stood up. So did Trent and Mildrey, ready to hop to it if Scott said "jump." Scott was suddenly afire with purpose and neither one of them thought it wise to cross him. "Where is Hosea now?" he demanded. "I got to talk to him."

"Last I saw him he was heading up the hill toward the barn," she said.

Scott slammed his hat on. "Come on, Trent. Miz Beldon, don't go anywhere till we come back."

"I don't aim to, Sheriff," she assured him.

Trenton Calder

Hosea saw us coming from a long way off, but he didn't bestir himself to come down the hill to meet us. Instead he sat down on an upturned barrel and commenced to whittling on a stick. We had to get pretty close before I could see that he was carving out one of them little whistles.

Scott put his hands on his hips when Hosea didn't even look up after we stopped in front of him. I could tell that Scott was put out. He never did hold with rude behavior. "Hosea," he said. Hosea shook the shavings off his little whistle and looked up at Scott from under his hat brim. His expression wasn't friendly.

"What do you want, Sheriff?"

"I come about your brother."

"Which one?

"You know which one. We're here because I have a notion that Jubal met with aggression on the road the night he died."

"That so? Well, it wouldn't surprise me."

"I been talking to your ma and she tells me that Wallace MacKenzie come by here looking for Jubal a couple of hours after he left here on Sunday evening."

Hosea looked interested in the implications of that question. "Yes, he did, him and that friend of his. He asked me where Jubal went off to, and I told him I didn't know, just like I told you."

"Did he say what he wanted?"

"Just said he had some business with Jubal. No more than that."

"Do you have an idea what the trouble was?"

Hosea's upper lip curled back enough to show the tips of his eye teeth. It was either a sneer or poor excuse for a smile. "He did not, but I expect it may have had something to do with the confabulation some of us boys had with his grandma and Ruth Tucker last week."

I was supposed to keep my mouth shut and let Scott do the questioning, but before I knew it, I said, "What? What confabulation?"

My reaction amused him. "Y'all didn't know about that? Why don't you ask your sweetie about it, Calder?"

Scott jumped in, impatient. He wasn't in the mood to pull two young bucks off of one another. "That's enough. We'll be talking to Miz MacKenzie. Hosea, your ma told us that you and Jubal never did get along."

Hosea went back to his carving. "Ma don't know nothing."

"Your ma also says that you and Jubal had yourselves a scuffle the day he got killed, and that you rode off somewhere shortly after MacKenzie left here and didn't come home until the middle of the night. We know, too, that Jubal and you both were at the Rusty Horseshoe that very night, one after the other. Mind telling me where you went when you left there?"

"None of your business."

"Well, until I find out who caused Jubal's death, I guarantee you it is my business. I suggest you save yourself some trouble and answer me before I arrest you and take you in for questioning."

His eyes flicked up again to give Scott a hostile look. "Are you hinting at something, Sheriff? I can't say I'm sorry Jubal's dead. But there ain't no way you can prove I did him in."

Scott didn't rise to the bait. Instead he smiled. "That's a good-looking carving knife you've got there."

"Glad you like it."

The smile disappeared and Scott backed up a step. "Hosea Beldon, I aim to take you into town for questioning about the death of your brother."

Hosea was calm. "I ain't going nowhere with you."

"Save yourself some grief…"

I don't know how Scott meant to end that sentence because he never got the chance. Hosea came up off that barrel like he was shot out of a gun. He grabbed Scott's right hand and slashed the knife right across Scott's neck.

It was so quick I hardly knew what was happening. I saw Hosea grab Scott's hand and a blur when he swung the knife. Blood spurted out of Scott's neck.

It was a pretty smart idea to grab for Scott's gun hand before he slashed, but there was one thing Hosea must not have noticed before he made his move.

Scott was left-handed.

My pistol was out of the holster but Scott was faster. He slapped leather and blew Hosea Beldon halfway across the barnyard. I didn't even get the chance to aim. Hosea landed on his back with his arms and legs flung out and the knife still in his hand, shot square in the chest and dead as Abraham.

Scott was still standing when I rushed over to him. His right hand was pressed up against his neck and blood was dripping onto his collar. But not squirting, so Hosea had missed cutting an artery, or even worse, Scott's windpipe.

He looked annoyed. "Dang," he said.

I don't know why that made me laugh. I guess I was so blamed glad he wasn't dead that I lost all sense of proper deportment. I leaned over Hosea and felt his neck for a pulse, but I already knew it was no use. Miz Beldon and Lovelle had come out of the house, but when they got close enough for the ma to see how things were, she grabbed the little girl by the hand and took her back inside. I could see a couple of the brothers running toward us from the field behind the barn. That made me nervous and I drew my pistol again, but when they reached us they just stood around with their mouths open, thunderstruck.

Miz Beldon came out of the house again and trudged up the hill, looking like the weight of the world was on her shoulders. She put her hands on her hips and looked down on her son. Her second bereavement in a week.

"Miz Beldon," Scott croaked, "I'm so sorry. He tried to…"

Mildrey cut him off. "Did Hosea kill Jubal?"

I could tell by how white his face was that Scott was beginning to feel the shock, so I was the one who answered. "We don't know, ma'am. The sheriff told him we were going to take him back to Boynton for questioning, and he just went crazy. If the sheriff hadn't have shot him, Hosea would have cut his throat. He tried, as you can see."

"Yes, Deputy, I was looking out the kitchen window at y'all. I seen what happened. Now, Mr. Tucker, come on back to the house and let me tend that cut. Boys, y'all carry your brother to the shed and cover him up. After that I reckon you'd better get to digging a second grave."

She took us back into the house and sat Scott down in a kitchen chair to doctor him. The cut was pretty superficial, thank the Lord, but it bled a lot. She cleaned him up, then put brown paper over the wound to stop the bleeding and bound it up with a cloth. Scott sat there like a stunned beast while she worked on him. I couldn't stop my hands from shaking, myself.

"I wish this hadn't happened," Scott said after a while. "I do wish it."

"Sheriff, Hosea always was an angry boy." Tears started to her eyes, which in truth made me feel better about her. She blinked them back. "Now maybe he'll have some peace." Mildrey turned her head to look through the door into the parlor. Her eyes softened as she watched Lovelle playing with her doll on the floor.

Her voice was soft when she spoke again, like she was talking to herself. "I always figured that God was testing me when he gave me six boys in a row. That's why I called them all names from the Bible. I wanted to show that I was faithful." She smiled a sad smile. "And I kind of wanted to signal God that I was on to him. I kept them warm, fed, and clothed, and handed them over to their daddy to finish raising as soon as they could be any use to him on the farm. I did what the Lord asked of me as best as I could, and at long last, he rewarded me with my angel. So you see, I bear a deal of the blame for the way them boys turned out. I didn't love them enough."

Alafair Tucker

Alafair waited until after breakfast, after Shaw and the children had left for their chores and it was only her and Grace in the house. Mr. Eichelberger had gone back out onto the newly repaired front porch to take his accustomed seat near the front door, where he could sit undisturbed and ponder his losses in silence.

After the dishes were washed and put away, Alafair picked up her mending, took Grace by the hand and joined the old man. It was another steamy day, but the scudding clouds were white and puffy. No threat of another storm on the horizon. She took a seat close to Eichelberger and sent Grace to play in the front yard.

She picked up a child's frock and examined it critically. Too ragged to save. She laid it aside. "Nice morning," she opened casually.

"A mite hot." Eichelberger noted.

"It is that. But it don't look like rain. You expect Abra Jane will be in today?"

"Wouldn't surprise me none. I hope so."

Alafair took a piece of paper from her apron pocket. "Mr. Eichelberger, I've been studying this map that Trent drew when he was here yesterday." She handed it to him and he eyed it curiously.

"Him and Scott figured out that Jubal Beldon left his ma's at around half past four or maybe five o'clock and wasn't seen again until at least six at the Rusty Horseshoe. I know that's about right because Gee Dub saw him there when he went to fetch my son-in-law Walter at the roadhouse. That must have been right in between six and seven. He left there before it was quite dark, say seven? Then nobody admits to ever seeing him alive again."

She looked up and cocked an eyebrow at Eichelberger, but all he said was, "Ain't that interesting?"

Alafair bit her lip. "See this line?" She tapped on the map. "It's the path of the twister. Trent thinks that Jubal Beldon's body was so torn up that it had to have been carried by the wind and battered about. He likely died somewhere along this storm path. Now, the twister tore from the roadhouse, past our house, and right through Phoebe and John Lee's. It went through your place, too, and the Bonds'. Gee Dub thinks he found Jubal's body right about here." She paused and looked at Eichelberger again. He was watching her, silent. "In this fallow field." Another pause. Eichelberger said nothing. "Directly behind your house."

The old man had no reaction. Alafair leaned back in her chair. She decided to try the direct approach. "Did Jubal come by your house that night?"

Eichelberger looked away.

Alafair tried again. "Trent told me that Jubal was seen with a lot of money Sunday evening. Did he get it from you?"

The look of hatred that crossed his face startled her. She hadn't realized that the gentle little man whom she had known for so many years was capable of such a poisonous emotion. "No. All he got from me was an earful of hellfire."

There was a long silence as they gazed at one another. Alafair's heart was pounding.

She broke the silence. "He came to see you that night?"

His expression changed in the blink of an eye. He emitted a gleeful cackle that scared her worse than the anger. Was he crazy? "Yes, he came by," he admitted. "He came by, and then he left."

Alafair was not surprised that she was right, but it still stunned her to hear him say it aloud. "Did you kill him?" she blurted.

"No."

"Why didn't you tell the sheriff?"

"Because the next day the twister took everything from me, and I forgot all about Beldon. He come by just before dark. I saw him turn in from the road. He was coming from the direction of his place, so I figured he was on his way to Boynton."

"Well, what did he want?"

Mr. Eichelberger looked amused by Alafair's flustered state. "For years Jubal's pa wanted the twenty acres of bottom land that I own over by Turkey Creek, but I never did want to sell. That's real good cotton land down there. Jubal threatened to spread an awful rumor about my family two years ago, but until that night he never did try to blackmail Maisie and me with his low down claptrap. Jubal liked having things over folks, but I reckon he finally figured out he could use his threats to get something that he wanted. He told me that if I didn't deed that plot over to him he'd see that everybody in town heard his vile rumor. I gave him a short answer. And before you ask, no, I ain't going to tell you what his lie was. It bears no relation."

Alafair wondered if Mr. Eichelberger's short answer involved a knife. Did Jubal finally go too far and the old man decided to shut him up for good?

He went on. "I told him to go to hell—excuse me, dear heart. He said I should reconsider that answer and left."

"Was he headed toward his farm?"

"I don't know. When I told him to go drown himself, he said to expect a visit from some white-robed friends of his. I watched him ride off until he got to the road. I turned around to go back in the house. Maisie was standing on the porch. I could tell that Jubal's threats had upset her. I tell you, Alafair, if I'da had the chance I might have killed him then."

"Did you see anybody else? Did he meet someone on the road in front of your place?"

Mr. Eicheberger hesitated. Alafair could feel her breathing speed up, because she knew that pause meant he had seen someone and he had to get up his gumption to say otherwise. The old man was not a natural liar. "It was getting dark by then," he said finally.

Alafair had to ask again. "Mr. Eichelberger, did you kill Jubal Beldon?"

When he answered, his gaze was straight and unwavering. "No, I did not. More's the pity."

At that moment, Alafair wanted to believe him more than anything. She pressed him. "Mr. Eichelberger, did you do it?"

"No, I didn't, Alafair. Believe me, if it had been me, I wouldn't be loath to tell you."

"You have to tell Scott what happened," she said.

"He'll think I done it."

"But you didn't."

"No, I did not."

"Who did do it, Mr. Eichelberger?" she urged.

This time he answered quickly. "I didn't say it was anybody, did I?

Alafair regretted her impatience, for she had just given him a route of escape. She decided to go for broke. "Mr. Eichelberger, I don't know for sure what salacious information Jubal thought he had about Rollo, but even if he did bruit a rumor about, everybody around here knew not to believe a thing he said. And everybody knows Rollo, too, what a good-hearted fellow he is." She put her hand on his arm. "And everybody knows that Sugar Welsh is an upstanding, virtuous girl." Marva's sister-in-law, Sugar Welsh, was a beautiful young woman who had worked off and on for Mrs. Eichelberger for years. Until suddenly she didn't.

Eichelberger said nothing for a moment, dumbfounded at Alafair's apparent ability to read his mind. "Nothing untoward ever happened betwixt Rollo and Sugar," he said. "She was just nice to him. I think she felt sorry…" He hesitated and checked Alafair's reaction. A colored girl feeling sorry for a white boy? Shocking!

Alafair was holding his hand, now, trying to reassure him of her good will. Or maybe to keep him from bolting. She tried again. "Mr. Eichelberger, do you know who killed Jubal Beldon?"

The old man snorted. "If somebody killed Jubal Beldon, he did his fellow man a service. So even if I did know, I wouldn't tell you, Alafair Tucker."

Trenton Calder

Scott was steady in the saddle, but he said nary a word all the way back to Boynton. I was worried about him so I was relieved when we finally got to town and I was able to turn Scott over to his wife Hattie, who nearly had a conniption when she saw what had happened. She left her hired girl to run the mercantile and hustled Scott back to their house so she could fuss over him properly. The fact that he let her carry on so told me how he was feeling about the whole thing.

Hattie sent Spike running for the doctor, and while we were waiting for him to come, Hattie sat Scott at the table to change his bandage. Miz Beldon had done a good job. The wound was only seeping.

"Trent, sit down here," Scott ordered while his wife fretted over him. "I want to talk to you." Hattie didn't look too happy about it, but she didn't protest when I did what I was told.

"Trent, you're going to have to take over for a while," he said. He told me to go by the Western Union first thing and send a telegram to the county sheriff and one to the circuit judge about what had happened to Hosea. He figured there'd have to be an inquest.

Next, he said, "What we have to find out is where Jubal went after he left the Rusty Horseshoe. If he met Hosea and that meeting led to his death, we will likely never know what happened. But before we jump to any conclusions, we have to find out what Wallace MacKenzie and his friend were doing out at the Beldon place. So you've got to talk to both of them."

"Scott, can't this wait?" Hattie sounded impatient.

He didn't look at her. "No, it can't. If those boys had something to do with Jubal's end I don't want them getting wind of my suspicions and doing a bolt."

"They already done a bolt," I pointed out. "They went to see Wallace's dad in Muskogee on the night Jubal died. But they came back. That does not bespeak a guilty conscience."

"Then they won't mind telling you everything they did that night and when they did it. I know they left town, along with Miz Beckie, and went to Muskogee. Then Miz Beckie came back the day of the storm, but Wallace and Randal didn't show up again for another couple of days. I want all the holes plugged before the judge gets here. Randal Wakefield is at the hotel. Bring him in and question him first. Lock him up before you go out to MacKenzie's so they can't put their heads together and come up with a story. Then see if the two of them tell you the same tale."

Alafair Tucker

Now what? Alafair was almost certain that Mr. Eichelberger had seen Jubal Beldon's killer. Whoever it was, the old man was determined not to tell. Was he protecting someone he cared for or did he hate Jubal so much that he was grateful to the killer whoever he was? He said that his wife Maisie was there when Jubal came by. Could it have been her? A quick stab with a kitchen knife. The idea made Alafair's skin crawl. Yet what wouldn't a mother do to protect her child? Or was Mr. Eichelberger himself Jubal Beldon's killer?

It was an miserable situation under any circumstances, and Alafair couldn't see a good outcome for Eichelberger.

She bustled around the kitchen, frying ham slices and making biscuits and gravy for the family's midday meal, and trying to decide what to do. Poor Mr. Eichelberger had already suffered so much. Yet, it wasn't for her to be judge and jury, and besides, if she kept her knowledge to herself she was as guilty after the fact as Mr. Eichelberger. She ought to tell Scott and be done with it. Yes, she had to go to the law with this.

However…

Who else had crossed paths with Jubal Beldon that night? Someone who hated or feared him enough to remove him from this earth. She ticked off the list of known sojourners that evening. Trent had discovered that Hosea and Jubal Beldon had barely missed meeting one another at the roadhouse. Had Hosea gone after Jubal with murder on his mind? His own mother had admitted that Hosea hated his brother.

Mr. or Mrs. Eichelberger? Rollo Eichelberger was a sweet boy, friendly to a fault. If he had been friendly with the wrong girl… there didn't have to be more to it than that. Just the suspicion of an interracial relationship would be disastrous for both him and Sugar Welsh.

What about the Welshes? That was a tight family, and proud. If one of their own was in danger of ruination, what might they do? She dismissed the idea of pursuing that notion. If it was even suspected that one of their number might have attacked a white man, no matter how good the reason, that would be the end of them. No, that was a thought that Alafair would never voice. Even if it had happened.

Wallace MacKenzie and Randal Wakefield? If what Ruth had unwittingly intimated about the young men was true, and Jubal Beldon knew it and had threatened to expose them, they had a powerful incentive to shut him up for good. The love that dare not speak its name would earn them prison terms and they would be ostracized from society for life. If they weren't beaten to death first.

If she could just check one more thing, she might be able to present Scott with a much more complete scenario. For she was beginning to form a picture in her mind of what must have happened that night.

Trenton Calder

I sent the telegram to the county sheriff in Muskogee and to the circuit judge's office, like Scott had told me to, but I wasn't happy about it. I thought an inquest was a waste of time since the shooting was self-defense pure and simple. However, nobody asked my opinion about that. Next I went hunting for Randal Wakefield. I knew he was staying in the American Hotel, because he had a room right down the hall from me. Hattie Tucker ran the hotel, and when folks came to check in, they did it at the mercantile then went next door and up the stairs to their rooms over the store. So there wasn't any lobby like in a big city hotel. I went up the stairs and right to Randal's door and knocked, but there was no answer.

I went ahead and turned the knob. It wasn't locked. No one thought to lock their doors these days. I stepped in, and sure enough Randal wasn't there. The bed was made, and his valise was sitting wide open on top of the dresser. I was sorely tempted to go through it, but if I found something incriminating I wouldn't be able to use it in a court of law. That didn't stop me so much as the thought that if Scott found out I snooped around without a warrant he'd skin me alive. So I left.

I stopped at the mercantile and asked the girl behind the counter, Ellen Ray, if she'd seen Randal that day, and she said she'd caught sight of him crossing the street toward the Newport Cafe. That made sense, since it was near dinner time, so I went on over there and found Randal sitting all by himself at a table, eating a roast beef sandwich and reading a book. I hung my hat on the hat rack by the door and sat down next to him. He looked up at me like I had two heads. I figure it took him a minute to remember who I was.

"Trenton Calder," he said. "Would you care to join me for luncheon?"

Since I hadn't eaten for a couple of hours, I was peckish. "Don't mind if I do." I waved at Miz Newport and she waved back. She didn't ask what I wanted. I always wanted the same thing; dark meat chicken, fried potatoes and cream gravy, and a glass of buttermilk.

Randal closed his book and smiled. "Judging by the proprietress' familiar greeting, I assume you're a regular customer. This is a nice place."

I leaned my elbows on the table. "Regular as clockwork. I saw you in here yesterday. I was wondering why you aren't staying out at MacKenzie's like you did before your little side trip to Muskogee."

"The house was damaged by the storm, as you know. I do not wish to be a burden to Miz MacKenzie."

"You're not helping Wallace fix the place up?"

Randal sat back. "I am not a competent carpenter. What is this about, Trenton Calder?"

"You know I'm deputy to the town sheriff, Mr. Tucker?"

"So I have been told." His voice sounded the littlest bit ironic.

"Sheriff Tucker sent me over to ask you a couple of questions about the night y'all went to Muskogee after the Christian Church picnic. We just heard from the Beldons that you and Wallace come out to their place looking for Jubal that afternoon before you left town."

Randal kind of shrunk when I said that, but he didn't look shocked that I knew. He picked up his fork and pushed his mashed potatoes around. "Have you asked Wallace about this?"

"I'm asking you."

Miz Newport brought my dinner so we quit talking long enough for Randal to think about what he wanted to tell me. "Yes, Deputy," he said, after she was out of earshot. "We went out there, but as I'm sure the Beldons told you, Jubal wasn't at home. So we headed out for Muskogee and didn't stop until we got to Wallace's father's house."

"What did y'all want with Jubal?"

"I didn't want to have anything to do with him. Wallace was angry about the incident at the church picnic earlier." He took a swallow of his tea and eyed me. "You were there. You saw that they exchanged words. Anyway, Jubal wasn't there. Wallace wanted to wait for him, but we were supposed to be on our way to Muskogee so we didn't linger. We turned around and headed right out."

"That's quite a detour. The Beldon place is way out of your way if y'all were going to Muskogee. You'd have had to go right back past the MacKenzie place again on the way out. You didn't stop in and pick up Miz MacKenzie and all leave for Muskogee together?"

"No. The trip was a spur of the moment thing on Wallace's part. Miz Beckie wanted to pack a few things. She told us to take the shay and she'd take the eight-thirty train in and drive the shay back when she came home in a couple of days."

"That seems unhandy. Wallace couldn't wait two hours and go on the train with his grandma?"

Randal looked away. "You know Wallace. Once he gets a thing into his head, he's got to do it right then." The way he said it gave me a prickle of suspicion.

He leveled his gaze at me again. "We left the Beldons' about six and made it in to Wallace's father's house in Muskogee around nine. It was well dark."

"I can check that timing pretty easy, you know." I was eating chicken at the time I said it, but Randal understood me just fine.

"I know you can."

"You didn't meet Jubal on the road betwixt the farm and Muskogee?"

"We did not."

"I thought y'all were going to start back out on your trip to Colorado. Why'd you end up coming back here?"

"We changed our minds about the trip. While we were in Muskogee, we enlisted in the Army. Then Miz Beckie sent a note to her son saying her house had been damaged, and Wallace volunteered to come back and help with repairs."

When he said "enlisted in the Army" I near to choked to death on my drumstick. The idea of Wallace MacKenzie the Third ever obeying orders and marching in step was beyond me. And Randal was far too high-class to sport a shaved head and combat boots. "What possessed y'all to join up?" I managed.

Randal shrugged. "You know that Congress has lately put all college men on standby in case of war, so we decided we might as well get a jump on things."

Not being a college man I hadn't known that, but I pretended like I did. It did occur to me that my compadre Gee Dub Tucker was in college, but he hadn't said a word about it. Maybe he didn't want his ma to know.

"When do y'all have to report for duty?"

"A couple of weeks. We'll leave from here and go to Fort Riley."

"Well, I hope this is all cleared up in time, because I reckon y'all may have to stick around until Scott figures out what happened. In fact, finish up your sandwich there, because I'm going to lock you up in the hoosegow for a spell while I go out to MacKenzie's and question Wallace."

Randal looked affronted. "On what charge, Deputy?"

"I don't need a charge to hold you for twenty-four hours, but let's say it's on the charge that I don't want you talking to Wallace before I do."

Alafair Tucker

The road to town was finally passable enough for the Tuckers' small rig, so after dinner, when the men and boys had gone back to work, Alafair rounded up Blanche, Sophronia, and Grace for a trip into town to visit Alice and see the new baby.

That was her story, anyway. And there was certainly truth to it. The girls hadn't met their new niece yet, and when Alafair suggested the trip at the dinner table all three of them went into paroxysms of squealing delight. Shaw didn't suspect that his wife might have an ulterior motive, but Mr. Eichelberger eyed her suspiciously. She paid him no mind. She couldn't reassure him since she didn't know herself what she was going to do.

When Alafair and the girls left the house, Eichelberger resumed his seat on the porch and said nothing. *He's resigned to his fate*, she thought, feeling guilty. Not guilty enough. She had not promised to keep Eichelberger's revelation a secret, and he hadn't asked her to.

The two-mile trip to Boynton was slow going. There were still obstacles to dodge and boggy places that had to be slogged through. Fortunately, the light buggy never became so mired down that Missy couldn't pull it out with a bit of effort.

The girls were properly enraptured by the new baby, and while they crowded around Alice's chair and cooed like a flock of doves, Martha drew her mother aside and told her what had happened to Scott. Mother and daughter perched on the settee with their heads together, speaking low to keep the news from shocking the children.

Alafair's hand went to her throat. "Oh, my, goodness! What next with this awful business? But you say he's not hurt bad?"

"Doc Addison says he's barely nicked," Martha assured her, "but he's mighty upset about having to shoot Hosea. I walked over there an hour or so ago and spoke to Hattie. Trent has taken over for the time being. All the boys and their families are there, and Scott's sister and dad, too. I declare, Mama, you couldn't stuff one more person into that house."

Alafair wasn't surprised to hear it. It was only natural for the family to gather around their wounded patriarch. "So! Hosea Beldon, you say. Well, that sure makes it sound like Hosea is the one who met up with Jubal in the dark of the night."

"It does, Ma, but now neither of them is alive to attest to it. That's not all, either. While they were out there, Miz Beldon told them that Wallace MacKenzie and his friend had come by that evening hunting for Jubal, but he wasn't there. Trent has gone out to question both of them about it." Martha sat back and shook her head. "It could have been them who met Jubal. It's quite a puzzle, what with no witness to the death."

Alafair eyed her look-alike eldest child and nodded, but didn't say that she thought there may have been a witness after all. "Is Trent over at the MacKenzies' now?"

Martha shrugged. "I don't know. But that's where Wallace is, so if Trent isn't there now he will be directly."

Alafair stood up. "Girls," she called to the group huddled around Alice and the baby, "I'm going to go out to Miz MacKenzie's and visit with Ruth for a little bit. Y'all stay here till I come back. Won't be but a tick."

Three-year-old Grace propelled herself out off the sofa where she had wedged herself in beside Alice. “I want to go with you!” She voiced her wishes in an ear-piercing shriek, and baby Linda gave a startled wail.

“Good gracious! All right then, you don’t need to deafen us!” Alafair picked the tot up and shot Alice an apologetic glance.

Alice laughed at the din. New motherhood had made her imperturbable. “Go on, Ma. These two will be fine.” She nodded at Blanche and Sophronia, who didn’t even look up.

“I’ll come with you, Ma,” Martha offered, but Alafair shook her head.

She leaned in and murmured in Martha’s ear. “I want to have a private word with Miz MacKenzie while we’re in town.”

Trenton Calder

After I locked up Randal Wakefield I headed for the MacKenzie place. I was about as anxious to set eyes on Ruth as I was to question Wallace. I was champing to tell Ruth all that happened at the Beldon place. I don’t know why I was so anxious to see her after such an awful thing as what happened to Hosea and to Scott, too. The whole episode had upset me no end, and I was as eager to lay my eyes upon her face as a thirsty man is eager for water. After the long trip out to the Beldon farm that morning, old Brownie wasn’t happy about setting out again. He tugged at the reins when I rode past the stable, but I jerked his head around and he headed back out of town with an ill-natured snort. Fortunately, the MacKenzie house was just barely up the road so it didn’t take us all that long to get there.

I could see Wallace and Coleman Welsh over around beside the house, cutting up cottonwood branches and piling them in the back of a wagon. There was a buggy parked by the front porch, so I figured Miz MacKenzie had company. I was disappointed that I probably wasn’t going to get to see Ruth, but I figured it was just as well that I didn’t have to go into the house where Miz MacKenzie could hear this. I didn’t relish the notion of having to take Wallace to jail with his grandma dragging on his leg all the way. Coleman straightened up and waved at me as I dismounted.

When I said his name, Wallace turned around and gave me the once over. "Hello, Trent. Come to join the construction crew?"

"I come to ask you about Jubal Beldon," I said.

He didn't bat an eye. He threw another limb into the wagon. "I hear he's dead."

I shot a glance at Coleman, who had stopped sawing and was listening to this exchange like his life depended on it. "Coleman," I said, "would you give us a minute, please?"

I could tell he didn't want to do it. He looked at Wallace, who said, "Stay if you want, Coleman. I got nothing to hide."

I didn't care. I went on. "All right then. Yes, Wallace, Jubal is dead. And I hear that you and Wakefield drove out to his place looking for him before you set out for Muskogee on Sunday night."

Wallace stopped tossing limbs and turned back around at that. He gave me a long look before he answered. "We did, but nothing came of it. Jubal wasn't there, so we left and went to Dad's. As you know."

"Why did you go out there, Wallace?"

He looked down, and then up again. "I intended to give him a piece of my mind."

"About what?"

"You were at the picnic. You saw the little set-to that occurred between us. It niggled at me, and I took a notion to let him know it before we left town. But when we discovered he wasn't home, Randal pointed out that in my state of mind it was just as well that I missed him. So we took off for Muskogee."

"And you never saw Jubal again?"

"I swear I did not," Wallace assured me.

I fell to thinking for a second. I was new to this interrogation business and didn't quite know what to say next. I glanced at Coleman. He looked quite diverted by the situation. Finally I came out with, "I'll tell Scott what you said. The circuit judge will be through here in a couple of days, so I'd advise y'all not to leave town until Scott says you can."

Wallace nodded. "I have no plans to go anywhere for the next couple of days, anyway. Why does Scott care if we made a detour before we left town?"

I wasn't sure how much I could tell them. "He has his reasons. He suspects that Jubal had a run-in with somebody on Sunday night that may have led to his death."

"Deputy," Wallace said, "Sheriff Tucker must not take his suspicion too seriously if he sent the likes of you out to question me. Is he trying to create a crime where none exists? Or is this your idea? Why is he not here himself?"

I heaved a sigh. Nobody could annoy me like Wallace MacKenzie. Wallace and Coleman listened in open-mouthed silence as I related how Hosea Beldon got shot dead and Scott sustained a wound that put me in charge of this investigation.

When I finished my tale they looked at one another, then at me, before Coleman finally piped up. "Why on earth do you think Hosea did it, Deputy? Do you think he killed his brother?"

"Maybe he did. Why else try to kill a lawman who ain't even accused you of anything yet?"

"It sounds like Hosea did think the sheriff was accusing him," Coleman pointed out.

"If Scott thinks Jubal's death was unnatural, surely after what Hosea did you need look no further for your culprit," Wallace said.

"Maybe," I admitted. "Their ma said they were always at each other about something. Though knowing Jubal, if y'all did run across him it could have turned into a killing matter real easy."

"Well, it didn't, Deputy." Wallace pushed a hank of his yellow hair back off his forehead. "It didn't because Randal and I never saw him again that evening. We did not stab him because we did not meet him on the road or anywhere else. I will swear it before the judge or God himself."

I never had a high opinion of Wallace MacKenzie. I thought he was a silly creature. But the look in his eyes when he said that to me was arrow straight. I believed him. That is until I was turning to go and it dawned on me that I hadn't said a word to Wallace about Jubal getting stabbed.

Alafair Tucker

Beckie sat in one of the two armchairs in the parlor and Alalfair sat in the other with Grace in her lap. They could hear the sound of scales being played by one of Ruth's students in the drawing room. Marva had left Coleman to his job and was banging around in the kitchen. The common, homey sounds were comforting.

For a while she and Beckie talked of the ordinary things. How long it would be before the storm damage was repaired. Who had died and who was wounded and who had lost everything and was moving on. Which of Beckie's students had resumed taking piano lessons. Ruth's budding friendship with Trent Calder. Everything, Alafair noticed, except Beckie's usual favorite topic—her grandson.

Beckie listened dumbstruck while Alafair told her how Hosea Beldon had tried to cut Scott's throat and ended up with a hole in his chest. Beckie was properly shocked by the information, so Alafair took some time to reassure her that Scott wasn't hurt very badly. They spent a few moments speculating on why Hosea would have done such a thing.

"It could have been him who killed Jubal," Alafair offered.

There was an inordinately long silence while Beckie digested this information. "I do declare," she murmured. "I do declare."

Alafair shifted a drowsing Grace to a more comfortable position. "Scott can't be sure, though."

"Well, no, if Hosea didn't admit to it. But why else would he do such an awful thing?"

"I'm not so sure, either," Alafair ventured. "Scott thinks there are more people than Hosea who had reason to kill Jubal Beldon, and until they are all cleared, he intends to continue to pursue the matter."

Beckie's pale blue eyes regarded her thoughtfully. "Alafair, I wish you would stop beating around the bush. I do believe you are trying to say something to me."

Alafair's eyes widened. So much for trying to be subtle. "Yes, ma'am. I hope you will forgive me for not being straight with you in the first place, but I do not relish being the bearer of unwelcome news. But what I was so delicately building up to is this; I'm afraid that Wallace is one of the suspects. At first I couldn't imagine what reason Wallace, more than anyone else, would have to kill Jubal. But I wonder if Jubal knew something…some hurtful information about Wallace and aimed to use it to his own advantage."

Beckie listened to this with no apparent emotion. "What information?"

Alafair hesitated before answering. "I don't know."

Beckie smiled, but her eyes were filled with sadness. "You are trying to spare my feelings. I appreciate it. However, I see that the wicked truth about my grandson will be known, no matter how one tries to keep it secret." She took a sip from her teacup before placing it carefully on the side table. She sat back and clasped her hands in her lap. "Alafair, what would you do if you found out something awful about one of your bairns?"

"Well, I've been so lucky up to now that I kind of expect to, one of these days."

"No, I mean something really horrible. Is there anything one of them could do that you could not forgive? Anything so bad that would make you stop loving them?"

Alafair was shocked at the question. She stroked Grace's hair, soft, warm, and dark as a starless night, and the child snuggled up with her head on her mother's heart. How could she not love her little fairy girl with a direct connection to heaven? "Surely you're joking, Miz Beckie. There isn't anything they could do that'd make me stop loving my children."

"I'm serious. Have you ever really thought about it? Is there any unforgivable sin that would make you disown one of your babies? Even something perverted and sick?"

Perverted and sick? So Miz Beckie was aware of the rumor about Wallace and Randal. Did she believe it? And even if it was true, Alafair could understand if Beckie wanted to protect her grandson from going to prison. But she could never understand if Beckie had stopped caring for him because of who he chose to love. Alafair considered what she could say to ease the older woman's heart.

"No, there isn't anything they could do that would make me disown them. I think sometimes about the news reports of young German soldiers stabbing little Belgian babies with their bayonets. Those boys have mamas. What if one of my boys did something like that?" She paused. Goose flesh rose on her arms, and she scrubbed at them with her hands. "I think I might chase him down to hell to get him back, because he'd sure be in hell. I'd trail him clean to the end of the world and besiege him until he repented. I'd spend the rest my life helping him to atone for his sins. Even if I learned that one of my young'uns was Satan himself, I couldn't help but still love them. Love ain't something that can be turned on and off."

Without warning, Beckie burst into tears. "My boy, my boy," she sobbed. "I love him more than anything in this life, Alafair."

Alafair reached across the space between the armchairs to grasp Beckie's hand. "I know. I know you do."

"He's the most wonderful boy, Alafair. How could he be so good, and yet indulge in such despicable behavior? How could God let it happen? How could God let it happen? I'm so ashamed, and yet I love him so."

Alafair wasn't sure what Miz Beckie was talking about. The rumor about Wallace and Randal or something much worse? "Miz Beckie, Scott knows that Wallace and his friend went out to the Beldon farm looking to confront Jubal before they left town on Sunday night. Miz Beldon told him so. She also said that Jubal wasn't there and Wallace left unsatisfied. Now Scott is wondering if the boys met by accident on the road and something passed between them that led to Jubal's death."

Beckie blinked at Alafair through her tears. "Scott truly suspects Wallace of murder?"

"I think he does."

"Don't be ridiculous, Alafair dear. Wallace didn't kill that horrid Jubal Beldon. Wallace wouldn't squash a flea."

"Miz Beckie, did Wallace confess to you after he got to Muskogee? Is that why he came back, because he knew he had nothing to fear from Jubal anymore? Trent told us how it must have happened. It sounds like his killer lashed out without thinking. I know he didn't mean it."

Beckie's expression was one of horror and disbelief. She tried to withdraw her hand from Alafair's grasp, but Alafair wouldn't let go. There was no getting away from the truth. "There is no way anyone can prove that Wallace did such a thing, Alafair Tucker. He didn't do such a thing. He couldn't!"

Beckie stood up, and Alafair followed suit with a sleep-befogged Grace clinging to her neck. Alafair spoke quickly before the older woman had a chance to escape. "Miz Beckie, I think Mr. Eichelberger knows who did it. Just this morning he confessed to me that after Jubal left the roadhouse on Sunday night he came to try and extort money from Mr. and Miz Eichelberger. I think Jubal met his end on the road in front of their farm and I think Mr. Eichelberger saw the whole thing."

Trenton Calder

It was Wallace MacKenzie who stabbed Jubal Beldon that night. All at once I was sure of it. Everything fit. Him and Jubal were both on the road that night, and Wallace admitted that he was looking for a fight. And on the day of the picnic—the day Jubal died—Wallace had shown up in that ridiculous get up with a knife stuck in his sock. That little blade could easily have made the wound Scott described on both Jubal's leg and on his horse.

But why? Wallace didn't strike me as somebody who cared what folks thought about him. Maybe Jubal had something bad on his grandma. Something that would shame Miz Beckie before the whole town. And whatever his faults, I don't think Wallace would let that happen. Or maybe it had something to do with his friend Randal who seemed to stick to him like flypaper.

The memory of that conversation I had had with Ruth fell on me like a boulder. Is that why she was asking me about sodomites?

Lord have mercy! If that was it, no wonder Wallace killed him.

When I turned back around, Wallace must have seen something in my face. He took a step back and nearly stumbled over a cottonwood branch.

I laid my hand on my pistol butt. The incident with Hosea was fresh on my mind. "I don't think you're telling me the truth, Wallace. I think you and your friend did meet Jubal that night. I think Jubal threatened you with ruination and you made sure he didn't have the chance to carry out his threat."

I expected Wallace to look scared or guilty or take off running or something, but he snorted. "Calder, as far as I know, Jubal Beldon threatened half the people in town."

"Does that include you and your friend Randal Wakefield?"

His eyes narrowed. He didn't answer. Coleman Welsh knew he was witnessing something he didn't want to get involved in and backed off a ways.

"Wallace," I said, "I know that Beldon was a skunk. If he thought he knew about you what I suspect he did, he'd have used it against you for sure, and got great pleasure out of seeing you ruined and your whole family to boot."

Wallace looked away.

"Was it you or your friend plunged that little Scotch knife into Jubal's horse?"

Wallace MacKenzie heaved a great sigh. "Deputy" he said, "Randal had nothing to do with it. I don't want my grandmother upset if it can be helped. Let's leave quietly." He beckoned to Coleman. "When my grandma asks, tell her that I've gone to get more supplies and may spend the night in town."

Coleman started to protest, but Wallace cut him off. "Please, do me this favor. There's nothing else you can do."

We left Coleman beside the wagon, looking unhappy, and I followed Wallace as he walked to the coach house to get his horse. "What is your grandmother going to think when you don't come back tomorrow?" I asked. "You can't keep this a secret from her."

He didn't look at me. "I'll figure that out when I have to. Let her have every minute of peace she can get until that happens."

Alafair Tucker

"What makes you think that poor dear Mr. Eichelberger saw anything that night, Alafair?"

"He refuses to say who met Jubal on the road. But he knows. 'Even if I knew, I wouldn't tell you.' That's what he said to me. Miz Beckie, I have to tell Trent about Mr. Eichelberger, and Trent is going to press him until he tells what he knows. I had to warn you, ma'am. In fact when I got to town this afternoon, I found out that Trent is already questioning Randal about that night, and plans to question Wallace next, if he ain't already. It's going to come out, who killed Jubal Beldon."

Beckie flopped back down in her armchair, hopeless. "No it isn't. The only thing that's going to come out is the wrong thing. Wallace didn't kill Jubal, but if the law confronts him he may say that he did. I know my grandson. He will protect someone he cares for."

Alafair's heart skipped a beat. "You know who it was? It was Randal?"

Beckie laughed at that. "I wish it had been. That would solve everything. No, Randal Wakefield didn't do it either. It was I who plunged the knife into that evil man's leg."

"Oh, Miz Beckie, no!" The two women started and turned to see Ruth standing in the parlor door, pale with shock and clutching a sheet of piano music to her chest. She was not having it. "Mama, she's lying! She's the one who's trying to protect Wallace. Tell her not to do it!"

"Ruth, hush!" Alafair scolded. "Miz Beckie, if you are trying to protect Wallace, it's a foolish thing to do. The truth always comes to light."

Beckie's smile had no humor behind it. "I know it does. Come in, Ruth dear. You may as well hear this."

Ruth sat stiffly on the ottoman at her mother's knee. Grace was wide awake now, sitting straight up on Alafair's lap with a look of interest, as though she understood the situation perfectly.

Beckie leaned back and got comfortable before she began her tale. There was no tension in her expression anymore. There was no point.

"You were right when you said that Jubal threatened my boy, Alafair. He came by the house Sunday afternoon and confronted Wallace and Randal in the backyard. Wallace gave him all the money he had saved for his trip, trying to buy his silence. I heard the entire exchange. After Jubal left, we figured he might go straight to the sheriff with his infamous insinuation, even though he had been paid. So we made a plan. Wallace and that friend of his took the shay and headed for Muskogee, where they could take the train out of state the next morning.

"I planned to walk into town and catch the eight-thirty to Muskogee myself. The boys were to leave the buggy at Wallace Junior's house, and get the first train out of Muskogee going anywhere far away. I had no idea they went looking for that evil man first. Thank God they didn't find him. I thought that after the boys were long gone, I'd tell my son that I intended to sell the house and move to Muskogee to be near him and his wife. He's been after me to do that very thing for a long time. I planned to suggest to Junior that one of his agents could take care of the sale and move my furniture so that I would never have to come back to Boynton again. I didn't want Junior to get wind of why we left so hastily. Him and his son don't get on that well in any event. He'd disown the boy if he believed the rumor was true. And I think he would believe it."

"Miz Beckie," Ruth interrupted, "what could Wallace have possibly done that is so bad his own father would disown him?"

"Never you mind, Ruth dear. Perhaps it isn't even true." Her expression said she feared it was true, though. "Nothing vicious or cruel, I assure you. I packed a bag and left the house for the station at about an hour before the train was due. Then when I got to the junction I turned right, toward the Beldon place, instead of going straight on into town. I don't know what I aimed to do. I didn't know for sure if Jubal would follow through on his threat, but I expected he would. It's miles to the Beldon place and I had a train to catch, but I had to try one more time to save my boy.

"Anyhow, it turned out that I didn't have to walk all that way after all. I had almost reached the junction to the Morris road when I saw Jubal on that roan of his, coming out of the Eichelberger farm. Like I said, I didn't have a plan. But he saw me and came toward me. I nearly lost my nerve, but then I figured what more could he do to me? Kill me? It would have been a relief.

"So he says to me, 'Howdy, Miz MacKenzie. I figured you'd be coming by to see me directly.'

"I asked him what he wanted to leave us alone. He told me that Wallace had given him two hundred dollars and a good idea, and he reckoned that if I was as eager to buy his silence, he might keep his newfound knowledge to himself. If he had enough money he might even decide to go to Chicago and live in style."

Alafair was listening to Beckie's story with a look of skepticism on her face. She still thought it likely that Beckie was attempting to take the blame for her grandson. But Beckie misinterpreted her expression.

"It's not like I believed him, Alafair. I knew that even if I gave Jubal every dollar I possess, he'd hold that scandalous libel over our heads for the rest of his life. But what could I do? I told him I'd pay him anything he wanted. I said I had near to twenty dollars on me and I could get more from the bank come Monday. Five hundred dollars, I said. I put my carpet bag on the ground and started digging around in my pocketbook for my money purse, and that's when I found it. My da's *sgian dubh*.

"I didn't even think. I pulled it out and stabbed that scoundrel in the thigh. He screeched like a banshee and I went to stab him again, but his horse shied and I stabbed the poor creature in the hip. He went to bucking like a wild unbroke mustang, and Jubal was flung right off on his head. He didn't even have time to brace himself. The horse took off across a field, and I never saw him more.

"Jubal broke his neck. I could tell right away he was dead. I stood there shocked to my soul at what I had done. I don't know how long I stood there, but the Eichelbergers must have heard the ruckus, because they both came running. I expected I was doomed, but you know, neither of them even asked me what happened. Mr. Eichelberger even laughed when he saw Jubal lying there dead. Dear Miz Eichelberger looked relieved. The worst part of it, Alafair dear, is that I was relieved, too. I came very near to falling on my knees to offer up a prayer of thanks for our delivery, but truth is I knew the Lord didn't approve of my action. I couldn't help myself, though. The three of us dragged the body back up the drive, and Mr. Eichelberger put him in one of his storage sheds. He told me not to fret myself about it for even one minute. He said he was going to dig a hole in the woods and bury the body where nobody would ever find it."

A feeling of uncertainly began to niggle at Alafair. Was Miz Beckie's story true after all? If Eichelberger had hidden the body in one of his sheds, and the shed was blown to bits in the storm, that would explain a lot.

"Miz Eichelberger asked me to come inside and rest my nerves, but I told them I had a train to catch and walked back home. I washed my face and hands and got to the station in time to get the train.

"When I got to my son's house a little after nine, the shay was parked behind his house. The boys had intended to resume their trip to Colorado that very night and didn't mean to tarry. But I pulled Wallace aside and told him what had happened. There was no reason to worry about Jubal Beldon anymore. I expect he talked it over with his friend Randal, and that's when they decided to join up while they were in Muskogee.

"I didn't have anything to say about that. I had a visit with Junior and my daughter-in-law and headed for home on Monday evening. Just in time to nearly get blown away.

"When I found out that the Eichelbergers' place was destroyed and that Jubal's body had been found in a field, I didn't imagine anyone would suspect me or my boy either. I figured the sheriff wouldn't think other than Jubal was killed in the storm."

She smiled. "I almost got away with it. But of course sin always comes to light. I'd do it again though, God forgive me. I don't care about myself. I'm old, but Wallace has his whole life ahead of him."

Alafair was stunned. She had been so certain that Wallace and his friend were the culprits and both Beckie and Mr. Eichelberger were covering for them. Could it really have been the other way around?

There was a long silence after Beckie finished, broken only by a sniffle from Ruth. Until Marva Welsh rushed into the room, breathless. "Miz Beckie, Coleman come in the kitchen and told me that Deputy Calder just arrested Mr. Wallace for stabbing Jubal Beldon! Mr. Wallace didn't want Coleman to tell you that he is in custody, but I figure you ought to know. Miz Beckie, I don't think he done it. I saw Mr. Wallace and his friend go by the house in a big hurry on Sunday evening, heading toward Muskogee in that yellow-topped shay. I was surprised to see them because I thought they were already long gone. Then at least two hours after that, Coleman and me saw Jubal Beldon on the road west of town. He was still alive after Mr. Wallace left town."

Beckie stood up, full of purpose. "Oh, that foolish boy! What is he thinking? Well, ladies, I hope you'll be so kind as to accompany me to the sheriff's office. It's time for me to clear this matter up."

Trenton Calder

I locked Wallace in the cell next to Randal and went back out into the front office to write up a report for Scott. I had barely sat down before a covey of ladies flocked through the door and arrayed themselves in front of the desk. Ruth was one of them, and Marva Coleman, and Miz Tucker, holding her littlest one, Grace, on her hip. It was Miz Beckie MacKenzie who stepped forward and laid out the whole story of how she stabbed Jubal Beldon.

I was thunderstruck, and at first I didn't believe her. Marva told me about seeing Jubal alive after Wallace had left town, but as far as I was concerned, that didn't prove anything. The boys could easily have circled back later. But then Miz Tucker told me what Mr. Eichelberger had said to her, and how she suspected he saw the whole incident, I began to reconsider. I told the ladies to sit themselves down while I went back to the cells and put the question to my prisoners. Miz MacKenzie wanted to protest, but Miz Tucker and Marva persuaded her that argument would do no good.

I opened the cell door and stepped in. Wallace stood up to meet me. I could tell that he was still resigned to a bad fate, and I was a little surprised. The boys had to have heard women's voices coming through the office, though they wouldn't have been able to understand what was being said. Still, it seemed to me that news flew on wings around Boynton, and everybody knew everything as fast as it happened.

"Wallace, your grandma is in the office along with Miz Tucker and Ruth, and Marva, too."

His spine stiffened as he braced himself. "So. What is Grandmother saying?"

In the next cell, Randal Wakefield stood up from his cot and came over to the bars to listen.

"Wallace, your grandma just now confessed that it was her who stuck Jubal Beldon that night."

He plopped himself back down on the cot like a bag of rocks. His eyes watered up, but he didn't let himself cry.

I moved up close so that I was standing over him. "What do you have to say about that?"

He looked at me with a quizzical expression, like he didn't have the foggiest idea what I meant. "It must be perfectly obvious even to you that she's trying to save me."

"Wallace, if you mean to take the blame for your grandmother, that does you credit. But there's no reason to protect her, now. I know that it was her who slid that knife into Beldon, and not you…"

"Don't be ridiculous," he interrupted, but I just went on like I hadn't heard.

"…because Mr. Eichelberger saw the whole thing." I fudged that fact a little bit. I didn't mention that Miz Tucker told me the old man wasn't talking. Not yet, anyway. "Did you really think your grandma would let you go to prison? You are the apple of her eye."

He drew back like I had slapped him in the face. "Mr. Eichelberger?" His voice was squeaky.

Randal gripped the bars. "Wallace…"

Wallace cut him off. "Shut up, Randy." He turned back to me. "They're in cahoots. All right, maybe Eichelberger saw something. My grandma somehow convinced him to say it was her. She's trying to take the blame, I'm telling you…"

"Like you're doing right now? And not very convincingly, either. Wallace, what's done is done. She was seen. And considering how it happened and why—and who got killed—I doubt your grandma will do much time. If any. Why don't you tell me what really happened when you went out to the Beldon place?"

It took him a long time to make up his mind. He looked up at his pal who was still standing in the next cell. I thought about asking Randal to tell me the truth, but I figured he was too loyal to say anything Wallace didn't want him to. I didn't have anywhere to go, so I just stood there like a dummy until Wallace finally began to speak.

"I meant to kill him, you know. I had a gun in my pocket." That was the first thing he said, then he clammed up for a while before the next sentence dribbled out. "He came to Grandmother's house after the picnic. I gave him a lot money and promised him a lot more. But I knew that wouldn't be the end of it."

He stopped talking again for a spell before he said, "Do I have to tell you what he threatened to tell the sheriff about us? Going to prison is bad enough. I don't want to do it wearing a suit of tar and feathers, too."

I knew what it was, of course, but I pretended like I didn't. Wallace was right about the suit of tar and feathers. If he had an inkling that some folks knew his secret, I didn't see how he'd ever be able to relax again. "I don't see why it's important anymore," I told him. "Unless y'all are German spies, that is."

He glanced at Randal then, and smiled. "That's one thing we assuredly are not." Then the dam broke and the story flowed out. "When Beldon came by the house, he confronted Randal and me in the backyard and I gave him the money. Then after he left, I found out that Gran had been sitting on the back veranda the whole time. You know what my first thought was? How much did Grandmother hear? Enough, as it turns out, and she believed it, too. I was a hundred times more devastated that Grandmother would hold me henceforth in contempt than worried about what the rest of the world thought of me."

His voice caught and he fell silent for a spell while he struggled to get control of himself. "Anyway, we made a plan for me and Randal to take the shay and head out for Muskogee then and there before Beldon could get to the sheriff. Granny would follow on the late train. Well, I couldn't let it go like that. Randal and I decided to find Beldon and put an end to it, but I told you the truth about what happened next. He wasn't home and as far as we knew he had gone directly to the sheriff. We lit out of town before y'all could catch up with us."

He stopped talking again. He looked at Randal, then at me. I could tell that he was at terrible odds with himself. His expression hardened. "What could Mr. Eichelberger have seen? I don't believe you. You're trying to trap me."

I felt myself droop. "Lord a'mighty, Wallace! I never heard of so many folks eager to take the blame for murder. What is wrong with y'all? Well, once Mr. Eichelberger tells his story to the judge, somebody will have to admit the truth. Then the judge can decide what to do with you, because, durn it, it's beyond me." I stood aside. "Now, go out and discuss the matter with your grandmother, and maybe she can convince you to come clean."

Wallace flushed, then rose abruptly and walked out of the cell and into the office without another word. I could hear him talking to his grandmother and the sound of her weeping. I figured the emotions were thick out there, so I sat down on the cot. I intended to let things calm down a bit before I had to go out there and make a decision about what to do next. I would have given a thousand dollars if the storm-damaged telephone lines were magically fixed, and I could have called Scott and asked him to take charge.

Randal Wakefield

Trent and Randal eyed one another in silence for a good while. Finally Trent said, "I'll unlock the cell and let you out directly. Unless you're in an all-fired hurry to join the congregation in the front office."

"I expect I can wait a few minutes for the flood to abate, Deputy."

Trent eyed his prisoner. He liked Randal Wakefield for his gentle, unassuming manner, if nothing else. But he was hard to figure. Now that Wallace was not in the room, Trent wondered if Randal would be any more forthcoming. "Are you really going to keep quiet and let Wallace say he did it even if he didn't? Or are you going to confess to the crime along with everybody else?"

Randal dropped his hands from the cell bars and slipped them into his trouser pockets. He chuckled. "I didn't stab Jubal, Trenton Calder. And no, I'm not going to let Wallace say he did it."

Trent sighed. "So it was her after all."

"That I don't know, Deputy. I only know that after Miz Beckie reached her son's house Sunday night, she drew Wallace aside and told him that he didn't have to worry about Jubal Beldon anymore. I don't know that she stabbed him. Perhaps it was Mr. Eichelberger, or Hosea Beldon. I only know that on Sunday night, Miz Beckie knew Jubal was dead."

"If this is the story you aim to tell the judge, Wallace won't be very happy with you," Trent said.

Randal gave him a slim smile. "I hope it won't be necessary for me to say anything. But I don't intend to let him swing for something he didn't do."

Trent leaned forward and draped his forearms across his knees. "Well, we'll let the judge decide when he gets here in a couple days. When were y'all planning to leave for basic?"

"We meant to leave next week, though if you arrest Wallace or his grandmother for murder, I expect we'll miss our train."

"If the hearing goes like I think it will, I expect y'all will be able to leave on time."

It took a moment for Randal to digest the implications of what the deputy had said to him. "Does this mean you don't intend to charge us with…anything else?"

Trent didn't let on that he knew perfectly well what Randal was asking him. "Since y'all didn't kill Jubal, there isn't anything else to charge you with."

The sound of weeping had abated and Trent could hear Alafair's voice, though he couldn't tell what she was saying. He stood up and went to unlock the other cell. Randal picked up his jacket off the cot. He turned to leave, but hesitated and gave the deputy an odd look out of the corner of his eye.

"You want to know the real irony of this situation, Trenton Calder?" He was almost whispering. "What Jubal said about us…it isn't even true."

Trent almost gasped. Considering all the trouble the rumor had caused, Randal's statement was the last thing he expected to hear. Neither man had made the slightest attempt to deny it. Of course it didn't matter whether it was a fact or not if people wanted to believe it. He opened his mouth to ask why on earth they hadn't at least enlightened Beckie and saved her so much grief. But then it dawned on him. "But you wish it was…"

"Yes, I wish it was. But it is not." Randal looked away. "Wallace has known about me practically from the moment we met at Vanderbilt, Trenton Calder, and from that moment he has accepted me and even championed my cause when the need arose. He has kept my secret at great cost to himself. Wallace

MacKenzie is without doubt the bravest man I know." His gaze was level when he looked at Trent again and answered the question he hadn't asked. "Wallace loves his grandmother, but I believe it hurt him deeply that her love for him seems to be conditional. He should have told her the truth. Don't worry, Deputy. Before we leave town, I will enlighten Miz Beckie. For her own peace of mind, if nothing else."

With that, he walked out and left Trent standing in the middle of the jailhouse floor, stunned. Trent had been taught that there was nothing good one could say about people who have amorous urges toward members of their own sex. But he was thinking that Randal Wakefield was pretty brave himself.

Trenton Calder

When I finally went back out into the front office, I found Randal sitting in one of the chairs under the front window with Miz Tucker and Grace on one side of him and Ruth and Marva Welsh on the other. Wallace and Miz Beckie were standing arm-in-arm by the desk, looking resigned.

I sat down behind the desk, trying to look official and keep my eyes off of Ruth. She smiled at me as she caught my gaze sliding toward her when my attention should have been on the business at hand. *I know what you're thinking,* her expression said. I could feel my face burning.

"Well, Miz MacKenzie, Wallace, Mr. Wakefield," I said, "I've already contacted the circuit judge and he should be here day after tomorrow. There will be a hearing, and he'll decide at that time whether or not to bind any of you over for trial. In the meantime, I'll have Lawyer Meriwether come round and see you this afternoon. I suggest that y'all tell *him* the truth, at least. Once he knows the whole story, I expect he'll be able to mount an effective defense for you. He'll have no trouble finding plenty of other folks with a strong motive to stab Jubal Beldon. If Jubal was stabbed at all and didn't just fall on something, that is. That's all for the time being. I reckon y'all can go home now."

Miz MacKenzie blinked at me. "You're not going to arrest me?"

"Do you aim to skip town, ma'am? ... I thought not. You just stay at home until you're told otherwise."

She still looked as though she couldn't believe her ears. "And Wallace is free to go as well?"

"Yes, ma'am. I have no particular reason to keep him locked up."

She shot Randal a stern glance. "And the other matter?"

"What other matter is that, Miz MacKenzie?"

Wallace barked out a laugh, though it sounded a little like a sob. "Come on, Gran, let's get out of here before Deputy Calder changes his mind."

Marva jumped up. "Now, Miz Beckie, you listen to what Mr. Wallace says. Let's go on back to the house and I'll fix y'all up a nice supper."

Miz MacKenzie still looked like she'd been slapped when Wallace and Marva dragged her out of the office. Randal shook my hand, then went back to the hotel. But not before Miz Tucker had invited him out to the farm for supper.

After he was gone, I turned around to see Miz Tucker standing there with little Grace on her hip, grinning so big that her face was like to split. "Trent, you ought to come for supper, too. I may not have bedrooms at the moment, but I've still got a kitchen and folks have brought us more food than I know what to do with."

"Thank you, ma'am, but since Scott is out of commission, it depends on if I can get Butch to do my rounds for me tonight."

"Well, I hope he will. Ruth, are you going to stay at Miz Beckie's house tonight?"

"Yes, Mama, I want to be whatever help I can. Besides, Martha and I decided we'd just as soon wait to come home until there's a place for us to sleep."

Miz Tucker nodded. "Well, Grace and me better go relieve Alice of her little sisters and get home. If Trent manages to get free this evening, maybe he'll ferry some of you girls out to the farm and back, and we'll all be together and have a right old feast tonight."

When she said that I knew that I'd be free if I had to kidnap Butch Tucker and tie him to a chair right there in the sheriff's office.

After Miz Tucker left, it was just me and Ruth in the office. She was still in the chair under the window, sitting real straight with her hands folded in her lap, her curly hair caught up in a yellow ribbon. The ribbon made her eyes take on a golden bronze hue, like asters in full bloom. She looked me up and down like she wanted to say something, but didn't know quite what it was. I knew the feeling.

"Do you think Miz Beckie did it, or is she trying to save Wallace?" she finally asked.

"I don't know, Ruthie. They may all be trying to save each other. But her story fits the best. Once Mr. Eichelberger talks, we'll know for sure."

"If it was her, will Miz Beckie go to prison?"

"The MacKenzies can afford the best defense. Besides, if anybody on the jury was acquainted with Jubal Beldon, I imagine she'd get off light."

"It's awful that nobody in the world is going to mourn Jubal's passing."

That made me smile. "You're generous to say so."

"What do you think Scott will say about your letting Miz Beckie and Wallace go home?"

"That it was justice, I hope."

That was the first of a thousand times since that I looked in those chameleon eyes and knew that I had done right.

Alafair Tucker

The morning star was just fading when Shaw caught sight of Alafair walking up the path from Mary's house. The sky was still the color of tarnished silver with a strip of pearl on the eastern horizon, and since Alafair was coming from the west, her silhouette was no more than a dark outline against a darker ground. Shaw put down the feed sack he had slung across his shoulders and stepped out into the barnyard to meet her, worried.

Kurt Lukenbach had shown up on horseback in the middle of the night and announced that Phoebe was in labor and needed her mother. That had been less than five hours ago. "What are you doing back here so soon?" he asked. "Is Phoebe all right?"

She came up to the corral fence and draped her elbows over the top rail. The twist of dark hair at her crown was askew and her eyes were drooping with fatigue, but she grinned at him. "Phoebe's fine. Everything is fine. She gave birth to that child easy as pie. It's a boy."

Shaw blinked at her, not sure he had heard her correctly. "A what?"

Alafair laughed. "Pull your eyeballs back in, honey. It's a boy! Hair as black as coal and eyes so blue I reckon they'll stay that way. He's a good squaller, too. Our boys will bust with joy when they hear." She put her hand on Shaw's arm. "John Lee says they aim to name him Shaw Tucker Day."

Shaw couldn't help but gape. He could hardly take in so many unexpected pieces of information at once. "What in the…" He smiled, then frowned, then smiled again. "That poor child!"

"John Lee said they're going to call him Tucker. I figure that's because one Shaw is all we can handle in this family. Doctor Ann almost didn't make it in time, but she's there right now, and I'm so dog tired that I figured I'd come home for a spell and get some sleep. Now that Martha's home she can get breakfast. We can go back over to Mary's later. I thought we could bring Zeltha home with us then. Mary and Kurt have enough to do what with little Judy, baby Tucker, and two invalids to take care of. I offered to take Chase as well, but Mary said he's a good helper and she'd just as soon he stay. I thought he'd pop his buttons when he heard that."

"Who'd have thought it of Chase Kemp?"

"Well, he just needed a place to fit in, and he fits in here with us just fine."

Trenton Calder

It took a long time for the town of Boynton to get over that twister. People were digging trash out of their yards for years, things like forks and bloomers and broken lamps. To this day folks around here love to tell tales of all the strange things they saw, like eggs flying for miles and landing unbroken in somebody's yard. Or how Oscar Smith's hay store caught on fire from a lightning strike, but when they went to put it out him and his sons discovered that the twister had sucked all the water out of the farm pond. Fortunately a downpour of rain put the fire out before everything burned to the ground. Things of that nature. I admit that the tales did get taller as the years went by.

Everybody lost something or somebody, but everybody helped their neighbors, too. Gee Dub and Charlie and me spent some time going around to neighbors to offer help with cleanup and repair. Like Gee Dub said, "I reckon I know how to lay shingles, at least." Once I went with Ruth over to her grandma's to help gather quilts and blankets to carry out to them who needed them. I enjoyed that task. Besides getting to spend time with Ruth, I liked delivering Miz McBride's quilts. It was nice for folks to have something to wrap in that smelled good, not like an old wet dog. I knew three or four families who figured it was just too big a task to rebuild so they sold out and moved on.

The circuit judge did order an investigation into the death of Jubal Beldon, but nobody was ever charged with his murder. The county sheriff must have interviewed a hundred people, but he decided that Wallace and Miz Beckie could have been covering up for each other, Mr. Eichelberger wasn't talking, there were too many folks who benefitted from Jubal's demise, and on top of it all, it was possible that Jubal simply fell off his horse. In the end he said there just wasn't enough hard evidence to bring anybody to trial.

It was whispered around town for years that Miz Beckie MacKenzie had most likely been the one to plunge her knife into the scoundrel's thigh. Nobody seemed to hold it much against her. She kept teaching piano to the local children and lived out her life in the house she loved. The Beldons sold their farm for taxes and moved away. I don't know what happened to them.

What with all that had happened to them, I reckon the Beldons forgot all about Jubal's horse, for none of them ever claimed him from the Luckenbachs. The animal finally calmed down enough that you could ride him, but every once in a while, out of the blue, he'd remember all the injustices that had been visited on him and go off his nut. Mr. Tucker was still of a mind to shoot him, but he was a fine piece of horseflesh, so Charlie said he'd take him over. Mr. Tucker said all right, but if the roan ever come near to hurting anybody again, Charlie would have to put him down.

John Lee Day recovered, but he never did walk quite right again. For a long time, he covered the bare patches on his head by wearing hats and bandannas around his head, as well as an eye patch for his sore eye. The children teased him a lot about looking like a pirate. When his new hair grew in it stuck out stiff like black straw.

Rollo Eichelberger moved back to the farm with his daddy and with the help of the neighbors, the two of them built a nice little house. I understand that Mr. Eichelberger was able to pay cash for the materials. Must have set him back close to two hundred dollars.

Mr. Tucker's brother Charles who owned a sawmill over in Okmulgee supplied all the lumber at a discount for the folks who had been hurt by the twister, so there was a lot of building going on around Boynton for months. By the time John Lee and Phoebe Day were both well enough to look after themselves, their house and barn had been rebuilt and furnished with dribs and drabs from nearly every family in Boynton. In fact, it was about six weeks after the storm and a bunch of us were hammering away at the Days' new house when Scott showed up with a man in tow and called Kurt Lukenbach aside. Mr. Tucker and I climbed down from the roof and joined them, because Scott and the old man were both looking mighty grim.

"Kurt," Scott said, "this here is Mr. Patrick Mitchell. He's come up from Mina, Arkansas, in response to the telegram we sent to the sheriff there about the young couple that got killed in the storm. From the description I gave him, he's pretty sure they were his son and daughter-in-law and the little gal Mary found is his granddaughter."

Mr. Patrick Mitchell from Mina, Arkansas, was a tall, thin, leathery, old man with faded blue eyes, dressed in overalls and a homespun cotton shirt. We all stood there for the longest time without anybody saying a word. Kurt was looking at Mr. Mitchell like he was the Grim Reaper himself. I didn't blame him any. We all knew what this was going to do to Mary.

Since nobody else was going to say anything, Scott went on. "Mr. Mitchell tells me his son's family was on their way down to Texas to homestead a plot outside of Fort Worth, but they never got there. He identified most of the items we were able to save from the wreckage of the wagon as theirs. I think there's little question that the deceased were Mr. Mitchell's kin."

After another long pause, he turned to Kurt. "I reckon we'd better head over to your place." *I'm sorry, but best to get this over with*, his expression said.

There wasn't any reason for any of us but Kurt to go, but Mr. Tucker came for support and I tagged along because it was my fault for figuring out where to send the telegram. We all trooped over to the Lukenbach farm in silence. You'd think somebody had just died.

Mary was mighty brave about the whole thing, but she couldn't help but weep when she brought the baby into the parlor to show her to Mr. Mitchell. Phoebe followed right along behind her. She was crying, too.

The old fellow stood up to get a close look at the girl, but he didn't try to take her out of Mary's arms or touch her. He stared at little Judy for a long time, and Judy stared right back, interested and unaware that any minute her life was likely to change forever. Mr. Mitchell's gaze shifted from the baby to Mary, then back to the baby. "Looks like you've been taking good care of her, Miz Lukenbach."

Mary's voice caught when she answered. "We love her like our own, Mr. Mitchell."

"Is this your granddaughter?" Scott asked.

Mitchell looked back over his shoulder at Scott. "She favors my son some, but I can't be sure."

"What is your granddaughter's name?"

"I never knew," Mitchell admitted.

Scott persevered. "Mr. Mitchell, is this your granddaughter or not?"

The old man took a step back. "I can't rightly say. Maybe. Maybe not."

Kurt reached out and put his hand on Mary's shoulder.

Scott wasn't satisfied with Mitchell's answer. "Mr. Mitchell, do you want to take responsibility for this child? Tell me now."

Mr. Patrick Mitchell looked like a man who had had a tough life. Sometimes that makes you hard and sometimes that makes you wise. He turned to Kurt. "She don't need me. I reckon she's all right where she is." Then he walked right out of the house.

We were all so dumbfounded that it took a minute to dawn on us what Mitchell had said. Phoebe finally made a squeaky noise, and Mary burst into tears of joy. We all did, to tell you the truth.

Scott shook himself and started after the old man, but Kurt grabbed his arm. "Sheriff, Mary and I want to keep the baby. Can we adopt her now? How shall we go about it?"

Scott looked like he still couldn't fathom what had just happened, but he said. "When we get back to town Mr. Mitchell and I will go see Lawyer Meriwether. I'll let you know what to do next."

And that's how Kurt and Mary got their first one. God blew her in on the wind.

The Boynton Index, **November 12, 1918**

Wallace Bruce MacKenzie III, grandson of Boynton resident Mrs. Wallace Bruce MacKenzie Sr., was severely wounded on October 20, 1918, at Meuse-Argonne, while leading a charge against a German machine gun emplacement. His commanding officer, Col. Michael Stone, reported that Lt. MacKenzie put himself between the incessant barrage and his comrades, saving the lives of the rest of the squad and allowing them to complete their mission and destroy the machine gun nest. Lt. MacKenzie had already been awarded the Bronze Star and the French *Croix de Guerre* for heroism in the field, and had recently refused a transfer to a rear position in order to remain with his unit. Col. Stone informed this reporter that he has recommended Lt. MacKenzie for the Medal of Honor.

According to Col. Stone, Lt. MacKenzie survived the battle only because of a small knife he was wearing on a leather thong around his neck, under his uniform blouse. The knife, a family heirloom which was given to him as a good luck charm by his grandmother, deflected two bullets which otherwise would have pierced his heart. Lt. MacKenzie is fighting for his life at the military hospital in Neuilly, France. His ultimate survival is in question.

The Boynton Index joins every citizen of the town in expressing our profound gratitude to Wallace MacKenzie for his sacrifice, and offers our prayers, support, and sincere best wishes to his parents, Mr. and Mrs. Wallace Bruce MacKenzie Jr. of Muskogee.

Glossary

Blue laws—Laws created to enforce moral behavior, especially on Sunday. There have been blue laws in America since the first British settlements, and they are still on the books in many local jurisdictions in the United States. In Oklahoma in 1916, it was illegal to conduct certain types of business on Sunday, including any venue where dancing or gaming took place. Since Oklahoma came into the Union in 1907 as a "dry" state, the sale of alcoholic beverages was prohibited at all times.

fashed—upset

feile-beag—pronounced *FIL-uh-beg*—"Little kilt,, the modern version of the Scottish kilt, made of seven or eight yards of pleated tartan material, as opposed to the older *feile-mohr (FIL-uh-mor),* or "great kilt" made of eighteen yards of material wrapped loosely around the wearer's middle and belted, with the surplus end thrown over the shoulder like a cloak.

half a section—320 acres. One section of land equals one square mile, or 640 acres.

Saddle skirts—two pieces of sheepskin-lined leather attached to the underside of a saddle to cushion the horse's back from the saddle bars. They also keep the rider from getting wet with horse sweat.

sgian dubh—pronounced *skeen doo*—"Black knife," a small knife kept in the top of a man's kilt hose or boot.

two bits—fifty cents. A 'bit' is a quarter dollar.

Alafair's Recipes

Scratch Cooking

If you are not used to cooking from scratch, simply following a recipe is not going to get you the same results your grandmother got when she cooked. Take simple biscuits, for instance. If you throw all the ingredients together in a bowl, stir them up, cut them out and cook them, you're liable to end up with little rocks rather than the delectable, melt-in-your-mouth morsels that Alafair made for her family every day of her married life. There is a science behind it, and every home cook was a chemist.

Buttermilk Biscuits

2 cups flour
1/2 tsp salt
4 tsp. baking powder* plus 1/2 tsp soda
5 Tbsp of shortening (vegetable shortening, butter, or—let's be brave—lard.)
1 cup buttermilk

First, sift the dry ingredients together into a bowl. This will aerate the biscuits and make them lighter. One problem modern cooks often have is that unless they are professional or gourmet cooks, they may not own the same utensils Alafair would have had at hand.

Do you own a sifter, Dear Reader?

If you do, congratulations, and don't forget to use it. If you don't, you can still sift your flour, baking soda, and salt together by shaking it through a wire mesh sieve.

Second, cut the shortening into the flour until the mixture looks like coarse crumbs. If you skip this step and mix the fat and flour into one big wad before adding the liquid, you will end up with the aforementioned rocks. How about using a pastry blender? This is a utensil that looks like a letter "D"; a straight handle with four or five curved metal blades attached. However, if you don't own a pastry blender, do not despair. You can do it with two ordinary case knives or even your hands. In fact, using your hands is an intimate, loving, time-honored technique. If you work biscuits with your hands as many times as Alafair did, you will develop a magical sense in you fingertips that will tell you the instant the dough is ready for the next step.

Next, make a well in the middle of the flour mixture and pour in all the milk at once, then stir it up with a fork or a big wooden spoon just until the dough begins to follow the spoon around the bowl.

STOP!

Turn the dough out onto a floured surface (a cutting board, or your clean cabinet is fine) and knead it with your hands for about half a minute. A little kneading makes the biscuits flakier.

STOP!

Pat the dough out with your hands or roll it out with a rolling pin until it's about half an inch thick. Be gentle!

The secret is that too much handling makes the biscuits tough. This is why your grandma could mix up a batch of biscuits in five minutes flat.

Cut the biscuits out with a biscuit cutter (or with the floured mouth of a drinking glass) and place them on an ungreased cookie sheet. If you like them crusty, place them about half an inch apart. If you like them softer, place them on the sheet so they are just touching. Then bake them in a very hot oven (450 degrees) for twelve to fifteen minutes. A very hot oven will make them poof up and develop a nice crust on top. Be sure that the oven is pre-heated before you put the biscuits in.

**Alafair would have used two parts cream of tartar mixed with one part baking soda. Baking powder is basically the same thing.*

Fried Green Tomatoes

Nothing is easier or tastier. Cut green tomatoes into slices about half an inch thick. Dip each slice into flour, salt and pepper, or a beaten egg then yellow cornmeal. Fry the slices slowly in a skillet in a little hot fat until they are browned to your satisfaction. Turn them over and brown them on the other side. Until the latter part of the twentieth century, "hot fat" would have been just that; the melted fat left over in the skillet after cooking meat, which your grandma saved in a grease jar that she kept next to the stove. Sometime in the 1970s or '80s, we got wise, and now when we say "hot fat," we really mean "hot non-hydrogenated vegetable oil."

Green Beans and Fatback

We denizens of the early twenty-first century are used to preparing our green beans so that they retain their snap. An early twentieth century chef would wonder what was the point of going to all the trouble of steaming or otherwise flash-cooking your green beans if you were going to eat them half raw anyway. Green beans used to be boiled in water along with a big hunk of pork fat or other fatty scrap meat for an hour or two until they were soft and limp and floating in a succulent meat and vegetable infused soup.

Pork Chops and Pan Dressing

Imagine this: It's 95 degrees outside with 90% humidity. Your house has no air conditioning. On top of it all, the only way you can cook is to start an actual fire with real live flames inside a giant iron stove, the surface of which will heat up enough to brand you if you touch it with your bare hand. Now you have an inkling of why an early twentieth century family cook preferred to make dishes in the summer which either required no cooking or were cooked on top of the stove as quickly as possible.

Because it spoiled more quickly in the heat, meat served in the summer either had to be from a freshly killed animal, or preserved, like ham, sausage, and bacon. It was the availability of artificial refrigeration which expanded the "fresh meat season" into the summer. Even so, for a long time people were wary of fresh meat in the summer unless they had killed the animal themselves. Pork is especially iffy, and had to be thoroughly cooked before eating.

Alafair would have cooked her chops in a cast iron skillet, which distributes the heat evenly and when covered tightly, works like a hot oven.

The Chops

Melt some butter in the pan (or meat drippings from the jar, if you're brave). Pat the chops dry and sprinkle them with salt and pepper, then sear each side in the fat over high heat, a minute or two per side. Then when the chops are browned, lower the heat, cover the pan, and cook about five minutes on each side. Stick a knife into the middle of the chop and when the juices run clear, the meat is done.

The Dressing

This is the same sort of bread dressing that one would use as a side with turkey on Thanksgiving, except it is cooked on top of the stove instead of baked in the oven. Every family in this country has its favorite dressing recipe, so feel free to use whatever ingredients you like best. Alafair would have used whatever she had to hand, so the dressing would have been different every time. The following recipe is just a suggestion. There's no hard and fast rule about measuring ingredients, either. With scratch cooking you eyeball it, taste it, stick your finger in it to see if it feels right. When it's hot enough, has cooked long enough to kill anything that might hurt you, and delicious enough to satisfy you, it's done.

1 small minced onion

Two or three celery stalks (if in season) with the leaves, chopped. If you'd rather, two or three small summer squash, like yellow crookneck, sliced thin or cut into small cubes, are good, too.

4 cups of dry bread cut into small cubes OR a pan of dry cornbread OR a combination of both.

Salt and pepper and dried herbs to taste. Sage is traditional. Garlic is good, as is thyme, parsley, savory, and basil. Whatever you like.

1 cup chicken or beef (or veggie) broth

1/4 cup melted butter

While the chops are cooking, mix the bread, herbs, broth, and butter in a large bowl and squish around with your hands. Set aside. When the chops are done. remove them from the skillet, leaving the juices, and put them on a platter. Scrape up all the delicious brown bits from the bottom of your cast iron skillet and stir them around in the meat juice. Saute the onion and celery in the pan juices until soft, then add the rest of the dressing and mix well with the celery and onion. Heat through. If the mixture seems too dry, add more broth or butter. Return the chops to the pan on top of the dressing and simmer with the lid on for a few minutes until everything is nice and hot. Serve immediately.

This is really good with chopped apples cooked in the dressing, or sliced and pan fried in butter as an accompaniment.

Creamed Onions

If you're into onions, this is one of the most delectable side dishes ever conceived.

Here is the original recipe as handed down in the family:

> *Boil the onions until tender, then pour off the water and add a teacup full of milk, a piece of butter the size of an egg, pepper and salt. Stir in a heaping tablespoon of flour until it is creamy, then let it all boil up once and serve it hot in a nice dish.*

Here is the recipe interpreted for those of us who don't know exactly what we're doing:

3 medium onions or half a dozen small onions
(or a couple of handfuls of pearl onions)
3 tablespoons of butter
2 tablespoons of flour
1/4 tsp salt
Pepper to taste
1 1/3 cups of milk
1 cup of shredded cheese, if desired

If you are using very small onions, cut off the top and bottom and remove the first layer of skin. If you are using large onions, peel and quarter them. Put the onions in cold salted water to cover, bring to a boil, and boil until almost tender. Length of boiling time depends on size. Usually about ten minutes for small onions. They will start to look opaque. You can stick a sharp knife into one to see if they're done. Drain off the water. In a saucepan, melt a hunk of butter, blend in flour, salt and pepper, and stir until smooth. Add the milk all at once and stir until thickened and bubbling. If you desire, you can add about a cup of shredded cheese to the roux right at the end and stir until blended. Stir in the drained onions and heat through.

To receive a free catalog of Poisoned Pen Press titles, please contact us in one of the following ways:

Phone: 1-800-421-3976
Facsimile: 1-480-949-1707
Email: info@poisonedpenpress.com
Website: www.poisonedpenpress.com

Poisoned Pen Press
6962 E. First Ave. Ste 103
Scottsdale, AZ 85251